SERPENTINE
Barry Napier

SERPENTINE

ISBN: 978-1-925342-86-4

PART ONE

FIRST
DAY
OF
SUMMER

ONE

George sat back in his chair, staring at the computer screen. The e-mail he had opened ten minutes ago consisted of only three words and a salutation. It remained on the screen, simple and to the point.

Wilkins is dead.

−KC

He closed the e-mail and signed out of his account. Shafts of early morning sunlight crept through the blinds, casting rectangles of white across the floor. *Wilkins is dead*, he thought. He stared up to the ceiling and tried to picture the face of Jimmy Wilkins, one of the men he had spent seven weeks with while studying the Aleutian Trench eighty miles off the coast of Siberia. It was odd—six of them had shared the cramped space within the submarine for those seven weeks, but George could not remember their faces.

He, Wilkins, and KC were the only ones that had made it home alive. The other three had died while underwater and he still wasn't sure what had happened. What George *did* remember was being retrieved by government vessels with most of the submarine's interior covered in blood and gore.

Even if he wanted to forget that part of it all, he couldn't. It was cemented into his brain, popping up in nightmares when he tried to sleep.

George swiveled in his chair and looked to the sunlight on the floor. The blinds sliced the light into segments that reminded him of the dance of light and water along the hull of the sub when Wilkins, KC, and himself had been rescued.

He belched, tasting the coffee he has just finished. Immediately following the belch, he felt something tickling the back of his throat. It felt like a thick trail of phlegm that refused to come up. He cleared his throat, but that urgent tickling remained.

He left his office and walked slowly into the bathroom. He studied his reflection in the mirror above the sink, frowning at

1

what he saw. His eyes were hollow and his face lacked any sort of color. He looked like a ghost. He sometimes wondered if he *had* died in that sub with the three other men.

But there was no fooling himself into believing that he was dead. The ache that had been growing within his stomach for the last three days was an indication of that, as was the prominent cough.

As he studied his reflection, he was assaulted by one of the fits of coughing that had plagued him since returning to land. How long had that been, anyway? Nine days? Ten? It didn't seem like that long.

He didn't bother covering his mouth. He hunkered down in the floor and hugged the toilet, coughing violently. The coughs were dry and raspy, each one making his chest burn. He coughed into the bowl and saw that there was a pinkish hue to his spit. He coughed a few more times, knowing that it would not stop until the…the *things* came up. He felt them climbing up his throat like tiny bugs. He spit into the toilet, grimacing.

Four small black shells fell from his mouth and made tiny *plink* sounds in the water. They were the size of pepper flakes but had the solidity of pebbles. Whatever they were, they appeared to be alive. They writhed in the toilet for a moment and then died.

George watched the small shapes until he was sure they were all dead. He flushed the toilet and watched them swirl down.

He tasted the faintest traces of blood and something else that tasted slightly like cabbage. He found this odd since all he had eaten for breakfast was toast, oatmeal and two cups of coffee.

His stomach lurched a bit at the peculiar taste but he paid it no mind. His stomach had been acting up for three days and he hadn't gotten sick yet. It would simply churn, almost as if he had gas. But after the churning passed, it would vanish completely. He kept trying to tell himself that there was nothing to worry about. It was probably just some side effect from whatever happened in the sub.

He'd been warned about the tension headaches and he had meds to ease them. The doctors had also warned about potential nose bleeds, but there had only been one minor episode since returning home. But then the black flea-like things had started coming from his throat when he coughed. That had happened almost right away, even before they had left Siberia. And as of last night, there was that tickling in his throat, something so prominent that he had felt as if his throat may close up.

He wondered if KC was going through this, too. Why else would he be sending such brief e-mails?

Wilkins is dead.

Well, how had Wilkins died? George wanted to reply to KC's e-mail, but he knew that it would be dangerous to do so. He felt certain that KC was putting himself at great risk to get his messages out. Surely after what had happened in the trench, they were being monitored somehow.

Well what the hell happened in the trench, anyway?

George couldn't remember, and trying to recall the memories only frustrated him.

On his way to the kitchen for a glass of water, he went into another coughing fit. This time the black creatures came up right away. George felt them swarming in his mouth, clicking against his teeth. There were eight of them this time, six of which were dead by the time they hit the floor.

He tracked the other two down and stepped on them. They made a crunching sound beneath his foot. When he removed his foot, he saw that they left a clear fluid when their bodies were smashed.

George poured himself a glass of water and downed it. He then refilled the glass and went back into his office. There was a folder full of paperwork on his desk, contracts and documents that he, Wilkins, and KC had been forced to sign after being rescued. He fished through these and found the medical reports. One of the doctors had stapled his business card to one of the reports and had instructed them to call if things got really bad.

George wasn't sure if his current state was considered *bad* to these doctors, but he punched the number in anyway.

The phone rang nine times before it was picked up. The man on the other end sounded confused.

"Hello?"

"I'm looking for Dr. Kagle," George said.

"Speaking. But this is a private number. How did you get this?"

"My name is George Galworth. You examined me three weeks ago after my sub was rescued off of the coast of Siberia."

"Of course, of course! George, it's nice to hear from you." His tone and the waver in his voice indicated that this was a lie. "Is something wrong? Can I do anything for you today?"

"I've got this really bad cough," George said. "I'm spitting up these black things. And ever since last night, I get the feeling that there's something else. Like, when I cough, there's this larger thing trying to come up."

"That certainly sounds bizarre," Kagle said. "Are these black things harming you in any way?"

"No. But the coughing won't stop and I was told to contact you if things got bad."

"Exactly. And I'm glad you've called. But there's nothing I can do about it, I'm afraid. You were exposed to some nasty stuff down there, all of which is still being researched and studied. The best I can do is suggest that you try to bottle one of these things up for me and contact your supervising officer. They'll get it to me. And if things get worse, your supervising officer can have you picked up and brought back to our facility."

"That's it?"

"Yes, George. I'm sorry. But to be quite honest, this is frankly very much over my head. I can prescribe something for the cough, but your own local family doctor could do that much."

"I understand," George said.

But he didn't. When they had examined the three of them after the rescue, there had been a great deal of interest in them. But now they seemed to be nothing more than an afterthought, a necessary sacrifice in the name of discovery.

"Doctor Kagle," he said. "Did you know that Wilkins died? Do you think that maybe what I'm going through killed Wilkins?"

"Wilkins is dead?" Kagle sounded genuinely surprised.

"Yes."

"Who told you this?"

George nearly answered but decided not to at the last moment. Instead, he hung the phone up without saying another word. He sat in his chair and felt his stomach lurch. This time it was stronger, almost insistent. He wondered if this is what it felt like to a woman when a baby turned in the womb.

George signed back into his e-mail. He'd have to take the risk and send KC and e-mail.

He was a bit surprised to see that he had a new mail from KC awaiting him.

He opened the mail and read it. The message was in KC's typical quick and to-the-point fashion.

It needs water.

KC

This led George to two conclusions. The first was that KC was also experiencing this madness. He was keeping the e-mails vague so that anyone that might be spying on them wouldn't be able to immediately figure out what was going on. The second thing George realized was that Kagle was probably lying to him.

Had the doctors sent the three of them home only to die? During the medical exams after the rescue, had the doctors seen something of interest but kept them in the dark about it?

He tried to recover his memories, tried to remember what could have happened in the sub. What had they found in the trench? What had caused the interior of the sub to be caked in blood upon their retrieval?

He had no idea.

It needs water.

George's stomach lurched again. He began to cough and this time he tasted blood right away. It came out of his mouth in a red burst, splattering onto his desk and his pants. His mouth filled with a horde of the tiny black creatures and the noise they made against his teeth was almost like music. He felt them coursing down his chin, riding the flow of his blood as he ran to the bathroom.

His stomach lurched again, almost violently this time. He cried out against the sensation as he leaned over the toilet. He was certain that he would vomit, the churning in his stomach now at an impossible strength.

He hung his head over the bowl and only managed to cough up more blood and the black creatures. But he could feel that other thing, perhaps a larger one of the creatures or maybe just a large amount of bile, riding up the course of his digestive track. With another cough and shudder of his chest, he felt it rise further up into his throat.

He tasted that faint trace of cabbage again, weaker now because of the blood in his mouth. He coughed again and that other thing finally came up his throat, filling his mouth. He felt it on his tongue, something solid, something moving.

Whatever it was, it was crawling.

And it was huge.

George felt like his throat might split in half as the thing made its exit and cut off his wind supply. Forgetting about the toilet, George fell back against the wall, clutching at his throat. He gagged instinctively as the thing continued to crawl forward.

It pushed its way out of his mouth and worked its way down to his shirt where it swung weakly back and forth. George crossed his eyes in an attempt to see it but all he saw was a blur of his own blood. Several wet retching noises came from his throat, but they were choked off and weak.

Fighting for breath, George scrambled to his feet. As he did so, he knocked the towel rack from the wall and wasn't aware of it. All he knew in that moment was that there was something enormous coming out of his mouth, and he couldn't breathe.

He stood in front of the mirror and stared himself down. Had his throat and mouth not been filled with this foreign mass, he would have screamed.

There was a large grey tentacle protruding from his face, hanging out of his mouth like an enormous tongue. Several pucker-like abnormalities seemed to flex along its underside, as if trying to swim.

It poured from his mouth like a vine over the edge of a flower pot. The tentacle ended in a crude point at his chest where it congregated with the carcasses of the small black things. The tentacle swayed from side to side as if looking for something to grasp.

George felt himself on the verge of blacking out. He didn't know if it was from a lack of oxygen or from the shock of seeing something so absurd, but the darkness was coming and he feared that if he didn't do something to ward it off, he may never return to the light.

His first impulse was to run upstairs, grab a knife, and cut the tentacle away. But as he continued to gag, he could feel its length inside of him and he feared that no amount of pulling would free it.

It needs water.

KC's last e-mail didn't make a lot of sense, but he didn't think his friend would lie to him about such a thing. And in light of his current situation, he was willing to try anything.

George stumbled to the bathtub, the muscles in his throat aching. His hands seemed miles away as he cut the water on. The whole time, the tentacle hung from his mouth, filling it completely, its curled end slapping against his shirt.

As soon as the water began to gather in the bottom of the tub, George could feel the tentacle reaching for it. He could feel it all the way down to his gut and imagined the source of the peculiar appendage trying to crawl out of his body.

George climbed into the tub with his clothes on and was amazed to find that the moment the tentacle touched the water, he was able to breathe. He could feel the air entering his nostrils but where it went after that, he wasn't sure. He saw something in the tentacle, almost like a pulse, a widening and then a thinning along its surface that moved in perfect unison with the panicked breaths that he took. A thin whine of despair leaked from the corners of his mouth.

The tentacle rested calmly in the water, floating and drifting effortlessly like a snake while still hanging out of his mouth. As George did his best to get accustomed to his predicament, he studied the tentacle as best as he could. Its underside was white, freckled with spots of red. The little puckers on its underside seemed calm and at ease now, responding to the comfort of the water. A series of ridges and bumps ran horizontally across its glossy surface. Taking all of this in, the tentacle resembled that of a squid.

A brief flash suddenly rushed through his head, a memory of his work in the trench. They had seen hundreds of squid there, most of them small, but a few of them rather gigantic. Hadn't Wilkins commented on how odd it had seemed that after a certain point, the only aquatic life within the trench had been squids? And there was something else too, something that Wilkins had said…he had been a marine biologist, so they had taken everything he'd said as gospel. But damn it, George could hardly remember any of it.

Especially not now, as he lay in his bathtub with a tentacle having erupted from his mouth. He would have wept if he could have mustered the emotional capacity to do so. But as he lay there with water pouring from the faucet, rational thoughts seemed a thing of the past.

He wasn't sure how long he sat in the tub but at some point his wet clothes had started itching, so he took them off. Working his shirt over the tentacle was difficult, but it seemed to know what he was attempting to do. It clung close to his body and did not move as he pulled his shirt off. It moved of its own accord, operating separately from George's body.

Time crawled by slowly and George could feel lunacy creeping up on him. He could actually feel it at the edges of his mind and it brought to mind how a corner of bread would go soggy if left in a bowl of soup.

After several hours, the water turned cold. The tentacle seemed to prefer this. As the water grew colder, it moved more actively and a bit more was freed from George's mouth. When he had originally crawled into the tub, there had been perhaps two feet of it hanging out. Now, roughly four hours later, nearly three and a half feet of it had freed itself.

The corners of his mouth ached to the point where they were nearly numb. His tongue was nothing more than a sore lump trapped under the tentacle. His skull felt as if it was splitting down the middle and his lips felt as if they had been pulled from his skin by pliers.

George considered getting out of the tub and going to the phone, but recalled that he had been unable to breathe when the tentacle had been out of the water. He'd probably suffocate on his way to the phone. And even if he *did* make it to the phone, how was he supposed to say anything?

Forgetting this idea, he simply sat slumped against the porcelain, letting the tentacle explore the bathwater and his body.

It studied his legs, his genitalia, and his chest, where it lingered for an extended period of time.

Somehow, much later, George fell asleep.

When he awoke, it was to a loud crashing from somewhere close by. A series of loud footsteps filled the house like thunder. Someone screamed out, *"Clear,"* and someone else bellowed, *"Move it!"*

George sat up instantly and tried to scream but was, of course, unable to. He looked down to the tentacle and was suddenly alarmed. There was now at least four and a half feet of it taking up the tub. George also saw that hundreds of those small black things were clamoring over the surface of the tentacle, clinging to it even when it was submerged in the water.

George turned towards the open bathroom door as the footsteps grew louder, looking down the hall towards the living room. He watched as several men in body armor entered the hallway and began running towards him. George wondered how these men knew of his situation and then recalled the conversation he had shared with Dr. Kagle. This made sense, and proved his theory that he, as well as KC and Wilkins, had been lied to. The military and their doctors had known that something was wrong with them all along. They had been used to gestate these things.

As he watched the men rush down the hall with guns drawn, he thought of Wilkins and suddenly remembered something he had said inside the sub that had spooked them all.

"That has *to be some mutated species of squid,"* he had told them when they had found a fossilized oddity compacted into the side of the trench. *"Or maybe prehistoric. I'm not sure."*

And then, not too long after that, there had been darkness.

And screaming.

Something had enveloped the sub. Something had...

There had been much more, but it was all nothing more than a bloody blur of terror.

His memories were shattered as three men came into the bathroom with assault rifles raised. George tried to get to his feet but slipped and went splashing into the water. The tentacle seemed aggravated at this and began to churn within the water, splashing in a frenzy. George tried to stand again but was pushed down by one of the soldiers.

"Stay down," the soldier said. He raised the barrel of his rifle to George's head to punctuate this.

A few more men entered the room, all armed and dressed in some sort of dark-colored military fatigues. They parted right away to let two other men inside. These men wore medical garb and carried a large case with them. They knelt on the floor and opened the case. There were scalpels, saws, syringes and vials of fluid packed neatly inside.

George's eyes grew wide and, almost as if following his panic, the tentacle rose from the water and darted out of the tub with incredible speed. It struck one of the doctors squarely in the face and the man's head exploded in a shower of red.

"Hostile actions," one of the soldiers screamed. "Sir, just give the order."

In the half a second between the soldier's request and his superior's answer, the tentacle had found the other doctor. It wrapped around his neck and seemed to pass directly through it. The doctor's head tilted for a moment and then fell to the floor where it rolled to rest at the sink.

"*Fire,*" came the command.

The bathroom was filled with the deafening report of gunfire. George saw the flashes come but they didn't distress him as much as what he felt within his body. He felt the tentacle writhing madly in his stomach, surging forward in all directions within his frame.

It leaped from his mouth with such force that he felt several of his teeth splinter. He felt it trying to find exits within his nose, within his chest, under his navel.

The pain was immense. When George saw a bullet tear into the porcelain of the tub, he prayed that one would take him in the head. He felt the tentacle pushing his intestines aside as it continued to erupt from his mouth.

Seconds later, George's prayer was answered. A bullet hit him squarely in the neck. Almost instantaneously, his mouth was torn open as the tentacle pushed the last of itself out.

Despite the pain, George was fully aware that the tentacle had left his body. Blood poured from a ragged tear in his left cheek but it was the sweetest relief he had ever felt. The thing was finally out.

His body relaxed and sank down, sliding along the bottom of the tub. His chin caught the edge of the tub and his hazy eyes caught glimpses of what was happening as the darkness closed in on him.

The tentacle was its own creature. There was no body to which it was designated, yet the end that George assumed to be its tail looked incomplete, as if there was something much larger to which this monstrosity should be attached.

It looked like a leech when it stood on its own, only much faster and far more deadly. It was about five feet long and moved with a speed that betrayed its appearance. It was covered in glistening mucus that seemed to help it move with impossible speed along the bathroom floor.

George's weakening eyes saw it plow through the soldiers, tearing and squeezing in a blur of blood and gunfire. The tentacle took numerous shots to its body but the holes that tore through it seemed to heal immediately. George saw men torn in half, heard their screams of terror and watched the tentacle in something like awe.

George felt the weight of the rest of his body pulling his head back down into the water that his blood had turned red.

He stared at the ceiling, waiting for the rapidly approaching darkness to take him. The light of the world was fading away, dancing like the sun on water, like the play of light along the hull of the sub.

Wilkins is dead.

This had happened to Wilkins. And if KC had known that the things needed water, then chances were good that he was also dead.

Moments later, George noticed with a dulled realization that the gunshots and screaming had stopped. But somewhere else in his house, something crashed to the floor, followed by the sound of glass breaking—and that was the last thing he heard.

George looked to the bloodied water in the tub and then the darkness swallowed the light.

TWO

Wayne Crosby was on his fifth beer of the evening when the two black vans went speeding down the dirt road in front of his house. He'd been sitting out in the sun, ready to watch the tourists like he did every summer. But he hadn't expected this. He'd never seen vehicles move so quickly down Kerr Lane, the dirt road that connected the majority of the vacation rentals.

The vans kicked up dust, taking the dirt road with treacherous speed. Wayne raised an eyebrow, as well as his beer to his mouth, but didn't bother getting up out of his chair.

This was the first summer of his retirement and he planned to spend a great deal of it on his front porch—probably drunk most of the time—to watch the vacationers come and go. They came every year like clockwork, on the first weekend of summer. Some of the more ambitious ones came before then (usually retirees like himself from upstate) to get ready for a summer at Clarkton Lake.

Twenty years ago, the vacation traffic had been minor. But a few years back, someone had posted a news article on a travel website about the great fishing and quaint small-town charm of Clarkton Lake. And that had been that. The hive-mind of the internet had started and someone's unique experience at the lake had become another generic vacation for families that didn't want to bother with hauling their whining kids to overpopulated beaches.

Wayne watched the black vans pass by, the thick clouds of dust puffing up into the lower-hanging branches of the trees that cradled the road. He sat up in his chair and watched them go barreling further down Kerr Lane. Wayne considered getting in his truck to follow behind them to see what was going on. But he'd had just enough beer to allow his laziness to win out over his curiosity.

As the dust clouds settled, Wayne heard his phone ringing from inside the house. He was tempted to just let it ring but he thought it might be someone else from on the Lane with information about why those black vans were here and in such a hurry.

He got up, giving the dust clouds one last look, and walked inside the small lake house that he had been calling home ever since his wife had walked out five years ago. He left the door standing open, allowing the beautiful June sunshine to spill into the otherwise musty house.

He grabbed the phone on the fifth ring. "Hello?"

"Wayne!" It was the excited voice of Al Crabtree, the only real friend he had left around Clarkton Lake. "What are you doing right now?"

"Calculus," Wayne snapped. "It's the first day of summer. What do you think I'm doing?"

"Same as me," Al said. "On your way to tomorrow's hangover."

"I'm sure your wife is so proud."

"When I drink, it means I leave her alone. Everyone is happy."

"Well, then…cheers. What's up?"

"Did you catch a glimpse of those black vans?" Al asked. "They were hauling ass down your road. I just caught a glimpse of them when I was outside brushing up the horseshoe pit."

"Yeah, I saw 'em. They kicked up a huge cloud of dust."

"Where do you think they were headed?" It was clear by the speed of his voice that Al hadn't been kidding; he was indeed doing the exact same thing Wayne was doing—drinking away the first day of summer.

"Who knows?" Wayne said. "With all of these vacationing people on their way down here, it's probably some emergency cleaning crew or something. Most of the houses on that end of the road are in bad shape."

"I hear that," Al said with a laugh. "So, you want to head out to The Wharf with me tonight?"

"Yeah, I can do that," Wayne said. "But when you start hitting on young girls again, I'm cutting you off and dragging you home."

"Great. That means I'll be in bed by nine o' clock."

"Something else for your wife to be proud of."

"She loves me for my many complexities."

Wayne rolled his eyes. "Bye, Al."

He hung up the phone and walked back out onto his front porch. He reclaimed his seat, killed off his beer, and popped the top on the small cooler at the foot of his chair. He fished another beer out and twisted off the cap. He tossed it into the little silver pail beside the cooler where the caps of his other empties sat waiting for more company.

As he put the bottle to his lips, he thought he heard something in the distance. He thought it was a woodpecker at first, tapping away at a tree, but that didn't seem quite right. He paused, the beer held to his mouth, and concentrated.

There it was again—a hollow popping noise. Fireworks from some kids that were eager to get the summer started, maybe?

The noise came again and then again. He heard it six more times before it stopped. By the time he heard it for the second time, he was pretty sure he knew what it was.

Gunshots.

He took a gulp of his beer and began to feel uneasy. That sound had certainly been more of a gunshot sound than a friendly firecracker noise. On the heels of having seen those black vans racing down Kerr Lane, it suddenly seemed like a particularly nasty noise.

Wayne drove it out of his mind, though. He took his new beer back inside, taking the small cooler with him. He sat on his couch and fell asleep while listening to a John Prine CD.

It wouldn't be until two days later when he'd realize that although he'd easily noticed the black vans racing down Kerr Lane, he never saw them leave.

PART TWO

SUMMERTIME BLUES

THREE

When he caught his first glimpse of the lake, Joe was unimpressed.

He watched it roll by from his seat in the back of his dad's car as they crossed a bridge. The bridge carried them high over the water and while the bridge itself was sort of cool, Joe was not at all moved by the sparkling sunlit landscape. There were a few fishing boats scattered here and there, casting tiny silver glints of sunlight across the water. A single speedboat blazed by with a skier connected to the back. On the tiny speck of shoreline he could see, three boys splashed about in the water.

Everywhere else, though, there were trees, trees, and more trees. They surrounded the lake like some weird barrier and, as far as Joe was concerned, made the lake seem boring.

A muddy lake, and trees. That was it.

Ahead and behind, there was only the rural town of Clarkton. There were boat shops, tractor supply stores, bait and tackle shops, fast-food restaurants, and convenience stores. They were spread out as if each building gave off its own vibe, the brick of each business too scared of the next to get too close. Joe had heard his dad talk about this little town repeatedly over the last month or so as he had tried to get his family excited about their trip…but when it came to Joe, it had fallen on deaf ears.

Beside him, his sister looked out at it all with a wide-eyed fascination. But she was only eight years old. She still thought One Direction was good music and thought there was a fat dude in a red suit that came to see her every Christmas. It didn't take much to fascinate her.

Joe rolled his eyes, still looking out to the rural scene. The sun sat fat and hot in the sky, doing little to enhance the scene. Clarkton Lake looked like any other lake he had ever seen. And that was being generous.

His parents sat in the front, his mother craning her neck to get a better look at a boat that was speeding across the water about one hundred feet below. A slight smile touched her lips.

"It's cute," she said without much enthusiasm.

"Yeah, it's not too bad," his dad said.

This irritated Joe to no end. His dad was usually a pretty straight-laced guy as far as dads went. To see him so desperately trying to make himself like this place was sort of sad. Drew Evans was not the type of person to fake something just to make someone else happy. As his fourteen-year-old son, Joe knew this all too well.

As for his mom...well, Joe knew that she was going to agree with just about anything her husband said while in front of the kids. In his fourteen years under their roof, Joe had pieced that together. But he knew they argued; they just waited until they thought the kids were asleep.

And now here they were, Drew and Amy Evans, a united front trying to sell their children on their family vacation for the summer. Meanwhile, Joe was sitting in the back with his dud of a sister, trying to figure out why his life sucked so much.

He'd had enough. He knew it would probably cause some drama if he opened his mouth, but he was fine with that. It would finally add some flair to what had, so far, been a boring twelve-hour drive from New York.

"Whatever," Joe said. "It looks like a big mud hole."

Joe had never been one to soften his words. His dad had told him that he'd grow out of his smart mouth and that it was something most males suffered from until the age of twenty-five or so.

Beside Joe, his sister made a dramatic show of disgust, shaking her head. "No way," Mackenzie Evans—"Mac" to her friends and family—said. "I think it's cool. Daddy, are you gonna teach me to ski?"

"We'll see, honey," Drew said.

Even Joe knew that their dad had no intentions at all of teaching Mac to ski. She was only eight years old and the thought of getting her out onto the water terrified both of his parents; he could tell by simply looking at their faces every time the topic had been mentioned over the last two weeks or so. Besides, their dad had only driven a boat once before and that had not gone well. Joe knew that this was one of those conversations his folks would have behind closed doors when they thought he and Mac were asleep.

"You can barely ride your new bike," Joe said. "How do you expect to ski?"

"I ride my bike just fine!"

"Yeah, for a crash test dummy."

"Hey," Drew said, peering in the back at them. "Cut it out. Let's not start our vacation like this, okay?"

"This isn't a vacation," Joe said. "This is like a two-month family rehab."

"You're right," Amy said sarcastically. "Maybe A&E will contact us about doing a show."

Joe knew that when his mom started using sarcasm as a defense, it was best to shut up. He puffed out his chest, folded his arms, and looked out of the window again.

Joe saw his dad give him a chagrined look in the rear view before turning his attention back to the lake. Only now, the lake was being hidden by more trees as Drew brought the car to the end of the bridge and came to a stop sign. Joe peered ahead and saw that the trees only grew thicker and thicker.

It was unsettling to know that this was where he'd spend the next two months of his life. Yet hidden behind his angst-laden teenage exterior, he knew that this vacation was sort of necessary for his family. He knew that his dad had ultimately rented a lake cabin in Clarkton for a low-profile vacation that would hopefully help bring their family closer together. With the turmoil and infighting they'd been working through in the last few months, it was certainly needed.

But if his first impression of Clarkton Lake was any indication, Joe didn't know it was going to work. More than that, he had a feeling that it was going to be the sort of environment that was going to set his parents off. Isolated and out in the middle of nowhere, Joe didn't see how they were going to make it out alive. He knew that they had been bickering lot lately but, of course, he hadn't let them know that he was on to them.

Still looking out of the window, Joe watched his dad pull out the sheet of paper that his agent had given him just before they had left town. Joe had read it a few times himself during the long drive down here. He'd read it over and over again, trying to envision where directions like the ones his dad was following might lead them.

Joe recited them in his head as his dad read them from the driver's seat. *At stop sign, turn left. Look for dirt road on right two miles ahead. Turn.*

Drew came to the stop sign in question and took a left. For a moment, the lake was completely blocked from their view by a copse of trees. As drove down the thin, unmarked road for two miles, Joe noticed the forest growing thicker all around them.

Joe suddenly found it very easy to imagine a series of rough dirt roads winding through the trees and leading to only God knew where. His mind conjured up serial killer scenarios or maybe a horror movie type thing where rednecks and inbred country folks would assault them with machetes and pitchforks.

As the trees grew thicker and the road became darkened by their shadows, the entire Evans family went silent. Joe didn't know if it was because they were instantly uncomfortable with their surroundings or if it was the calm before the storm, a warning of an impending argument.

Never one to handle silence well, Joe responded to it in the only way he knew.

"This stinks. My iPhone doesn't even have any service out here," he said, pulling his phone from his pocket. "Look...I have two bars. Now one. Nope, now two again...and back to one."

"My God," Drew said. "How will Facebook ever operate without the insights of a fourteen year old to keep it lively?"

"I *would* like to call some of my friends this summer, you know," Joe said.

"I know," Drew said. "Look, we'll get it figured out. Let's just give it a chance before you get upset."

Joe frowned but he was secretly hopeful. There was something in his dad's voice that indicated that he wasn't a huge fan of this vacation so far, either.

It had all sprung out of Joe discovering that his parents had been discussing a divorce. He'd overheard a heated conversation one night while sitting halfway down the stairs (something he did to sneakily watch *Game of Thrones* since his parents wouldn't let him watch it) and had not taken it well. He'd started acting out in school, doing incredibly stupid things like spray-painting a penis in the girl's locker room and being intentionally rude to his teachers.

Joe had gone so far as to tell Mackenzie what may potentially be happening to their parents but she had ignored him. She had responded by informing Joe that their parents were like the princes and princesses in Disney movies and that divorce was an ugly and stupid thing.

Joe found her attitude towards this both naïve and irritating. It was one of the many reasons he thought his little sister might have a legitimate mental condition.

The dirt road that had been called out in the directions—Kerr Lane—appeared as if by magic to the right. When Drew turned onto it, the car bucked a bit. Joe watched as his sister peered out to it all like a girl that had been sucked into a fairytale. All she had ever seen were the crowded streets and buildings of Manhattan (with the exception of their Disney vacation two years ago), so Drew was sure that driving down a dirt road must be surreal to her. Joe had seen similar wooded area during camp for the last two years, so he wasn't all that impressed.

Well, maybe not *entirely* impressed. While he'd never let either of his parents know his real thoughts, there *was* something sort of cool and ominous about the overhanging branches scraping at the roof of the car and how the woods seemed to go on forever.

Maybe this is going to turn out alright, after all, Joe thought.

Immediately after that thought, the car struck a small rut and he let out a surprised shout. His mom laughed at him but he saw that she was sitting rigid in her seat. She looked like she was strapped into a roller coaster rather than the same car the Evans family had owned for the last six years.

Finally, after what felt like forever, Joe saw the house for the first time. The boyhood wonder in him loved it at once, but the anger-ridden teen hated it. It was marked by a simple wooden plank that was bolted into a pine tree, boasting a simple painted 31 to mark the address. His view cleared a bit when his dad pulled the car into the thin driveway. There was no gravel on the driveway— just dirt and fallen pine needles. Joe studied the house with a skeptical eye, trying to imagine himself living here for eight weeks.

From the passenger seat, Amy Evans mother responded predictably. "Isn't it charming?" she asked in a sugar-coated way that made Joe wonder if she was being genuine or making some underhanded jab at her husband.

"What is this?" Joe said. "Some painting in an old woman's house?"

"Zip it," Drew said, killing the engine.

Slowly, the Evans family unloaded from the car. Mac wasted no time in running around the shaded yard, kicking up dust and pine needles. Meanwhile, Joe leaned defiantly against the side of the car, scrolling with this thumb on his iPhone. He could feel his dad's eyes on him but was pretty sure the old man wouldn't say anything to him. Joe knew his dad did not want to start an argument so soon after getting here. And he was right—his dad took his mom by the hand and they walked to the house, ignoring his defiance completely.

With his parents turned away from him, Joe took a chance to check the place out. The house was actually very quaint but he still stood by his original thought; given the wooded lot and the cabin-like appearance of the house, it *did* look like something from a painting in an old woman's house or a dentist's office. Looking at it, Joe felt like he was actually standing in a painting. It didn't seem real to him. He was used to the business of New York City, the buildings and the foot traffic, the honking and the chatter.

This was like another world. There was a crispness to this place, a rich earthy smell that he had never experienced before. There was a trace of grilling meat in the air, wafting on the slight summer breeze from one of the other summer homes along the road.

It's not so bad, Joe thought. *But I bet it'll get boring really fast.*

He sighed and watched his parents heading for the porch. Joe wondered how long he'd be able to get away with being a smart-ass. He'd seen his dad go from chill to berserk in a few seconds but Joe didn't think he'd do such a thing on vacation...would he?

"When will the truck get here?" Mac asked, coming alongside her parents and taking her mother's free hand. "I want my toys!"

"In about two hours," Drew said.

"So that gives us plenty of time to check the place out," Amy said, leading Mac towards the house.

As they neared the front porch—complete with a porch swing that looked like it might collapse if a fly landed on it—Mac gasped. She clapped her hands together and started cheering. Joe was curious as to what had made her so happy, but then she pointed towards the back of the house and he saw it.

To the right of the house, snaking out from the back porch, was a thin dirt track bordered by stones. It wound down a slight hill where it then disappeared. Beyond this drop in the ground, Joe saw the lake glimmering through the trees. A small floating dock sat at the edge of the property on a tiny crescent of beach.

"Is that *ours?*" Mac asked, jumping with excitement. Her little blonde curls bounced on her shoulder and she looked eerily like her mother as she smiled widely.

"For the next two months, yes," Drew said.

"Awesome," she yelled.

Joe, finally joining them as they climbed the porch steps, said nothing. He looked out to the lake and the faintest trace of interest bloomed in his eyes. He noticed that his dad was looking and instantly wiped the interest from his face. They shared an awkward little glance that fell flat in the midst of Mac's enthusiasm for the lake.

Drew reached into his pocket and took out the key that the realtor had snail mailed him a week ago. He inserted it into the old brass lock on the front door and turned it. With that, the Evans family officially began their summer vacation.

FOUR

Joe knew that he had to tread carefully. Was he excited to be away from home, spending two months in the backwoods of Virginia? Surprisingly, yes. There was something cool about it that he couldn't quite describe. Maybe it was the sense of isolation—knowing that the nearest stoplight or glass-covered multi-story building was hundreds of miles away. Whatever it was, something about the idea had appealed to him from the very first moment his dad had brought up the idea.

But there was no way he was going to let his parents know this. As far as he was concerned, he was going to do everything he could to make this vacation miserable for them. It was bratty thing to do and he felt like such a clichéd teenager by doing it, but he thought it was his duty nonetheless. He'd miss most of the summer with his friends, and that *was* a legitimate complaint. But other than that…this might not be too bad.

Unlike Mac, he was pretty sure knew the real purpose behind the vacation. Well, actually, there were two reasons behind it. The one that his dad was pushing very hard was that he had landed a great job scoring an independent film that was already getting great positive buzz. He was going to use these two months in the wilderness as inspiration to get the score done. He talked about it a lot, sometimes going so far as to ramble on and on about it even when it was clear that no one was listening. This, Joe knew, meant that it was something that his father was actually excited about. And *excited* was something that he rarely saw from his father.

But then there was a second reason: there was something wrong with his parents. He'd heard them talking about divorce and had noticed how they didn't talk as much as they used to. He wasn't sure *why* his parents were getting a divorce. He didn't think either of his parents had it in them to have an affair and he was pretty sure their finances weren't at the root of it. In fact, from what he

23

had gathered, his dad's recent contract with for this film score had put them in a pretty great spot as far as money went.

He supposed *that* could be the cause of the turmoil. He'd heard his dad talking about maybe moving to California where he'd be better connected and there would maybe be more opportunities for his work. And when he had mentioned it, his mother had shut him down. Joe knew they had tons of conversations in private, and he'd never heard an extended version of this argument—just a few muffled complaints from his roost on the stairs late at night.

So maybe the one mention he'd heard about divorce wasn't anything to be too worried about. Maybe, he hoped, this trip was to squash their feelings about a potential divorce. Joe certainly hoped that was the case. He liked his parents and although it pained him to admit it, they were really good together.

Whatever the real reason for the divorce-talks might be, all Joe knew for sure was that it meant that he and Mac had a rough and awkward summer ahead of them if things didn't go well between their folks.

Joe thought it was selfish of them. But then again, he also knew that there was much about marriage and being an adult that he didn't understand.

For instance...if this trip to Clarkton Lake for the summer was indeed a thinly veiled attempt at his parents reconciling their differences, how did they plan to get any talking done with both of their kids around all of the time? If they had been dumb enough to bring their kids along while trying to patch things up, Joe thought they deserved a little hostility from their teenage son.

He gathered up more hostility when he saw that the cabin only had two bedrooms. He stood in front of the door of the bedroom he and Mac had been assigned, staring hard at his little sister as she set her stuffed animals up on the bed along the right wall.

"You're kidding me, right?" Joe said loudly, making sure his parents heard him.

His mom came up behind him and gave him her best smile. "A problem?" she asked.

"You didn't tell me I was going to have to share a room with her," he said coldly.

"It's your sister," she said. "It's two months. You'll survive."

"This sucks," Joe said.

Mac turned to him, a pink and purple stuffed elephant in her arms. "I'm not thrilled about sharing a room with you, either," she said. She stuck out her tongue to emphasize this point.

"This *sucks,"* Joe said again and stomped away.

He stormed through the cabin, using it as an excuse to check the place out. Truth be told, it was sort of awesome. The front door opened up on a large living area that was decked out with a huge flat screen TV that was mounted over a fireplace. The door to the master bedroom sat beyond the fireplace. Joe had only peeked in there and saw that it was huge. But he didn't take the time to check the master bedroom out because he found it creepy to pay much attention to where his parents would be sleeping together.

A wide hallway connected the living room and a kitchen that looked out onto a gorgeous view of the lake. The bedroom that he and Mac would be sharing for eight straight weeks sat along this hallway. When he passed it, he cast a scowling glance into the room where Mac and their mom were putting away Mac's clothes. He hurried away and entered the kitchen, admiring the immaculately clean marble countertops.

Joe stood at the kitchen table and looked through the picture window. He took in the sight of the lake and the endless trees that bordered it. He had said the lake looked like a big mud hole when they had arrived, but the fact of the matter was that he couldn't wait to get his swimming trunks on and head down to that dock.

I don't know if I'm going to be able to fake this mad crap much longer, he thought as he looked down across the back yard and to the water beyond. *Maybe I should just suck it up and actually enjoy it all. Maybe we could actually have a great vacation.*

It was a tempting thought. But if he didn't have some sort of chip on his shoulder about being away from his friends for two months while his parents sorted out their stupid issues, who would? Again, that sense of stubborn teenage duty gave him a reassuring pat on the back.

"What are you thinking about?"

Joe jumped a little and turned to find his dad standing in the entrance to the kitchen. He was looking out to the same scenery as

Joe. He wore a smile that was both sincere and tired at the same time.

"This isn't so bad," Joe said softly. He didn't care if his dad knew how he felt…not really. But there was no way he wanted Mac to hear.

"Glad to hear it," Drew said and stepped forward. He rustled his son's hair and gave him a lazy one-armed hug as they stood together and looked out towards the lake.

"I know you have questions about what you heard me and your mom talking about a few weeks ago," Drew said. He spoke quietly and confidentially. It made Joe feel older, like someone that his father respected.

"What?" Joe asked, feigning shock.

"The stairs creak, kiddo. We know you come down to listen to *Game of Thrones*. And every now and then, we know when you're there, listening to us talk."

Joe looked to the floor, mortified.

"It's okay," his dad said. "So anyway…you have questions, yes?"

"Yeah. I do."

"You're a smart kid and I'm sure you want to know *why*. At some point, we'll talk to you about it while we're here."

Joe nodded. "Do you think you're going to….you know. Are you going to get one?"

"No," Drew said. "My work has gotten unexpectedly huge all of a sudden and there's a lot to deal with. More money, more duties, and different goals between us. Really, it's a good problem to have but…well, it's still a problem. But we're hoping this trip will reveal some things for us"

"Like what?"

Drew only shrugged. It was a shrug that Joe had seen a lot over the last three or four years. It was his dad's answer to just about everything. Joe had come to realize that it wasn't an *I don't know* shrug, but an *I don't want to talk about it anymore* shrug.

As if timed perfectly to help get his father out of an uncomfortable conversation, a loud horn honked from the front of the house. It sounded strange to Joe, hearing such a loud horn blast without the usual mix of congested traffic and towering buildings to all sides.

"That must be the U-Haul," Drew said. "Lend me a hand, would you?"

"Sure, Dad," Joe said.

He started walking away before his dad could say anything else. It was just as well; Joe didn't feel like talking about it right now, either. They had all summer to obsess over their family's problems. What was the point in unpacking them all right now?

They walked outside where two men were already at the back of the U-Haul, pulling out the ramp. For the next forty minutes, Joe helped his dad haul in the few boxes of things they had packed for the summer. It was just hot enough to work up a sweat and the shade of the trees in the yard provided some additional comfort.

As they finished up, watching the truck pull back out into the dusty road, Joe realized that the forty minutes they had spent unloading the truck was the most uninterrupted time he had spent with his dad in several months.

He looked out to the lake and felt his father standing beside him. Without a gesture or a single word shared, Joe felt close to him. It was a guy thing, Joe thought—the ability to communicate a job well done in absolute silence.

A smile touched his lips. It was an unfamiliar feeling, but he welcomed it past the false wall he had placed around the feelings for his family.

Maybe, Joe thought. *Maybe this summer won't be so bad after all.*

FIVE

Wayne had grown up in rural Virginia and had long ago grown accustomed to the music of long country summers. Near the lake, that music consisted of the distant insect-like hum of speed boats on the water, the ghostly noise of children laughing from deeper down the lanes where the summer rentals were packed in, and the rustling sounds of the forest.

But as of late, especially since he had become good friends with Al, there was another noise that defined his summers. It was the distinct *clink* of a horseshoe striking the post after he'd thrown it. The exasperated sigh coming from Al made the *clink* that much sweeter.

Currently, Wayne was enjoying that sound as he rang up his fifth ringer of the afternoon. He raised up his hands in victory (one clasping a lukewarm can of beer) to celebrate his third win of the day.

"It doesn't seem right," Al said from his post. "You seem to get better the more you drink."

"It's like that with bowling, too," Wayne said. "It's always been that way."

"Remind me to never go bowling with you, then."

"Losing hurts, huh?"

"Shut up."

Wayne and Al had settled into a routine over the last five years. When Wayne's wife had walked out on him right around that same time, he had become something of a staple at Al's house. Kathy, Al's wife, had taken it in stride, understanding that Wayne needed a friend in his time of pain. But Wayne had quickly taken to the bottle, something he had done earlier in his life and had easily run back to within a month of his wife leaving.

Because Kathy was too kind-hearted to say anything and Al didn't have many friends since retiring two years before, she hadn't made too much of a fuss about Wayne hanging around so much. For the most part, Wayne did a good job of recognizing boundaries. But when summer came, he tended to drink more than usual and there were plenty of days where Wayne and Al were in their own little world. The boundaries he usually recognized became only blurred lines that could be easily pushed. Wayne was well aware of this and he wondered just how long Kathy was going to put up with him.

Most days, it wasn't so bad. Wayne and Al were usually either playing horseshoes in the pit behind Al's house or sitting on Wayne's porch watching the vacationer's amble up and down the road. On occasion, they'd take Al's little speed boat out to one of the nearby coves to catch fish and gossip like old women.

Wayne was well aware that Kathy often kept a close eye on him. He didn't know if she simply didn't care for him or if she worried that his influence would rub off on Al. He didn't blame her; he knew that Al and Kathy had a strong marriage and had always been close. To Kathy, he was really just like the neighborhood kid that came by far too often to ask if Al could come out and play. He caught glimpses of her spying on them through the kitchen window or around the corner of the house while she was in the back yard, tending to her little vegetable garden. But he'd never mentioned this to Al. No sense in causing drama about it.

"Another round?" Al asked, picking the horseshoes up from the pit.

"Sure," Wayne said. He took a sip from his can of beer and picked up the horseshoes on his end. "I can stay sober enough to destroy you one more time."

With the shoes picked up, they took their positions by their respective ends of the horseshoe pit. Wayne, having won the last round, went first. On his first throw, the horseshoe clipped the side of the post and lay in the sand beside it. Al instantly tossed the second one and it made that delightful *clink* sound as it wrapped the pole.

"Now we're getting somewhere," Al said, clapping.

Wayne threw his next horseshoe, but without much interest. It landed in the sand in front of the pole, a few inches shy of scoring a point.

"Do you remember those black vans we saw?" he asked out of nowhere.

"Yeah," Al said. "Did you ever find out what that was all about?"

"No. But the vans are parked in front of a house down on Kerr Lane. Second one from the very end of the road."

"That's a rental, right?"

"Sort of. That's the one that belongs to George Galworth. He rarely rents it out. It's a nice little house."

"And the vans are there? Have they been there since we saw them?"

"Yup."

"How long ago was that? Four days?"

"Yeah," Wayne said, taking a break to finish off his can of beer. "I saw them yesterday when I went down that way just riding around."

"Just riding around or trying to check out the pretty ladies on vacation?"

Wayne shrugged. "Six of one, half a dozen of the other."

"Those weren't plain old vans, were they?" Al asked.

"I didn't stop and look," Wayne said. "They're parked really close to the house, and the yard has a slope to it. But no, they didn't look like plain old vans. It looked almost like one of those newer FedEx vans, you know?"

"Locals?"

Wayne shook his head. "I don't think so. They had Virginia license plates, but I'm pretty sure they were government plates."

"That's weird."

"I thought so, too.

Al absently started taking his turn, tossing his horseshoes in lazy underhanded lobs. His mind, like Wayne's, was elsewhere now. After he threw his second turn, he looked to the left, towards the woods that hid away Kerr Lane.

"Probably just some guys from an environmental agency to check the water levels and crap," Al said.

"Maybe," Wayne said. "But don't you remember how fast they were going when they went through here?"

Al nodded, gripping the third horseshoe in his hand, all but forgotten now."I'm sure it'll be in the paper or something," he said.

Wayne didn't say anything. He set his empty can down by two others along the wooden planks that surrounded the post. He looked up to Wayne's porch and thought he saw Kathy looking out at them through the kitchen window.

He jumped a bit when a loud and unexpected *clink* filled the air. He looked down and saw that Al had tossed his third horseshoe and landed a ringer.

"Lucky shot," Wayne said.

"Not lucky. The word you're looking for is *skilled*."

They carried on with their game as the afternoon sun started to creep down towards the tree line. On occasion, they would look in the direction of Kerr Lane and get a certain thoughtful look in their eyes. It was a look that meant the same thing on all men, be it young mischievous boys or older retired men with nothing much to occupy their time.

It was a look that spoke of a curiosity that would not be satisfied until at least a little bit of trouble had been stirred up.

SIX

Five days after the Evans family had unpacked most of their belongings and the U-Haul was unloaded, Joe walked down to the dock behind the house for the first time. While he had done his best to remain grouchy and overbearing, he had found it not worth the effort. Besides, after five days of staring at it through the windows of the house—especially when Mac and his mom were splashing in a raft around the dock—it started to itch at him. There was only so much temptation a fourteen-year-old boy could take.

There was, of course, his mood to deal with. Several moments before he finally caved in and headed down to the water, he had been sitting at the kitchen table and looking through the window. Down on the lake, Mac and his mom were splashing lazily in the water.

Joe was holding his iPhone, reading and re-reading a single message over and over: DEVILSGUT! TONIGHT! ALREADY GOT THE TIX, SUCKA!

The text was from his best friend back home, a boy that neither of his parents cared for. They didn't care for Ricky Marshall because he was sixteen and had gotten Joe into the thrash metal scene. Because of Ricky's influence, Devilsgut was Joe's favorite band. He had downloaded everything they had ever released and often walked around the house growling the lyrics to songs like "Blood Bath" and "Parasite Alley." When they toured, though, it was usually on the stupid West Coast. They never came east.

Except for now. They were playing New York City tomorrow night, in a venue that was less than half an hour away from Joe's house.

And here he was, stuck at this stupid lake with his stupid family. To Joe, it almost seemed like he wasn't meant to enjoy this trip. Every time he talked himself into giving it a chance, something like this happened.

Joe read the text message again and then set the phone on the table, screen-side down. He stared back out the window and watched as his mom playfully threatened to tip Mac's raft over. The late morning sun sparkled in the water behind them. He could hear Mac's gleeful squeals through the glass and the itch to get down there and at least try to have some fun grew stronger.

With a thin smile, he shoved his pride aside and stood up from the table. He ran into the room that he and Mac shared and slid on a pair of swimming trunks. As he did, he could hear the soft hum of a synth noise filling the cabin. It sounded like wind coming from the far corner of the living room—the area his father had elected to set up his workspace. This was followed by a melody on his dad's keyboard that he had been toying with all morning. Hearing that keyboard did Joe a world of good. Back in their home in New York, the sounds of his dad at play on his keyboard had often carried Joe into sleep.

For some people, it was rain. For Joe, there was no better sound to fall asleep to than his father striking the keys and crafting a story with music. He was smiling again as he listened to his father's music and tied the elastic strings of his swim trunks.

"Dad," he yelled out as he ran for the back door on the other side of the kitchen. "I'm going out with Mom and Mac!"

"Have fun," his dad called back. He spoke as if he had been programmed to do so. He had always been great about remaining attentive when he was behind the keyboard, but his voice was usually flat and emotionless when he spoke.

Joe went out the back door, down the back porch steps and across the yard. He was still overwhelmed by the very presence of so much nature everywhere. Back home, he'd had to walk a few blocks to the nearest park just to get in a game of football with his friends. He couldn't imagine living in a place where you could walk outside and have ample space to do whatever you wanted without the risk of getting hit by a taxi or a bus.

It was nice, although he was hesitant to admit it—even to himself. He was pretty sure he would never be able to live in a place like this (hell, the two months they planned to stay here was pushing it), but he was quickly growing enamored with the forest.

He made his way down the flagstone path that led to the dock. When he stepped on it, Mac and his mom looked up at him in surprise.

"I'm glad you decided to join us," his mom said. She was wearing her sunglasses, lifting them up above her eyebrows and squinting at him.

"Yeah," Mac said as she reclined on her circular float. "I didn't think you were ever going to—"

Joe took two running strides along the dock and launched himself into the air. As he came down, he hugged his knees to his chest. He splashed down into the water with a perfect cannonball. He missed Mac's float by less than a foot and he felt her splashing into the water beside him, the float having tipped over.

He came up to find his mother giving him a scowl as Mac started angrily slapping at the water, trying to grab on to the edge of her float.

"You turd," she screamed as she pulled herself up. She sounded angry but it was apparent by the look on her face that she had enjoyed it.

"At least turds float," Joe said back as he swam a few feet away from the float. "Well, some *do* sink to the bottom. Like you, I guess."

Mac looked confused but was snickering at the topic of the current conversation.

"Can we not talk like that, please?" Amy asked her children.

Joe swam to the front of the dock and hung on to it. He was surprised at how refreshing and cool the water was. Yes, it *did* look muddy and discolored, especially around the wooden frame of the dock. But it wasn't as bad as he had been expecting. He pushed himself away from the dock and swam over to where Mac was once again in her float.

He began twirling the float around slowly, making her giggle. He looked over and saw a smile of approval and delight on his mother's face. It was a look that he had fawned over ever since kindergarten when he'd brought home his first assignment with a big red check in the top corner. The smile within that look reminded Joe just how pretty his mom was.

He thought briefly about the text message from Ricky Marshall and was surprised to find that most of the sting of it wasn't there anymore.

"How are you doing, Joe?" his mom asked from her float.

"Good."

"No more brooding?"

"No. I don't think so."

She gave him that smile again and then reclined her head back, relaxing and letting the sun soak into her skin.

Joe kept his eyes on her for a bit longer and tried to recall the last time he had seen his mother in a state where she had been able to relax. In the few months leading up to their trip to Clarkton Lake, he'd seen her angry and depressed far too often. To see her like this right now did him more good than he was able to understand.

"Faster!"

Joe snapped out of his thoughts at his sister's demands to be spun faster in her float. Joe obliged, listening to her peals of laughter. Within seconds, he was laughing right along with her, the sun shining down and the lake glistening in little sparks of afternoon sunlight all around them.

SEVEN

Scott Miles pulled his black sedan in beside the pair of vans and killed the engine. He looked to the house in front of him before getting out. From where he was parked, he could see the front door. The house had no porch, but one of those quaint little archways covering the front door. This one was made of pine posts and an arching row of stone-colored bricks.

The front door was closed but the doorknob was loose, hanging down slightly. This wasn't something that could be seen from the road, especially considering the row of trees that separated the front yard from the dirt road behind him.

Scott opened his door and stepped out. He approached the first black van and then the second. He performed a quick search of each one and found the exact same thing in each van. They were spotless and nearly featureless. There were no belongings in the glove compartment, not even a vehicle registration. In the back of each one there was a tiny cot-like stretcher. Twin straps hung from each one, hanging down away from the starch white sheet that covered the thin mattress.

Scott turned away from the vans and made his way to the house. He walked along the sidewalk as if he belonged there, maybe someone that wanted to rent this quaint little lakeside cabin for a few weeks. He'd seen only one vehicle on the road since turning off from the main highway and onto the winding series of dirt tracks that spread through the forests around Clarkton Lake. There was no real risk of being seen. And even if he was spotted, all he had to do was flash the badge he carried in his front pocket.

Scott was dressed in jeans and a simple button-down shirt, not in the usual suit and tie get-up the bureau usually had him wear on assignment. He had known from the start that this assignment was different, so he was letting himself enjoy the assignment as much as he could. Part of that included not having to wear the monkey suit.

The *bad* thing about this assignment was that it dealt with something truly bizarre. This was not the usual murder investigation or some underhanded back-room drama to cover up. He could handle those things all day, and he could handle them well.

But this was different...and therefore, he welcomed it.

Scott came to the front door of the cabin. When he reached out to push it open with his left hand, his right hand went to his service pistol. He withdrew his Sig Sauer P220 and inched inside, pushing the door open. As it eased open, the top hinge shrieked slightly. He looked up and saw that the hinge had been popped out from the side of the door. Whoever had come in here had done so with tremendous force. From the looks of the door, a battering ram had not been used. It had been good old strength—probably a well-delivered kick that had popped the front door open like a tin can.

He had been expecting to enter George Galworth's house to instantly see signs of a slaughter. But as he walked inside the front door and into the foyer, he saw nothing of the sort. The house was clean and quite cool. The only thing that unsettled Scott was the staleness in the air and the sheer quiet of everything.

He'd been told to expect the worst and that was exactly what he was waiting for as he took several steps across the foyer and into a short but wide hallway. A large den sat to his left, but he paid it no attention. Looking ahead, he saw the first signs of trouble.

The hallway stopped at a T-intersection in front him. There, protruding from behind the wall on the right, was someone's arm. The arm was dressed in a black sleeve, the hand wearing the type of glove that covered everything but the fingers. Scott saw that the fingers were permanently curled.

He quietly approached the end of the hallway, his eyes still on that arm. When he came to the corner, he swept around it, holding his gun out at chest level.

That's when he saw the carnage he had been expecting.

For starters, the arm he had seen was just that—an arm. It had been severed from its body, which was lying in a pool of dried blood a few feet away. Six other bodies lay strewn about around it.

They were all dressed in black outfits that resembled SWAT gear. Military-grade automatic rifles were scattered along the floor, one of which looked as if it had been saturated in blood.

A cloud of flies hovered over the bodies, up and down from the blood-drenched bodies and then into the air.

Scott tried to look past the bodies and towards the room that sat a few feet in front of the bloodbath. As he looked that way, his eyes locked on the face of one of the dead men. His face was frozen in a state of terror, his eyes wide and his jaw set. Whatever had killed him had done it very quickly. Gauging from the look of the man, that death had come in the form of a severely traumatic wound to the chest and neck. His head was barely attached to the rest of his body.

Scott had to take a moment to gather himself. It was by far the grisliest scene he had come across during his decade with the FBI. Even in the last three years, when he had been promoted to the hush-hush position of a "clean-up man," he hadn't seen anything this bad.

Once he had his wits about him, he crept through the carnage as best he could. There was no way to avoid stepping in the blood and he almost had to literally jump over one of the corpses.

Scott came to the room at the end of the hall, the doorway of which was partially blocked by the final mangled corpse. The blood from this body trailed out onto the floor of the bathroom beyond, mostly dried on the white tile.

When he looked into the bathroom, it took Scott's eyes a moment to understand what he was seeing.

There was blood everywhere. It was on the walls, on the ceiling, splattered over the toilet, and covering all of the white porcelain of the tub. There was a body inside the tub, collapsed back against the far right corner where a few bottles of shampoo floated in water that looked like cherry Kool-Aid.

This, Scott assumed, was George Galworth.

The lower part of his face was dislodged from the rest. His jaw had been pulverized and hung down like hot taffy. The corners of his mouth had been torn and a few of his teeth looked like they had exploded from his gums. As Scoot took in the scene, he saw a fragment of one of these teeth standing out in the maroon coating along the tile floor.

"My God," Scott breathed.

If there were any clues to be found in the bathroom, he wasn't going to be able to find it in all of this blood. Besides...based on what he knew about what had happened here, it seemed clear to Scott that whatever had been resting in George's body had come out.

He also knew that there had been seven agents that had come to retrieve the thing that had been in George's body. The seven massacred bodies behind him in George's hallway told him that the mission had been a failure and there were no survivors.

That, of course, left the obvious question: what exactly had killed these men and where was it now?

Scott's instructions had been clear. He was to find out why the team had not reported back and, if there were casualties and the *specimen* was missing, he was supposed to find it. His priorities were to capture it alive but, if that wasn't possible, to kill it.

Looking back to the seven dead agents behind him, Scott wasn't sure that was going to be so easy.

He looked beyond the dead men and the mess around them, looking down the hall. He saw a few streaks of blood further down, smeared on the wooden floor. He managed his way back around the bodies, passed the place where the hallway broke into the T-intersection, and walked further into the house. He looked down to the smears of blood and saw that they didn't seem to be just random splotches of blood that had been strewn during the melee in the bathroom.

There was a pattern to it—a shape, almost.

He followed the streaks down the hallway and into a modestly sized kitchen. On the tiled kitchen floor, it was easier to see the movement and motion to the streaks. To Scott, it looked as if something had been dragged across the floor. Or, based on what he knew of this peculiar case, something had likely crawled or slithered across the floor.

The streaks went around the kitchen island a few times and then seemed to head in the direction of an elaborate screened-in back porch that was connected to the kitchen through a door that stood open. Scott walked out onto the porch and lost track of the blood streaks. The porch was carpeted and decorated with expensive patio furniture.

A single screen door led off of the porch and to a small wooden walkway that led down to the back yard. Beyond the yard, there was an unobstructed view of the lake. A single dock sat on a small crescent of beach. A speed boat was tied to it, bobbing in the water.

Scott started for the door to the walkway outside and stopped mid-stride. He looked to the door and saw what he had feared the most.

A hole had been torn in the bottom of the door's screen. The hole was about eight inches in length and equally tall. The screen was shredded around it, suggesting that something had torn its way out.

The door was locked from the inside, making that hole seem all the more dangerous. Looking out to the wooden walkway, Scott unlatched the lock. He stepped outside and looked for any signs that whatever had made the streaks on the floor inside had been out here. The wood along the walkway seemed to be untouched. There wasn't a single streak of blood anywhere to be seen.

This, of course, meant nothing. Whatever had torn its way through the agents and exited George Galworth's house had probably managed to lose all traces of its victims' blood while crawling around on the floor.

The ground beneath the wooden walkway was made up of well-maintained grass. If anything had wound through it recently, there were no signs.

The walkway ended in a series of three steps that led onto a small trail. This trail led out to the segment of beach twenty feet further out. Scott checked the stairs (even peering under them) and made his way down the trail, but there was no sign of—well, of *what,* he wasn't sure.

He made his way down to the water, walking out onto George Galworth's dock, and looked out onto the lake. The afternoon was bright, the water sparkling and tranquil.

He vaguely knew what he was up against. He had been sent a brief file on the case along with his explicit instructions. Part of that file had been the intercepted e-mails that George Galworth had sent out and received on the day the agents had been dispatched to the lake house.

The contents of one of those mails haunted Scott has he stared out at the lake.

It needs water.

That mail had been sent to George Galworth from KC Doughtry. And thinking of what it implied sent a chill through Scott as he stared out to the huge lake before him.

The report had told Scott that Clarkton Lake covered an area of a little less than ninety square miles. So there was plenty of water, that was for sure.

The question that made Scott uneasy was what, exactly, was he looking for.

He left the dock and headed back up the yard, across the walkway and back to the porch. He looked through the kitchen door, thinking of the bodies just down the hall.

He pulled his cellphone from his pocket and pulled up a number he didn't want to call. It rang only once before the other end was answered.

"Yeah?" came a voice that Scott had come to hate over the years. It was the voice of Roger Lowry, his direct supervisor. Roger was the type that held his position over those beneath him with an abundance of cockiness and fabricated power. The ideas of compassion and leading by example never seemed to cross Roger Lowry's mind.

"I'm here," Scott said. "And it's bad."

"The agents?"

"All dead."

"And George Galworth?"

"Deader than the rest."

"And what about the specimen?"

Scott paused a beat here, letting the conversation slow down. Roger had a bad habit of running a conversation at such a high speed that Scott would often end up confused and frustrated. From what he had seen in George's house so far, he knew that either of those emotions could make things harder than they had to be.

"Gone," Scott said. "Nowhere to be found."

"Well, then," Roger said, as if discussing how the weather had negatively impacted his plans to play a round of golf. "I suggest you find it pretty damn quick."

"I don't even know what I'm looking for."

"We're getting information as soon as it comes to us," Roger said. "Right now, we know just about the same as you. Whatever it is, it needs water to live. And it's highly likely that it is the same type creature that killed most of George's crew on that submarine. As soon as I get new information, you'll be the first to know."

"Okay."

"Anything else?" Roger asked, clearly annoyed that he was being questioned.

"No. Got it."

"Good. Now go find this thing."

"Yes, sir," Scott said, looking back out to the lake.

But the other line was already dead.

EIGHT

It would be another three months before Joe would turn fifteen, but he was pretty sure he was finally starting to understand how the family dynamic worked. When he was being a gigantic dick to his family, he tended to get treated like a child. There had been times in the past where it had seemed that Mac had gotten more freedoms than he had just because she was a genuinely sweet and kindhearted child.

On the other hand, when he actually acted his age and stopped being so difficult, his parents treated him with something very much like respect. They gave him more freedom and treated him almost as an equal.

He'd sensed it ever since he had spent so much time with Mac down at the lake yesterday afternoon. His mother had warmed to him instantly. Then, over dinner, the entire family had all sat on the back porch, looking out to the lake over grilled hamburgers. There had been much laughter, and they had all enjoyed each other in a way that rarely happened.

That was why he had no reservations about testing the limits of that perceived freedom after dinner, only one day removed from such a milestone. Mac was watching a Disney movie, already in her pajamas and ready for bed even before the sun was down, when Joe went out onto the back porch. Both of his parents were sitting there in wooden Adirondack chairs, drinking beer and looking out to the lake.

"What's up, buddy?" Drew asked him.

"Nothing. I really don't feel like watching *Frozen* for the millionth time."

"I hear that," Drew said.

"That's mean, guys," Amy said. "You just have to let it go. *Let it g—*"

"Don't you *even* start that," Drew said, shaking his head.

They all laughed at this, trying to keep it down as to not let Mac know that they were having too much fun at her favorite movie's expense. There was something magical about it—something that once again made Joe feel like more of an adult.

"I was wondering," Joe said. "Since we *did* pack my bike up on the U-Haul, I'd like to take it out for a ride."

Both parents looked at him at the same time, studying him. He felt like an ant under a microscope, but he didn't miss the fact that they seemed to be working together...as a unit. No fighting, no grudges, no cold shoulders. It was worth the awkwardness of having them stare him down.

They then looked to each other and shrugged at almost the same time before his dad turned back to him and nodded.

"That's fine," Drew said. "But make sure you take your phone. I want you back in an hour. Less would be better. And stay on the dirt roads. Don't go back near the gravel and don't even *think* about going to a main road."

"Sure, Dad."

"One hour," Amy echoed. "If you're gone for an hour and two minutes, there will be trouble."

"Got it. Thanks, guys."

Joe turned and headed down the steps before they had time to change their minds. He made his way around the edge of the house and took his bike from its place by the porch. He took his phone out of his pocket, checked the time, and then hopped on the bike.

He came to the end of the driveway and took a right. He had never been down that end of Kerr Lane and the shadowed road seemed to invite him further down. He wondered just how far down these vacation rentals went, finding it easy to imagine them winding all the way around the lake, tucked back in the seemingly endless forests. He pedaled slowly, enjoying the scenery. Kerr Lane was mostly straight, branching off on occasion for thinner roads that led to mobile homes that Joe could see from his perch on his bike.

He passed several cabins that looked incredibly similar to the one his family was staying in. Most of the license plates on the cars he saw in the driveways were from Virginia, but he also saw North Carolina plates, a few from Maryland and even one from

Texas. He saw one family playing with a Frisbee in the front yard and, on more than one occasion, he could hear the laughter of children from behind the cabins as they splashed about in the lake.

He also heard the now-familiar buzzing of distant boat motors out on the water. He had been trying to come up with a clever way to subtly drop the hint to his dad that he'd like to go out on the water on such a boat. Joe had seen the brochures lying around the cabin and knew that there were a few places in Clarkton that rented out boats. His dad had been mostly cool as of late and the thought that Joe might be able to convince him wasn't *totally* absurd.

Joe brought his bike to a four-way intersection that looked ominous in the shadows of the trees. Straight ahead, Kerr Lane kept venturing forward deeper into the woods. Another dirt road cut across it. A dusty road sign identified this road as Tucker Lane. Not wanting to veer too far off course and end up getting sidetracked or lost, Joe kept forward down Kerr Lane.

Twenty seconds later, when he first caught sight of the girl, he was very glad he had chosen to stay on course.

She was walking further up the road and closing in fast as Joe's bike barreled forward. He gently tapped the brakes, not wanting to go rocketing past her, but also not wanting to creep by her like some perverted stalker.

From behind, all Joe could tell was that she had raven black hair that was put up into a messy ponytail. She wore a spaghetti-strapped shirt that showed her small tanned shoulders and a pair of shorts that wouldn't pass any school's dress code. Even without seeing her from the front, Joe assumed that she must be sixteen or older. Far out of his league, for sure.

He caught up to her and she apparently heard his bike as it neared. She turned around slightly, still not breaking stride from her walk. She gave him a slight smile, waved, and then turned back to face the direction she was headed.

Joe saw at once that she was younger than he had thought. Her face looked young, but sort of defined in a way that he had started to notice in most of the girls in his grade. It was the sort of thing teenaged boys that weren't quite obsessed with sex just yet were still able to pick up on.

She's my age, he thought. *She's my age, and—*

The thought came to an abrupt stop as his bicycle seemed to hiccup, stop, and tilt forward. Joe was taken off-guard and went sailing forward, flying over the handlebars. As he did a half-flip forward and felt himself momentarily suspended in the air, he barely had time to think: *what the hell was that?*

Then he hit the ground on his back. The air whooshed out of him and he heard a gasping sound escape his throat. He was barely aware of his bike clattering to the ground beside him.

As he whooped for breath and started to try getting up, he felt blood trickling down his hand. He looked at his left palm and saw that he had skinned it up pretty badly. He blinked at the sight of the blood and then noticed the figure that slowly started to come into focus to his right. He blinked once more, wondering if his vision was blurring from the impact, but then he remembered the girl he had been ogling over just before he'd crashed.

Oh my God, he thought, *that's so embarrassing, that's so—*

"If you had have landed on your feet," the girl said, "that would have been awesome."

Joe gave her a perplexed look as he tried sucking air in. Although he took a moment to search for the right words, the only thing that came out of his mouth, through a strangled gasp for breath, was *"Huh?"*

"Are you okay?" she asked.

Her face started to come into focus. She was smiling down at him, her dark eyes sparkling with mischief. It was clear that she wasn't yet sure if she should be concerned for him or if she was allowed to laugh. Joe knew he had better say or do something quickly or he'd lose her.

"I'm good," he said, sitting up slowly. He looked behind him to see what had caused the crash. It was nothing more than a stray branch that had fallen from one of the overhanging trees.

"You sure?" she asked. She offered her hand and Joe looked at it oddly for a moment. He made sure not to reach out with his bloody hand and then took it. She helped him to his feet and he dusted off his shirt and pants.

"Well that was embarrassing," he said.

"I've seen worse," she said. "You should really pay attention, though."

"I know," Joe said. *Oh God, she caught me staring at her,* he thought.

But if this was true, she made no mention of it. She gave him a smile and then nodded to his bleeding hand.

"Got somewhere to get that fixed up?" she asked.

"Yeah. My family is staying in a cabin further back down the road. I'll clean it up there."

"Ah, an out-of-towner," the girl said.

"You're not?" he asked.

"Nope. Born and raised about an hour away from here. My dad brings us out here every summer as a cheap vacation. I wanted Hawaii but I got this. I've gotten this every year for as long as I can remember."

Joe nodded, doing what he could to not blatantly stare at her. She was pretty in a way that he wasn't used to. There was nothing extraordinary about her at all, but several small qualities seemed to jab him in the heart all at once: the way the one loose strand of hair bobbed over the side of her head, the way she rolled her eyes when she said *but I got this,* and the way she had no problem standing so close to a bleeding boy she had just met.

"So where are you visiting from?" she asked.

"New York," he said. "My name is Joe."

He sounded like some weird robot when he gave his name, but he sensed that the conversation was either going to lead much further ahead or stall out within just a few seconds. Giving his name seemed like the most natural way to keep it going.

God, he thought, *am I really this bad at talking to girls?*

"Hello, Joe from New York," she said. "I'm Valerie. From…well, too close to here."

"Where are you guys staying?" Joe asked.

Valerie pointed down the way Joe had been headed. "Just a bit further down that way."

"And you're just out walking around?" Joe asked.

"I am. Dad is watching baseball. I hate baseball. So I went walking. It's sort of funny to see the vacationers. No offense. Some of them seem so out of place here. Last summer I met this old lady that said she had been coming here for almost ten years because her therapist had recommended it."

"There does seem to be a nice mixture of locals and vacation people, huh?"

"Yeah," Valerie said. She then looked awkwardly to his bike and frowned. "Do you think you messed it up?" she asked.

Joe leaned over and pulled the bike back up onto its wheels. He rolled it back and forth and gave it a once-over. Other than a slight dent along the handlebars, it seemed to be unscathed.

"Seems fine," he said.

Valerie started walking and waved him on to follow. When Joe obeyed the hand gesture, he tried not to seem overly enthusiastic.

"So," Valerie said. "New York. New York *City?*"

"Yeah. Manhattan."

"That's awesome. Why the hell did your family come out here if you live in New York City?"

"My dad just signed a contract to compose the score to a movie that everyone thinks could be pretty big. Having meetings all of the time was burning him out. Stifling his creativity or whatever. So his agent suggested we leave the state, go somewhere secluded."

He nearly added in the bit of the tension between his parents but caught it at the last minute. He wasn't going to go there with this cute and interesting girl.

"And your dad chose *here?*"

"I think his agent did. I'm not sure."

"That's cool…that your dad is a musician, I mean."

"You'd think so," Joe said. "But he can really get wrapped up in it at times." He sensed the conversation leaning towards his parents after all, so he swerved it as quickly as he could. "How about your dad?" he asked. "What's he do?"

"He owns a small engine repair shop. But he also does home repair on the side. He doesn't need to, though. He makes good money. My mom died three years ago and even though he hasn't told me, I know we got a nice chunk of money from the insurance. He says we need the extra cash so I can go to college."

"Cool," Joe said, mainly because he didn't know what else to say. Valerie had just dropped a bomb about the death of a parent and her family's financial state. It had gotten very awkward very fast. "Not about your mom, I mean," he added. "But about… yeah…"

She smiled at him and shrugged. "It's okay."

They walked on in silence for another twenty seconds. Joe glanced to her several times, taking her in as much as he could without being too obvious.

"That's me," Valerie said, pointing to a grove within the trees ahead. A pick-up truck sat parked in the driveway of a cabin that was a bit smaller than the one Joe was staying in.

"You calling it a day?" Joe asked.

"Yeah. Dad is going to take me out on the lake tomorrow. He's going to try to teach me how to ski. He wants to get started early. Also, if he saw me out here talking to a strange boy, he'd kill you first and make me watch. Then he'd kill me."

"My parents are the same way," he said even though, in all honesty, they weren't.

She nodded and they looked at one another, letting an uncomfortable silence grow between them. It was awkward, but Joe relished every minute of it.

"So what are you doing after skiing tomorrow?" Joe asked.

"Nothing that I know of. If the stupid Orioles are playing tomorrow, Dad will probably watch. Which means I'll be out walking or something."

"Want some company?" The boldness of the question shocked him and when it was out, his mouth snapped shut quickly.

Did I seriously just ask her that?

He barely caught the flicker of a smile on her face. She then shrugged and said, "Sure. That could be cool. How about three o' clock? Meet me where you fell off your bike."

"I didn't fall. I was…distracted."

Again, that smile. It killed Joe in the most glorious way.

This time the smile stayed on her face. Joe felt a surge of heat rocket through him and he wondered if he was blushing. Before giving himself enough time to become a stupid stuttering mess, he smiled back and turned his bike around, headed back towards his cabin.

"See you then," he said.

"Bye, Joe from New York" she called back.

Joe took one look over his shoulder and saw that Valerie had a little bob in her step as she walked towards the driveway she had pointed to moments ago. He then turned back around and started to pick up speed again, pedaling with a new energy in his legs. Moments later, he took a wide swooping turn around the branch in the road that he had struck earlier.

He grinned as he passed the stray branch. Without that branch's interference, he may have never spoken to Valerie. Sure, his left hand was hurting like hell—a stark reminder of his clumsiness— but it was worth it.

Joe drove on, recalling Valerie's face to his mind at least once every ten seconds. He had never been one to develop fast crushes but he knew almost at once that it was happening to him now.

It was a little alarming, but he welcomed it all the same. Without Ricky Marshall and his friends from back home to ridicule him or make slanderous and dirty jokes about him, it felt safe. With a smile on his face, Joe pedaled leisurely back to his cabin, catching glimpses of the afternoon sun on the lake as he blazed by the trees.

NINE

As dusk started to settle on Clarkton Lake, a small fishing boat slowly crept out towards the center of the lake's southernmost tip. It was an unremarkable little aluminum boat, pushed along by its only occupant, a twenty-three year old local named Brett Yates. He rowed the boat with precision, as he had done four days a week for the last two months, towards his favorite spot.

When he reached his spot, he brought the paddles in and tossed out his small anchor. He watched the chain spool out link by link until it stopped. The water here was about twenty feet deep. He had gone through this so many times that he had come to anticipate when the anchor would hit. He nodded to the chain at the exact moment it stopped unspooling.

Brett took off his shirt and sat it on the little boat's rear seat. On the other rear seat there was a towel and a bottle of water. He opened the water and took a sip as he looked out to the water. A little more than two hundred yards in front of him there was a small bank. He kept his eyes on the sand and the trees over there as he arched his back. Then, with a motion that felt almost mechanical, he took a single step to the front of the boat and leaped into the water in a perfect dive.

He came up right away and swam for the bank two hundred yards ahead.

Some people liked to run. It was summer now and Brett had already seen several clueless tourists jogging down the trails that wound around the lake. They were sweating, huffing and puffing to get over the next hill so they could get back to their rented houses and cabins to put salves and lotions on their newly acquired bug bites.

But Brett preferred to swim. He had always enjoyed swimming as far back as he could remember. His mother had once joked that when he was a baby, it was impossible to get him out of the tub. He had always liked the water.

He'd never joined a team—not in high school (not that his backwoods high school had offered a swimming team) and not during the two years of college that he still considered a waste of his time. He had never seen the point in joining a team. To him, swimming was relaxing. It no longer even felt like exercise to Brett. He did it now because he enjoyed it and he knew that it kept his body in superb shape. He hadn't bedded many women but the handful that he had slept with had all commented on his body, asking if he worked out.

No, he would always say. *I just swim.*

He thought about those women as he made his way swiftly to the bank. Maybe he'd head out to The Wharf tonight to see if he could get lucky. It was a gorgeous afternoon and the water was at an absolute perfect temperature. He was in a great mood, and it only improved with each stroke.

He swam with the mechanics and speed of someone training for the Olympics. He was oblivious to everything as he reached the bank, dug his feet into the murky bottom, and then kicked back off towards the boat.

He'd started this routine two months back, a little sooner than most people usually preferred to go back out into the lake after the chill of spring. The water had been very brisk then, but not too cold. Brett liked it that way; he felt like he knew the lake better than anyone, feeling the changes in its temperature every couple of days.

He approached his boat, tapped the side, and pushed off, headed back to the bank again. He would go two more times before ending his session—three, if he started to get that pleasant little burn in his lungs and shoulders. He liked pushing himself. It made him stronger, built up his endurance.

He glanced ahead as he sliced through the water. The bank was drawing close, its trees darkening as dusk slowly pulled in the night. He lowered his head and swam on.

In mid-stroke, he felt something brush along his stomach. It was soft and brief, but it had been enough to startle him. He stopped swimming to allow his nerves to settle and looked around for signs of the brave little fish that had wanted to join him for a swim.

Not seeing any sign of it, Brett stretched back out and picked up the pace again.

He made it a few yard ahead before he felt something at his leg.

He thought it was the same fish again and almost smiled at the idea. But before a smile could touch his lips, he felt pressure on his leg as something grabbed him and pulled him down.

He cried out once, his head going under and his mouth filling with water. He kicked at whatever had his leg and it let go right away.

Brett kicked to the surface, aware of a slight sting along his left leg where he had been grabbed.

What the hell was that?

He couldn't think of anything in the lake that would attack in such a way. If it was a snake, he didn't think it would have the strength to actually pull him under. The only thing with that sort of strength would be one of the monstrous catfish that he heard about from time to time, but they were supposed to live at the bottom of the lake in much deeper regions.

Whatever it was, it had effectively ruined his blissful swim. With his heart hammering his chest, Brett quickly turned back for the boat. No longer concerned with poise or technique, he swam as fast as he could.

His arms moved like pistons, his legs like propellers. He swam forward frantically, unable to remember *any* time he had ever been afraid to be in the water. He looked up to the boat. It was twenty feet away, drawing closer with every stroke.

Brett put a bit more energy into his stroke, dipping his arms under and bringing them back up as fast as he could. Right, left, right, left, his legs kicking the whole time. Right, left, right—

A sudden burning pain tore through his right arm as it was submerged. It was unlike any pain he had ever felt in his life. He felt his consciousness being pulled away but he fought to reclaim it, desperate to get back to the boat. The pain rocketed through his body and he thought he might throw up.

He screamed and tried to jerk his arm out of the water, but it wouldn't come. He tugged again and felt panic surge through him when he realized that he couldn't feel his arm. That panic intensified when he saw the water around him growing red and the smell of blood reached his nostrils.

He tried swimming forward but flapped around, unable to feel his right arm. He looked in that direction and screamed.

He couldn't feel his arm because it was no longer attached to his body.

Everything from four inches below his shoulder was missing, replaced by a grisly mess of red and a speck of white where his bone had been severed.

The world tried to float away. He saw white spots in his vision and his body suddenly felt as if it were floating—not in the water of the lake, but on some tide that wanted to carry him somewhere else entirely.

He made a feeble kick towards the boat that got him nowhere. He tried to cry out but even that wasn't easy. He was too weak. He was too—

He felt something wrap around his waist so tightly that he fully expected his hips to snap. He let out a moan that came out in a thick, wet gurgle.

There was a pause and then a violent pull from beneath him. It was so fast that Brett didn't understand what was happening until his mouth was filling with water.

His last glimpse of the world above the surface was his boat, rocking gently back and forth in the gathering night.

TEN

As someone that had lived in the town of Clarkton his entire life, Wayne was always happy to see a local business thrive. As is the case with small towns—Clarkton boasting a population of just over three thousand—it was never a surprise to see a new local business open, only to close its doors less than two years later.

But the one establishment that had always fared well in Clarkton was The Wharf. It was the town's only bar and it did well all year long. Even when summer wasn't luring in the tourists, the live music on most weekends brought people in from nearby towns during the non-summer months. And, of course, there were locals like Wayne and Al that kept the place busy.

But The Wharf was almost like a totally different place during the summer. When the tourists came into town, the place seemed fancier. The same cheap beer was on tap (although they did spring for a few summer ales and a wider variety of wine during the span between May and September) and the menu didn't change very much. But still, there was something about the way the owners advertised their specials and decorated the place like a cheap man's Margaritaville during the summer that gave The Wharf a charming sort of quality it didn't have during the rest of the year.

One thing that *didn't* change about The Wharf during the summer was its reliability as a source of local gossip. As a general rule, Wayne had always ignored gossip; his ex-wife had been at the center of the Clarkton grapevine and had often seeded its rotten fruit.

But ever since he and Al had briefly discussed those mysterious black vans parked in the driveway of a rental cabin on Kerr Lane, he'd considered heading to The Wharf to see if there was any low-hanging fruit to be plucked.

Using drinking as an excuse to gather any gossip was highly believable when it came to Wayne. He was a regular at The Wharf, the type that didn't even have to place an order because the bartender knew him so well. Wayne knew that this was nothing to be proud of but it still made him feel cozy in a weird sort of way.

He was feeling this coziness as he and Al sat at the bar on Thursday night, four days after they had first discussed the black vans while playing horseshoes. They were only on their second round of drinks when he overheard the first snippet of conversation that made him think of that house of Kerr Lane.

The snippet in question had come from another of The Wharf's regulars, Jimmy Fitz. Jimmy worked for the highway department and was widely known as one of the two men that were occasionally sent down into the dirt tracks that wound through the rental properties in the summer. It was well-known in Clarkton that if you wanted gossip on the tourists—who was rich, who was hot and single, and things of that sort—Jimmy Fitz was the man to see.

Wayne had caught the tail end of one of Jimmy's sentences as he spoke to a woman that sat beside him. She looked too old to be Jimmy's date and Wayne hadn't seen her at The Wharf before. She was probably on vacation and enjoying The Wharf's staged atmosphere.

"...the same as every other year," Jimmy was telling the woman. "He said that every single rental house and cabin is booked all the way through summer. All but one, anyway. A house at the end of Kerr Lane that no one is being allowed to rent out."

Wayne didn't bother trying to be polite or pretend that he hadn't been eavesdropping. He leaned over and nudged Jimmy Fitz in a good natured buddy-buddy sort of way.

"Who was telling you that?" he asked.

Jimmy seemed peeved that Wayne had interrupted his conversation with the lovely lady, but it was also apparent that he liked the feeling of having information that others were interested in. Jimmy looked to the woman, gave her a smile that was far too confident for his pudgy face, and then turned fully to Wayne.

"Stephen Collins," Jimmy said. "One of the realtors down at Lakeside Rentals. You know him?"

"A bit," Wayne said. "That one house on Kerr Lane...do you know which one it is?"

Jimmy shook his head. "No. I asked Stephen the same thing and he seemed like he didn't want to talk about it. I'm pretty sure he said it was one of those properties that the owner usually stays in, though."

"Like us," Wayne said with a chuckle, elbowing Al.

"Exactly," Jimmy said. "Anyway, the fella that owns the house is nowhere to be seen. And since it's not rented out, I assumed that means that there was some sort of structural damage or some other expensive reason that needs to be fixed up before anyone can rent it out. I guess because the rent money goes to the owner and not Lakeside Rentals, Stephen didn't really know enough about it. He was just nosy because it's one property that he can't shove tourists in."

"Oh, I know," Wayne said. "I live down that way. I see the vacationers come and go all summer long. Lakeside has to make a fortune off of them."

"Oh, absolutely," Jimmy said.

The conversation lulled at that point. Jimmy Fitz turned back to the woman he had been speaking with. Wayne thought this bit of information over for a bit and then turned back to Al.

"Well now," Wayne said. "That seems pretty damn interesting, doesn't it?"

"It does," Al said. "But not enough to keep snooping." He then looked around the bar, leaned in closer to Wayne, and whispered. "Especially not if you think you saw government plates on those vans."

Wayne nodded and sipped from his beer. He took the last bit from the glass and set it on the bar. He considered ordering another one, but his mind was already elsewhere.

"You know," he told Al, "those vans aren't there anymore."

"And how might you know that?" Al asked, irritated.

"I drove by yesterday. The vans are gone. So is George Galworth's truck."

"So?"

Wayne smirked and looked across the bar, through the milling locals and vacationers, towards the door. "So, I think it's getting stuffy in here. I think it's time to head out."

"For what?" Al asked suspiciously.

Now it was Wayne that leaned in to whisper. "Let's go have a look. If they aren't renting that house out, I can guarantee you that the government was up to a lot more than studying the water levels or the spawning habits of fish or whatever the hell those environmentalists do."

Al rolled his eyes, but Wayne knew that he had won his friend over. What else did Al have to do on a Friday night? Also, there *was* some mystery to this entire scenario one way or the other. If Wayne and Al hadn't seen those black vans rocketing down the dirt road on that first day of summer, it might have been easier to ignore it. But there was *something* going on in regards to that vacant house. If it turned out to be something small and unimportant, then at least their curiosity would be satisfied.

And if it was something bigger, the worst that could happen would be that they'd get a slap on the wrist from local law enforcement.

Wayne could see that these and similar thoughts were going through Al's mind. Al slowly finished the rest of his beer and the motioned for the bartender. He paid for both men's tabs and then turned on his barstool to face Wayne.

"Let's go then," he said in a playfully defeated voice. "But I need to be home by ten or so or Kathy will start to worry."

"You'll be fine," Wayne said. "You'll be with me."

"That's exactly what she's worried about."

They left the bar, Wayne clapping Jimmy Fitz on the shoulder as they made their way out.

***

As Al drove his truck down Kerr Lane, Wayne sat in the passenger seat and watched the night-shrouded trails pass by in the flicker of headlights. The roads out here along the rental properties seemed totally abandoned and emptied on most nights, the houses illuminated only by a few lights inside or an occasional porch light. They passed a single yard on their way in where people were gathered around a car that had a Randy Travis song coming out of its speakers. The folks were speaking loudly and no doubt drinking beer.

As they passed by Al's house, Wayne saw his friend cast a wary look at the driveway.

"Kathy really doesn't care much for me, does she?" Wayne asked.

"It's not like that."

"I think it sort if *is* like that. And that's fine. I get it."

Al seemed to think about something before finally saying, "She worries about you, that's all. And because she worries about you, she worries about me when I hang out with you."

"Does she want you to find some new friends?" Wayne asked with a chuckle.

"No. She thinks I'm good for you."

Wayne cracked up with laughter at this, slapping at the dashboard. He knew that Al *was* good for him. Without a good friend to hang out with and rely on after his wife had left, Wayne knew that he would have drunk himself into a stupor. He would have become one of those sad old men that walked around the streets with five dollars burning in their pocket to buy a six pack of cheap beer or a bottle of that disgusting malt liquor from the mini mart. There was a very good chance that's what his life would have become after retirement and the divorce if Al had not been there.

They'd done nothing more than fish, sit on Wayne's porch swatting at mosquitoes, and play endless rounds of horseshoes, but it had been exactly what he had needed. Spending that time with Al had occupied Wayne's time and kept him busy. He was sure this was obvious to Kathy as well. And although Wayne knew that she didn't like him, he had always been grateful to her for putting up with him.

Sure, a great deal of the time Wayne and Al spent together was spent drinking, but Al had always managed to put a limit on it without coming off as holier-than-thou or like some deranged wanna-be big brother. Wayne had known Al since their early twenties; he respected Al and trusted him more than anyone he had ever met.

Wayne's laughter, which was a disguise for the sting of blunt truth, tapered off as they reached the end of Kerr Lane. The empty house sat just ahead, its driveway totally vacant just as Wayne had said. Al slowed the truck, killed the headlights, and crept into the driveway.

They sat in the quiet for a moment. They could hear crickets and loons through the small cracks in their windows. The house sat ahead of them, nothing more than a forgotten prop from someone's summer vacation.

"Now what?" Al said.

Wayne shrugged and opened up his door. He stepped out into the night, the air humid but not staggeringly so. Al followed him, making an effort to keep quiet. The two men met in front of the truck and started walking towards the house.

"What are we supposed to be looking for?" Al asked.

"I don't know. Anything out of place, I guess."

But as they reached the house, it began to dawn on Wayne just how pointless this little expedition truly was. What *were* they supposed to be looking for? If there had been something fishy going on out here, what was the likelihood that the government had left behind any clues?

It was too late now, though. They were here, hidden in the dark, and Wayne felt that they had to at least take a look around.

"Got a flashlight?" Wayne asked.

"Yeah," Al said. "I keep it in my glove box right beside my lock pick and badge."

"Smart ass."

They walked slowly towards the front door, the night humid and thick around them. Wayne tried the knob but found it locked. He then walked to the windows and tried peering in, but it was too dark to see anything.

"You might have been right," Wayne said. "Maybe this wasn't the best idea."

"Of course I was right," Al said.

Wayne stepped away from the window and looked to the side of the house. If they had indeed over-reacted to the speeding vans on that first day of summer and there really was nothing going on but some daft environmental stuff, there might be evidence of it around the back of the house, maybe down by the water. He figured he might as well check it out while they were here or his big dumb curiosity would keep pestering him about it all summer long.

He started around the side of the house, hearing Al hissing a whisper behind him.

"Where the hell are you going?" Al asked.

"Around back. I want to see if there's any equipment lying around. Maybe they *are* just checking water levels or something."

"How do you expect to see *anything* in the dark?" Al said.

It was a good question, but not one that Wayne felt like answering. As a matter of fact, as the yard started descending into a slight hill, he started to get antsy. He could see the ground directly in front of him, as well as the faint sparkle of moonlight on the lake several yards ahead of him. But if there was a sudden stop to the yard or some random hole, he was going to break his ankle.

He looked back once to see if Al was following and saw his silhouette a few feet behind him. *Good old Al,* he thought.

When he found himself standing in the back yard, Wayne felt something very much like doubt. What was he doing? What could he hope to possibly achieve by snooping around the yard of this empty house at night?

He suddenly wanted to get out of there as quickly as possible. He wasn't scared, but felt out of place. And if there *was* something going on here that involved the government, did he really want to be trespassing?

This thought stopped him as he came to the decorative rock wall that separated the back yard from the small stretch of beach. He peered out onto the lake and was reminded again of why he loved it out here. On still nights when the weather wasn't stifling hot, there was a simple beauty to moonlight on a lake that was almost hypnotic.

"Wayne?" Al's voice was soft and ghost-like behind him.

"Yeah?"

"Look at that."

Wayne turned around and saw Al directly behind him, pointing to the water's edge.

"I don't see anything."

"About three feet from the water, slightly to the right."

Wayne carefully stepped over the rock wall and trained his eyes in that direction. He saw something there, a weird shape in the sand that was barely visible in the weak moonlight. It looked like someone had dragged a large stick over the sand and had drawn a straight line that was interrupted by a slight curve.

"A snake, maybe?" Al asked, coming over the low rock wall and joining Wayne on the sand.

"That would be a huge snake," Wayne said. "It would have to be heavy to leave a print like that. It would also be wide as hell."

As Wayne hunkered down and looked at the vague print in the sand—headed from the sand and into the water, from the looks of it—he thought his friend might be right. Still, he couldn't think of anything else that might leave such an indentation in the sand.

"It does look serpentine," Al said, now hunkered down by Wayne. "But the shape isn't right."

They looked at it for a moment longer in silence. They two men knew each other well enough to know what the other was thinking…and as it just so happened, their thoughts were identical.

Whatever this print was, it was certainly made much more interesting by the fact that there had been government vehicles parked in front of this house for several days.

Wayne and Al stood back up in unison. Wayne looked away from the suspicious print and then out onto the water.

"Any ideas?" Wayne asked.

"Yeah," Al said.

"What?"

"That it's time to get the hell out of here and head back home."

Wayne didn't argue. His eyes lingered on the water for a moment longer before they returned to the snake-like imprint in the sand. It was barely there at all and was maybe a few days old if he had to guess. Still, it was pronounced enough to make him feel uneasy.

"Yeah, good idea," he said, and started back towards the rock wall and the dark yard beyond.

ELEVEN

Scott woke up at seven thirty, feeling more refreshed than he had in quite some time. He had fully expected to have a hard time sleeping in the country, with the dead silence of the forest interrupted only by crickets and tree frogs. But the exact opposite had happened. For the two nights he had been renting out the cabin two lots over from where George Galworth and several FBI agents had died, Scott had slept like a baby.

He walked out onto the cabin's back patio with a cup of coffee and a plate of scrambled eggs. He took a seat at the patio table and looked out onto Clarkton Lake. The sun had been up long enough to evaporate the ghostly mist that rose up from the water in the morning but the scene still looked ethereal. He looked to the right and could just barely see the edge of the little beach that sat behind George Galworth's old cabin.

He'd gotten a call from the real estate agent yesterday while he'd been inside Galworth's cabin. The call had come from a boisterous and rather loud fellow named Stephen Collins. Collins had wanted to know when the government might be done with the Galworth cabin, so they could better update their listings and availability. Scott had assured Collins that the government would compensate him above and beyond his usual prices for his full cooperation. While he had spoken to Collins, there had been three other field agents behind him inside the property, taking notes, repairing the front door discreetly moving the corpses of the agents that had come before them, and fixing up all other damages.

Collins had also asked when George Galworth would be able to speak with him. All Scott had said in reply was that it was all classified information and that he would be updated as soon as possible.

The fact of the matter was that Scott had no idea how long this would take. He had no resources, no real help from the outside (except for the grunts that had come to help clean the property), and he didn't expect to get any. He never really got excessive information on any of his cases. He was a specialist of sorts, coming in to clean up high-profile messes that other agencies had left behind. These were typically messes that had high risks associated with them. He'd been called the Ghost by some, because he was usually in and out in of a case quickly. His work often involved talking to and roughing up witnesses, removing evidence, or finishing a job that those originally assigned to the job had been unable to complete.

But this one was going to be different. For starters, he had no idea what he was looking for. All he knew was that it was highly suspected that George Galworth and the crew he had been working with had been attacked while doing research in the Aleutian Trench. It was being speculated that whatever attacked them had infected (or, rather, *impregnated*) Jimmy Wilkins and KC Doughtry while killing the other three men on the crew.

Galworth, Doughtry, and Wilkins had died less than two weeks after having been rescued from the trench and cleared by medical teams. From what Scott knew based on the reports he had been given, Doughtry and Wilkins had been killed when a creature had erupted from their bodies like something straight out of a sci-fi movie. The creature had come out of their mouths, shattering their jaws and, in Doughtry's case, literally splitting his skull with the force behind it.

As of now, that's all Scott knew. He assumed that the creature that had sprung out of George Galworth had escaped, as evidenced by the blood trails he had seen on the floor. Furthermore, he was also certain that the creature was now living in Clarkton Lake. Scott was keeping his eyes and ears open for any local news about sightings or any attacks in the lake but so far, he had heard nothing.

As if the universe were in tune with Scott's troubles, his cellphone rang as he ran through all of this in his head. He tore his eyes away from the sight of the lake and headed inside through the sliding glass window where his cellphone sat on the kitchen counter. His display told him that it was Roger Lowry—not someone you wanted to speak to first thing in the morning.

Still, the hope that Roger might have updates that could help him get this nightmare assignment over made him actually *happy* that his supervisor was calling. He answered on the third ring, preparing himself for Roger's typical blunt candor.

"Good morning, sir," Scott said, trying to start on the conversation on a polite note.

"I've got some information for you," Roger said, getting straight to the point. "Based on what we can tell from data retrieved from submarine these poor bastards were working in, as well as the scraps of evidence from the Wilkins and Doughtry residences, we feel that we now have more of a complete story on what this thing is, what has happened so far, and how you can potentially find it."

"I'm listening, sir."

Roger started with the bits that Scott already knew: about how their sub had been compromised and something had killed three of the six crew members in a grisly fashion. He then went on to describe how events had occurred in the homes of Jimmy Wilkins and KC Doughtry.

The gentler of the accounts came from Jimmy Wilkins's residence in Sacramento, California. On the day he had died, his wife had gone to work like any other day while Wilkins remained home, complaining that he felt ill. Sometime before noon PST, Wilkins had died in his bedroom. It wasn't clear what had killed him first: the rupture to his skull or being suffocated by the creature that had hung three feet out of his mouth. Wilkins's wife had discovered him in that very state that afternoon—with a portion of the dead thing in her husband's mouth—and called 911.

About four hours later, the Wilkins residence received a phone call that was unanswered due to Wilkins's wife not being home. A message was left on the answering machine from KC Doughtry, whom at the time had no idea that Wilkins was dead, asking Wilkins to call him right away.

It still wasn't clear how Doughtry had learned about the death of Wilkins. But early in the morning nine days ago, Doughtry had sent an e-mail to George Galworth, stating simply: *Wilkins is dead.*

Sometime after this, Doughtry had locked himself in his bathroom. When his wife had unlocked the door to check on him, she was attacked by the creature that had erupted from his mouth. It choked her to death and, at some point, chewed off half of her right hand. This was all pieced together by the forensics team that had showed up about an hour later, just as their ten-year-old son was getting off of the bus.

"The kid was excited because the following day was the last day of school before summer vacation," Roger explained coldly.

"What about the creature?" Scott asked. "Was it recovered?"

"Yes. It apparently got confused and tried burrowing into the toilet. It was too big to fit, though. It got stuck and when it tried to attack the team that showed up to retrieve it, it was pretty slow and lethargic. They killed it easily."

"You think it was suffocating as it attacked?"

"Seems that way. Like a fish out of water for too long."

"What else do we know about it, sir?" Scott asked.

"There's nothing concrete, but the marine biologist that we're consulting has a few assumptions. First, the thing is going to grow very quickly. Based on the two carcasses she's studying, she believes the creatures are large to begin with, but are sort of compressed to stay inside the bodies they are grown in. The dead one at the Doughtry house was a little over four feet long when they recovered it. The one they pulled out of Jimmy Wilkins was about the same."

"What else?"

"The good news is that I can possibly narrow your search down. If what you told me the other day is true and this thing is capable of slithering around on the ground for small periods of time, the biologist thinks it might stay close to shore. But, on the other hand, that doesn't jive with the fact that the thing apparently originated in one of the deepest parts of the ocean. The marine biologist thinks a life form like this one would have hung around the cracks and crevices within the trench. That means your specimen is probably going to try to find the dankest, darkest, tightest places to live."

"Then why would it come to shore? If it likes tight dark places, wouldn't it want to stay *away* from the shore?"

"Yeah. Until it needs to eat."

Scott looked out to the lake, barely visible through the sliding glass doors from where he stood by the kitchen counter. To think that something very similar to the creature they were talking about could come upon that shore to kill vacationing tourists and unsuspecting locals was terrifying.

Scott wondered if it had already started and he simply hadn't heard anything about it yet.

"Another thing that might help," Roger said. "The experts here seem to think that as this thing gets bigger, it will lose some of its speed. So it might be easier to catch as it grows. But they say it's likely still going to be strong as hell."

"Should I get local law enforcement involved?" Scott asked.

"Not yet. Put that off as long as you can. In the meantime, I suggest you keep an ear out for any deaths on or near the water. Even if it just appears to be a simple drowning, I want you on it."

"Yes, sir."

"I want updates the moment you get them."

Scott opened his mouth to give another *Yes, sir,* but Roger had already hung up. Scott sighed, pocketed his phone, and walked back out onto the back porch.

He looked out to the water, over towards George Galworth's house again. He started to make a schedule for his day, doing his very best to busy himself with the details.

That way, it was a bit easier to pretend that he wasn't starting to get a little scared.

TWELVE

Joe had been surprised that his mother had let him take his bike back down the trails without at least some sort of argument. She seemed to be in a good mood when he asked, and that had been another plus. Usually when his mom was in a good mood, it meant that things were okay between his folks. And while he still wasn't sure what exactly was going on between them, seeing his mother smile always managed to put Joe in a good mood, too.

But it wasn't his mother's good mood that he was thinking of as he cruised down Kerr Lane. Instead, he was thinking of Valerie, the girl that he had met for a grand total of eight minutes yesterday—the girl he was somehow already developing a massive crush on.

He carefully checked the clock on his iPhone as he neared the place they had planned to meet. It was five minutes after three, which meant he was late. He hoped she hadn't given up on him. Or, worse yet, what if she had decided to not meet him after all? What if he had sort of creeped her out with his boldness?

And where had that boldness come from, anyway? He was *never* confident around girls and never knew what to say in those awkward situations when he knew he was expected to say *something*.

But Valerie had pulled it out of him and—

When he saw her standing in the spot where he had wrecked his bike the day before, he couldn't keep the smile from stretching across his face. She was standing in the center of the dirt road, giving him a sarcastic *slow down* gesture. And behind that gesture was a smile that made his entire body feel as if it had been flushed with heat.

Joe came to a stop directly beside her. He did everything he could to not stare her down like some crazed stalker...but he wasn't doing a very good job.

"I thought I'd make sure you came to a safe stop," she said. "I don't know that I could watch another ugly spill like yesterday."

"You're hilarious," Joe said.

"I know."

Joe dismounted from his bike, leaning against it as they stood in the center of the road. The shade of the overhanging trees kept the sunlight mostly away, creating a dusk-like atmosphere. Joe wasn't quite sure why, but it felt perfect for their little rendezvous.

"How was skiing?" he asked. He noted the way her hair was still slightly wet, presumably from spending time out on the water.

"It was fun," she said. "I'm not very good at it, though. I stayed up for about twenty seconds one time but bailed hard. How about you? You ever ski?"

"No."

"You should. It's fun."

"I can barely swim, much less ski," Joe said.

"Really? You don't swim, you don't ski and let's face it...you aren't very good at riding a bike. What do you do in New York?"

"Not much. I listen to music a lot. My folks will sometimes let me go to indie shows if it's an all-ages venue and I've been getting good grades. I also play football with some friends every now and then."

Valerie had started to walk as Joe spoke. He followed her as she led him further down Kerr Lane. He pushed his bike along, making sure to keep it on his left side so that he could walk directly beside her.

"What kind of music are you into?" she asked.

"Everything. But mostly metal. How about you? What do you do for fun?"

"Hold on one second," she said. She looked ahead and Joe realized that they were coming up on the driveway of the cabin that Valerie and her father were staying in.

"What is it?" Joe asked.

"I don't want Dad seeing you. I'm pretty sure he's half-drunk in front of the TV watching the game, but still...can't be too careful."

She stared at the house for a few moments and then started walking further down the road. She quickened her pace though, as if expecting her father to come out of the front door at any moment.

"It's safe," she said, waving Joe on. "Come on."

Joe followed, still pushing his bike along. When the cabin was behind them, Valerie slowed down, waiting for Joe to catch up.

"Is your dad really that strict?" Joe asked.

"Sometimes. It got worse when mom died. And now that there are boys calling the house for me sometimes, he gets really protective."

"You have boys calling your house?" Joe asked. The mere thought of it was like razorblades in his gut.

"Some," she said. "But nothing like that. No boyfriends. Why? You jealous?"

Joe only shrugged, caught off guard for the first time. He was sure he was blushing, so he looked down to the ground.

"What do you want to do?" Valerie asked.

"I don't know. What *is* there to do?"

"I know this place pretty well," she said. "Like I told you yesterday…me and Dad come here a lot. I can show you some secret places I've found."

"Like what?"

She gave him the same smile she'd shown him when giving him the slow-down gesture; it was a smile that Joe was coming to find was a weakness of his. It was like some weird Achilles heel that he had no guard against.

"Do you trust me?" she asked.

"I hardly know you," he said.

"That's now what I asked."

"I don't know."

"That hurts."

"Sure," Joe said with a shrug. "I guess I trust you. Why do you ask?"

"Just come with me. I want to show you something cool."

"I have to be back at the house by five o' clock."

"That's plenty of time," Valerie said. "I should be back by then, anyway. Dad will start to freak out if I'm gone for too long, especially if he keeps drinking."

"Then lead the way," Joe said.

They walked further down Kerr Lane, the road getting a bit rougher the further down they went. Joe started to regret bringing his stupid bike. Having to push it meant having his hands occupied. He wondered what it might be like to hold Valerie's hand. He wondered what she would do if he reached out and took it. Of course, it was a moot point because he had the damn bike to push along.

When they had walked a quarter of a mile or so away from Valerie's cabin, Valerie stepped off of the road and into the tree line. Ahead of her, the woods were relatively thin. The lake peeked through like a muddy promise through the trees. She started down that way, looking back over her shoulder to see if Joe was following along.

"Where are you going?" Joe asked.

"There's a trail down here," she said. "It's pretty short. Come on."

Joe didn't hesitate. He followed her into the woods, finally resting his bike on the ground (the kickstand long ago having fallen off) among leaves and other woodland debris.

As Joe followed Valerie into the woods, he was amazed at how different the environment seemed. Everything felt bigger, and the scents of the woods were thicker and somehow more alive. And above all, Valerie seemed more real. The road that led back to their cabins and their individual lives was behind them now. Here in the woods, there was just the two of them and that made Joe feel profoundly happy.

He walked close behind her and could smell some sort of lotion mingling with the very earthy combination of dirt and fish that seemed to emanate from the lake. He followed her footsteps as she merged onto a thin footpath that wound down a hill. Sitting at the bottom of the hill was an old wooden building. It was incredibly small and the roof looked like it might fall in at any moment.

"See?" she said, pointing happily to the building.

"This is one of your surprises?"

"Well, yeah," she said, as if he were an idiot for not instantly seeing the charm of the place.

He walked down to the building with her and tried to find something remarkable about it. The roof had a hole in it on the right side and the wall beneath it was buckled and bowed a bit. A doorway sat on the other side of the small shed-like building. A door sat crooked in the frame, the hinges so rusted they had turned completely brown. The door was partially open, revealing a dusty and neglected interior.

"What is it?" Joe asked.

"I'm not sure," she said, stepping up behind him. "I think it must have been like a shed for fishermen or something."

She walked by him, her back brushing his arm as he did so. She walked inside the building, pushing the door open a bit more as she entered. Joe watched as the dust motes floated up and caught the murky sunlight that came in through the doorway. Inside, the floor was rotten in most places, revealing packed dirt and rotted wooden boards underneath.

"This is what my mother would call a death trap," Joe said.

"There was a big black snake in here last summer," Valerie said. "I scared it away with a stick."

"And you come out here why?"

"Not the interior design, that's for sure," Valerie said.

Joe looked around the place. There was an old bench attached to the left wall, battered and worn. Along the front wall, there was what looked to have once been an old rack of some sort. An old neglected hammer hung from the wooden frame, along with a stripped fishing pole and an ancient-looking pitchfork. Old fishing line rested on the floor beneath it, tangled and forgotten.

Valerie walked out of the building as Joe looked around, again passing close enough by Joe so that they brushed against one another. Back outside, she headed around the dilapidated right side of the building. Joe followed dutifully behind her and saw a severe dip in the land. Several feet ahead of them and resting at the bottom the hill was a muddy bank and two old boats. One looked like an old canoe and the other was a basic cheap aluminum fishing boat. Neither of the boats looked like they had been used within the century. Beyond these boats, the muddy bank became muddy water that eventually joined with the not-quite-as-muddy lake.

"I took one of those boats out last week," she said. "But I almost didn't make it back. There was only one oar inside of it and

I suck at rowing. It's pretty hard to steer with one oar. Still, it was fun."

She looked at him expectantly, waiting for him to say something. He looked back at her for a solid three seconds, their eyes locked awkwardly, before he understood what she was getting at. She was asking him if he wanted to go out on the water with her in one of those rickety boats.

"That might not be such a good idea," he said.

"Scared?" she asked, her tone far too disappointed. "I mean, since you can't really swim and all."

"No, I'm not scared," he said. "I'm just not very coordinated, and if we're supposed to be back by five o' clock…"

"Good thinking," Valerie said. Still, she looked out to the boats longingly.

"What else do you do when you're not chasing snakes away or going out on the lake in the world's oldest boats?" Joe asked.

"Nothing much. I just walk around the woods, checking out the people on vacation. I especially like to watch them wreck their bikes."

"Funny."

They were standing two feet apart, Joe's posture as rigid as the trees around them. Valerie was swinging her arms nonchalantly, looking out to the lake. Joe wasn't sure, but he thought something was bothering her. She had a look in her eyes that his mother often got after his folks had a particularly heated argument. He wondered if Valerie's look had to do with her dad. Whenever she mentioned him, there seemed to be anger and annoyance in her voice.

"So what else do you do?" Joe asked. "For fun, I mean. I asked you before and you didn't answer because we were running by your cabin."

The confidence that he had managed to dredge up the day before was nowhere to be found now. He was very aware that this girl had some sort of hold on him even though he barely knew her. It was an uncomfortable thing to realize and it made his heart feel like it was boxing his tonsils. Despite that, it was also amazing in a way he had never expected.

"Oh. Well. I draw a lot," she said. "I don't think I'm good but my dad thinks so. He says I get it from my mom. He swiped one of my pictures and sent it to some contest earlier this year."

"Did you win?"

"Third place. Twenty-five bucks."

"Nice. Is that what you want to do for a job?"

"I'm not sure. What about you? What do you want to do after school?"

"No idea. I'd love to be in a band, but the chances of that are slim to none."

"Do you like music because your dad does it for a living?"

The question was so simple and direct that it caught him off guard. He'd considered this before, usually when he'd sit in the living room in their apartment and watch his dad tinkering with a keyboard. He would never tell his father, but he loved to watch the man work. When an idea hit him and he was able to execute it, there was little in the world that rivaled the joy Joe felt in seeing his father so focused and excited.

"I guess," he answered. "But I don't want to do the kind of music he does...slow boring stuff for movies." This actually wasn't true at all, but he thought it would probably make him look slightly more attractive to Valerie. He had no idea why and wished he hadn't have said it once it was out of his mouth.

The conversation went on like this for another twenty minutes, the two of them passing innocent and generic questions back and forth. They did nothing more than walk slow circles around the dilapidated little shack. On a few occasions, Joe looked out to the small boats along the shore and wished he had have taken her up on her offer.

Somehow, five o' clock snuck up on them. Joe had set an alarm on his phone and when it buzzed in his pocket, he jumped a bit. He and Valerie were sitting on a relatively clear spot on the ground several yards away from where the muddy water started to lap at the ground. The old boats bobbed there lazily, as if trying to lure them in.

As Joe fished his phone out of his pocket, Valerie giggled. "Is that an alarm clock in your pocket or are you just happy to see me?" she said.

"That's some weak humor," Joe replied, killing the alarm.

"Maybe," she said. "But you're turning red..."

He looked to the ground, ashamed and somehow aroused at the fact that she had caught him blushing at her harmless innuendo.

"It's been fun," Joe said. "But I'd like to see you again and if I don't get home when I'm supposed to, I may be killed."

"That would be unfortunate," Valerie said as they got to their feet and started back through the woods and towards Kerr Lane. "As for seeing me again...well, that might be tough. Dad and I are heading back home tomorrow. He has some rush job he has to do."

"When will you be back?" Joe asked, his heart suddenly sinking in his chest.

"Probably tomorrow night. But you know, we can meet here then. Like after hours, late at night. You ever chased fireflies before?"

"No."

"No surprise there, city boy," she said with a smile. "Can you sneak out and meet me here?"

"Yes," he said without bothering to think through it.

Joe knew that doing so would be risky. He hadn't really looked the place over for appropriate spots to get in and out without his parents finding out.

Of course, he hadn't been expecting to meet Valerie, either.

"What time?" he asked.

"Midnight. Seems fitting."

"Sure," Joe said, having no idea how he'd manage it.

They came to the edge of the forest where Joe's bike lay on the ground. He picked it up and watched Valerie go on ahead of him. She turned back to him to make sure he was coming and when she turned her back to him again, Joe allowed himself a sigh and a dumbfounded roll of the eyes.

What the hell is going on? he wondered.

He had no idea. A crush for sure, and certainly not love. But whatever this was, it was fast and somewhere in between those two categories. It made his stomach feel uneasy but was unlike anything he'd ever experienced.

He'd kissed one girl before...on a dare at a lame party. It had been nice. It had been warm, quick, and flat. But still, it had been a kiss. Now, trying to imagine what it would be like to kiss Valerie, the whole idea of that dared kiss was laughable. The mere thought of kissing Valerie had him leaping on his bike with energy that was almost frantic.

They made the short walk to her driveway without another word. He stopped short of the driveway so her father wouldn't see him with her if he happened to be out in the yard or on the porch. Apparently, single dads were very protective of their daughters. Joe certainly didn't want Valerie getting in trouble just because he was already busy setting a dreamlike sequence of events into motion that he hoped might happen tomorrow night.

Valerie gave him a slight wave and then started towards the cabin. "See you tomorrow night."

He returned the wave and said, "Yeah. Tomorrow night."

With that, he sped towards his cabin, suddenly happier than ever that his father had forced his family take this trip. Now if he could just hide his uncharacteristic giddiness from the rest of them, this might just be the best summer ever.

THIRTEEN

It was without a doubt the longest day in the history of Joe Evans's life.

He'd done everything he could to stay busy, hoping to make the day fly by, but nothing seemed to work. He swam with Mac, tinkered with one of his dad's spare keyboards and even did some fishing off of the dock with his dad. The attempt at fishing had been laughably terrible, as neither of them knew what they were doing, but he'd actually had a lot of fun. He'd stuck his finger three times in trying to properly bait a hook and wore the little scar with pride. They'd caught two fish, both very small and of a variety that Google taught them was called a crappie.

As the evening rolled on, he rode his bike up and down Kerr Lane and the adjoining Tucker Lane for what seemed like hours. He started to understand why Valerie enjoyed watching the tourists. They were extremely varied in the way they did just about everything. In one yard, Joe saw a mother hovering over her child in the yard, making sure the kid didn't wander too far. Yet, in another yard, two young kids—neither older than seven, for sure— roamed freely while their parents sat on the porch. Some yards were quite neat while others were littered with water toys, coolers, and fishing paraphernalia. Some waved at him while he passed while others gave a distrusting look.

After a while, seeing all of the vacationing families and locals along the lanes made him feel a little less special. It made him aware that he wasn't as isolated out here as he thought. It also made him feel as if the secret rendezvous with Valerie wasn't as private as he'd like it to be. Having had his fill of people-watching, he headed back to the Evans cabin, ready for dinner and wishing night would hurry up and get here already.

By the time dinner was set on the table—grilled burgers, green beans, and his mom's awesome homemade mac and cheese—Joe felt like he was going to burst with anticipation. There was some family time on the back porch that included a sing-along to his dad playing the acoustic guitar he used to sketch out the melodies to songs from time to time. Through it all, Joe found it hard to believe that he'd been such a spoiled little brat on the drive to the lake. It had been a *long* drive, sure…but he'd never even given it a chance.

He found it odd to think that kids from the city thought that other kids from the boondocks needed to get out and experience more of life. It was as if living in a city like New York made them feel like they were better or more educated. But coming out here to the middle of nowhere had shown Joe what a relationship with his parents *could* look like in just eight short days.

It had also showed him that being an annoying brat to everyone just because he wasn't always getting his way did nothing more than make him seem like an asshole.

Sure, thoughts of Valerie had lifted his spirits and there was very little that would detour his good mood, but there was something more to it. Joe wondered if there was something ingrained in every teenager that felt it was their responsibility to be a punk to their parents. As he sat in the gathering gloom of dusk and sang a medley of 80s songs with his family, he tried to pinpoint what his parents and Mac had ever done to piss him off so badly.

The answer was *nothing.*

Yet under it all was the unnamed reason his parents were fighting. He'd noticed that in the eight days they'd spent at the lake so far, his folks seemed to be gelling much better. Even as they sang on the back porch and looked out onto the lake, he saw his mother with her hand on his dad's shoulder. They were laughing together, having fun—something they had done very little of in New York.

But still, Joe kept fixating on what might be wrong. Over half of his friends had parents that were divorced. And he had definitely heard his own parents mention the word on one of the nights he had snooped on their conversation. He had not heard how they had actually *used* the word, but he had assumed the worst and let it rule his mood. Then of course, his father had all but confirmed it on their first day here, sneaking in a man-to-man talk with him as they'd stood by the picture window in the kitchen, looking out to the lake.

Maybe it's none of my business, he thought later in the day. Night had finally fallen over the lake, pushing midnight closer to Kerr Lane. Mac was giving him a kiss goodnight before climbing into bed and he was finding a whole new level of appreciation for his family as he wrestled with it all. *Mom and Dad would fill us in if something bad was going on, right? They're not the type to hide stuff.*

He sat in the darkness of the bedroom, looking at the digital clock and occupying himself with these thoughts, willing the time to pass. In the bed on the other side of the room, Mac had fallen asleep, her back to him and her breathing steady. Joe had his iPod playing the not-so-soothing tunes of Devilsgut in his ears as he watched the time trickle by.

10:35...10:42...11:07.

During the course of the day, he had managed to nonchalantly make a few laps around the house in search of his best escape route for the night. As it turned out, it had been easier than he had hoped: the best way to sneak out was from his very own room. Beneath the room's single window was a decorative wooden bench, bordered by two potted plants that sat along the back of the house. He'd have to sustain a bit of a drop and the bench looked like it might break with a strong win. Still, if he could land it right, it would be smooth sailing.

The trick of course, was to not wake up Mac. He'd played the scene out several times in his head. He could open the window and climb out without much of a problem. He'd checked the screens that sat outside of the glass and found they were simple to pop out. Getting them back in might cause a bit of a problem, but he'd worry about that when the time came.

When the clock read 11:45, he sat up and looked over to Mac's bed. She still had her back to him and was curled up like she usually was when she slept. He had no doubt that the stuffed bear she called Mr. Scraps would be tucked under her arm.

He quietly made his way across the room and slid the window up. It creaked a bit and made a faint whooshing noise in the frame. He then pulled the small plastic catches at the bottom corners of the screen and gently pushed outward. The clicking sound they made was a little loud but Mac didn't stir at all.

The screen came free easier than he expected. He lost his grip and the screen dropped from the frame and clattered to the ground outside.

He looked back to Mac and saw that she still hadn't budged. With a smile, Joe climbed into the window, carefully turned himself so that he was facing back into the room, and scaled down the side of the house. When his feet were dangling in the air roughly two feet away from the bench, he let go of the window frame before he could allow himself to chicken out. He landed on the bench perfectly, grimacing at the way it creaked under his one hundred and thirty-five pounds. He quickly hopped down onto the ground before the bench had a chance to break.

He picked up the screen and, with some effort, managed to balance himself along the bench and place it mostly back within the window frame. He made sure to leave the bottom corners free so he could pop it back out when he returned.

He opted to leave his bike, feeling that it would be easier to remain stealthy on foot. He ran down the driveway towards Kerr Lane and then headed right. He gave one hard look back towards his own cabin, deathly afraid that he'd see the light on in his parents' room. But there was nothing; the entire cabin was dark.

Joe reached Kerr Lane and kept straight, towards Valerie's cabin and the shed they had hung out around yesterday. He was a few steps into his speedy walk when he realized that he was all alone in the woods at night. He didn't know what sorts of animals lived out here and the thought suddenly had him scared. Were there bears? Cougars? He didn't think so, but he had no way of being certain.

He heard an owl hooting somewhere nearby and what seemed to be an infinite chorus of crickets and tree frogs. Hearing this and knowing that Valerie was waiting for him just up ahead dashed any fears he had of being mauled by some rural woodland creature or horror-movie maniac. He headed on with confidence in his step, suddenly finding the cooled night air and the vast darkness all around him exhilarating. The stars dotted the sky like stray salt on a dark tablecloth and the tree branches reached up, some blending with the night sky and others obscuring it. He took it all in, knowing that New York had much to offer, but nothing like this.

He noticed the flickering orange light of a few fireflies moments later. He'd never seen them before and couldn't help but smile. The way they floated and glowed in a weird orange-tinted light was almost comical, like something out of a cartoon. They glowed up ahead of him as if they were beckoning him on into the woods…which, he guessed, was more creepy than beautiful.

He didn't realize that he was passing Valerie's cabin until he was standing directly beside the driveway. He looked towards the cabin and saw that it was just as dark as the one he had left behind. He sped up and took his phone out of his pocket. It read 12:01.

He broke into a lazy sprint and started to look along the right edge of the road for the entrance to the thin footpath Valerie had led him down yesterday. After a few moments, he slowed a bit, fearing that he would miss it. When he sensed that he might have already gone too far, he stopped completely and peered out to the edge of the woods, sure that he had passed it.

He turned to walk back the way he had come, hoping he'd be able to see the trail if he used his phone as a makeshift nightlight. He took two steps in that direction, reaching for his phone, and then stopped cold in his tracks.

Something moved behind him. And as soon as he realized this, there was a hand around his mouth.

He tried to cry out, but the hand was tight against his lips.

"Don't move," a voice said from behind him. "You're dead."

His heart had started to gallop madly before he realized that the voice belonged to Valerie.

It started beating even faster when he realized that she was still holding him—one hand at his mouth, the other at his back—and speaking directly into his ear. He felt her breath on his neck and he was suddenly aware of an urgent stirring below his waist.

He chuckled nervously and she released his mouth. He turned to her, unsure of whether he should be glad to see her or pissed that she had almost made him scream.

"Sorry," she said. "I couldn't help it."

Although she was now two feet away from him, he could still feel her breath on his neck and along the lobe of his ear. His nerves seemed to soak it all up.

"It's okay," he said. "How long were you waiting to jump out at me like that?"

"Just a few minutes."

"Not cool," he said.

But it had been very cool. He could still feel her hand on his back and over his mouth. He licked his lips, thinking he might be able to taste her hand still there.

"Ready to catch some fireflies?" she asked.

"Sure."

"Then come on," she said. She reached out and grabbed his arm, leading him further down the lane.

"Where are we going?" he asked. Honestly, he didn't care. With her hand gently around his upper arm, he'd go wherever she took him.

"Just a bit further down this way," she answered. "There's a small field where they swarm. It's hard to catch them in the trees like this."

He didn't question her. He just let her lead him down the road and was suddenly very grateful that it was night. Anything remotely resembling fear was gone now, replaced with the idea that something about this was incredibly romantic. And while he'd usually cringe at the mention of anything being romantic, it was suddenly very exciting to him.

They passed another few darkened cabins and then Valerie led them down a road to the right. At first it looked like every other driveway on the lane but it quickly widened out into a larger expanse of dirt. This dirt was overtaken by weeds right away, as high as his chest his some areas. Throughout the small field, there were a few broken down old speed boats that looked to have been salvaged for their parts. The lake came into view behind all of this, sparkling in the moonlight almost as if it had snuck up on the land.

As Valerie had promised, the field was alive with fireflies. There were easily a hundred of them drifting in the darkness, flickering their orange light like little spaceships that floated through the weeds.

"Okay," Joe said, clearly impressed. "This is pretty cool."

"Isn't it?" Valerie said, smiling.

Joe walked slowly into the field and held his right hand out. He cupped it and brought it slowly up under two fireflies. When they were on his hand, he cupped his left hand over them and peered inside through the space between his thumb and forefinger. The flies didn't seem panicked at all; they simply lit up the darkness inside his closed hands with their otherworldly glow. He let out a tiny giggle at the way their legs and wings tickled the insides of his hands.

He looked to see if Valerie was also catching them, but she was walking further into the weeds alongside one of the gutted speedboats. He followed after her with the two fireflies still in his hand. Up ahead, he saw where the field dipped a bit, making way for a cracked concrete slab. The slab dropped into the lake at a slight angle. Joe guessed this was an old loading ramp of some kind. If Joe had to guess, the concrete ramp was probably as old as the broken down speedboats that occupied the field.

"Sort of creepy, isn't it?" Valerie asked.

"Yeah, I guess."

They walked across the length of the field, wading through the weeds, and came to the ramp. Joe watched as Valerie kicked off her shoes and walked carefully down the concrete ramp. Joe followed her, looking out over the lake just in time to see a fish jump out of the water some distance out, chasing after a daring nighttime insect skirting along the surface. He grinned at it, finally releasing the fireflies that had been held captive in his hands. They floated up and away slowly, almost in a dance.

Out in the water, the fish went back into the water with a delicate splash. As he watched this, Joe realized that the lake looked like a totally different place at night. This close to the water, it was easy to imagine that he and Valerie were standing on the banks of a body of water in some distant galaxy. With the weeds behind them, the shells of the boats, and nothing but forest and water to all sides, it felt like they were the only two people on the planet.

Joe was hesitant to take off his shoes, but he walked to the edge of the water and looked out. Valerie was walking into the water, her feet submerged as she followed the ramp down. She then walked out to where the water came to her knees, the legs of her shorts still a good three inches away from getting wet. Joe caught himself staring at her thin legs and jerked his attention back out to the water.

Another bank sat straight ahead, roughly one hundred yards out and barely visible in the dark. Porch lights glowed over there, dim and distant. To the left, the lake seemed to get choked out by the forest, the banks coming in and out to allow room for the cabins along Kerr Lane and the other winding roads that crept through the forest. To the left, though, the lake seemed to grow in size. The forest dropped away to all sides, giving an indication of Clarkton Lake's true size.

Joe hadn't had the chance to go out onto the lake yet but his dad kept promising that they'd rent a boat for a week or so and try some skiing or tubing. The idea was exciting but daunting at the same time. Joe had been to the beach before, but the lake was different somehow. The ocean kept going, spreading all around the globe until it came back around on itself. But the lake was confined, a hole in the earth that was much more peaceful and inviting than the thunderous roar of the ocean. It was sort of intimidating in terms of its isolation.

Valerie walked out another foot or so, the concrete boat ramp diving deeper under her feet. The water was now touching her shorts and when she turned back to smile at him, it took everything within Joe to not get in and join her.

"We need to go swimming sometime," Valerie said. "I'd invite you out on the boat with me and Dad sometime, but he'd kill you."

"He doesn't even know me."

"You're a male. That's enough for him."

"So you'll never be allowed to date at all?" Joe asked.

"Maybe when I'm off to college. Dad isn't mean...don't get that impression. He's just been very protective ever since mom died."

Not too protective, Joe thought. *He gets drunk in front of baseball games in the afternoon, leaves you unattended, and is oblivious when you sneak out at midnight.*

But he knew such thoughts weren't fair. He didn't know Valerie and her family history. After all, with some sort of drama lurking at the heart of his own parents' marriage, who was he to judge?

"Come on out," Valerie said, offering her hand. "The water is sort of chilly but it's nice. Just up to your knees. Come on."

Joe could technically do it. He was wearing a pair of mesh shorts, so he could get in up to his knees and there would be no evidence for his parents to discover that he had been out at night.

Her arm was still stretched out, offering her hand. Seeing her out there smiling at him, Joe couldn't resist. He kicked off his shoes and peeled off his socks. He reached out and took her hand, trying to play it as cool as possible when her fingers wrapped around his own.

As he took a step closer to her, he watched another fish break the surface of the water several feet behind them. It was sort of cool to see the lake at night, to see the quiet of it that most people forgot about during the day. It was—

Joe's eyes locked on the fish that had broken the water and gave it an uncertain glance. It had broken the surface of the water, but remained there, about fifteen feet away. It looked like it was just floating above the surface. Was it dead? Was it some weird fish that he'd never seen before?

"What is it?" Valerie asked.

She turned to look in the direction Joe was staring and took a sudden step backwards. As they watched, the thing that Joe had originally thought to be a fish swam along, breaking the water with a strange hump-like shape that appeared to be on its back. It swam quickly, going under and then breaking the surface again several times in a series of snake-like movements.

"Is it a snake?" Joe asked, already taking a nervous step back towards the top of the concrete ramp.

"No," Valerie answered. "That would be a *huge* snake."

Joe knew she was right. The thing was still moving out there, coasting along at the surface of the water with a large hump breaking the water. It made a turning motion and when it did, the single hump became two.

Joe's mind instantly brought up the images he had seen of the so-called Lochness Monster and its telltale humps breaking the water. And as comical as he found the possibility of the Lochness Monster to be, he was suddenly filled with bitter fear. It plummeted through him like a rock from a cliff.

But this was nothing like that certain fabled lake monster. First of all, it was much smaller. Secondly, Joe was pretty sure there was no sort of body attached to the thing; there was only the snake-like shape of it.

Also, it was moving fast. It was then, as he watched it and tried to make sense of its shape, that it put on extra speed and came straight towards them.

"Shit," Joe said, the word coming out in a whoosh of terrified breath.

Still holding Valerie's hand, he yanked her back at the exact same moment she had started to retreat. Their bodies collided as they started up the ramp and they went down in the shallow water in a tangle of arms and legs. There was a brief moment where Joe realized that his clothes were going to be soaked now and he'd have to come up with some lie to present to his folks.

But that thought was obliterated when he saw that the thing in the water had reached the place where he and Valerie had been standing less than three seconds ago. And it was still coming, not losing any speed.

Joe got to his feet, lake water splashing into his mouth. He reached out for Valerie and took her by the hand without thinking about it. He helped her to her feet and they once again started back towards the field.

As they made their way up the large concrete slab, Joe chanced a look back. What he saw drew a scream up in his throat but he was too terrified to let it out.

The thing had come mostly out of the water. It *did* look like a snake, but not like any snake Joe had ever seen. It was at least six or seven feet long and three feet across. Its skin looked to be rough on top, and white and soft underneath. He was able to see underneath the creature clearly as it raised the top half of its body. It reared back in a way that made Joe think of rubber, and then it lunged forward. In the split second that its underside was exposed, Joe saw a series of weird pucker-like things along its underside, but they paled in comparison to the slimy mouth that opened wide as it sprang towards him.

Joe's instincts hit a gear in his heart and mind that he didn't even know existed. Seeing the thing darting forward, he pushed Valerie to the left and followed after her with a panic-fueled leap into the weeds. The creature had been so close to striking Joe's leg that he could feel lake water spraying off of its body as it sailed towards him.

Valerie cried out as Joe landed hard on her leg. Joe again found himself tangled up in her arms and legs as they both scrambled back up to their feet. Joe found Valerie's hand, took it, and started to back further into the weeds behind them.

"Where is it?" Valerie asked in a frightened whisper.

Joe looked frantically around but couldn't see it. He supposed they were in a decent position to see the creature before it saw them, though; if it came barreling towards them, they'd see a clear indentation in the weeds, coming towards them. They stood quietly, roughly ten feet into the weeds. One of the old speedboats sat a few yards to their right, sitting on blocks.

In the quiet, Joe heard loons and the same owl that he had heard asking its ageless question as he had come down Kerr Lane by himself. But there was something else, too…something closer.

He could hear the thing moving, slithering along the ground in front of the boat ramp. In his mind's eye, he could still see the soft white underside of the thing as it had struck at them. The sound it made as it moved seemed to match that vision perfectly.

Valerie stepped closer to him, holding on to his arm. He felt her trembling, which was a feat in and of itself because he was shaking like a leaf, too. They both looked over the weeds, hoping to catch a glimpse of it.

That's when the weeds at the edge of the field started leaning in. They started falling slowly in a perfect path, directly towards them. Joe felt the muscles in his legs bunching up, wanting to run but soaked in fear and apparently immobile.

The moving path drew closer and closer, the slithering noise mingling with the dry scratchy sound of the weeds falling. Joe watched the path grow and suddenly felt the fear in his legs evaporate. He was ready to haul ass, to head back to Kerr Lane and hope they could outrun the thing.

The moving path in the weeds ahead of them came to a stop.

Time seemed to freeze as Joe and Valerie stared at the area where the creature had been sliding towards them. After a few seconds of silence, the sound of slithering and breaking weeds reached their ears again. Only this time, the sound was growing fainter. Another path broke out in the weeds directly by the first one, heading back towards the ramp.

Joe felt Valerie relaxing a bit beside him but noticed that she still held his arm. They stood motionless until the sound of slithering was gone completely. Joe strained his ears and was pretty sure he heard the moment when the thing made its way back into the water, easing in quickly but quietly.

"It's gone," he said.

"What the hell was it?" Valerie asked, her voice close to hysteria. Her hand traveled down his arm and found his hand. Joe took it, their hands interlacing.

"I don't know," Joe said.

Still holding her hand, he led her away from the woods by the ramp, heading further into the overgrowth that led back towards the dirt road. She went with him and although he was still shaking in terror, he realized that this was the first time he had led her anywhere. It felt good in a prideful way, but it also made him feel terribly lost.

"Did you see it?" she asked.

"Yeah. It looked like...I don't know. A mix between a snake and a slug. But it was too big to be either one."

He also recalled that slimy-coated black maw of a mouth but he decided to not terrify her with that bit of information.

When they reached the top of the field again, Valerie sat down heavily, as if exhausted. Joe sat down beside her. Somewhere along the way, he had released her hand but he sat so close to her that their legs were touching. They looked out towards the lake and said nothing.

"I'm going to ask a stupid question," Joe said.

"Yeah?"

"Is that some weird ass animal that's *supposed* to live in a lake?"

"I don't think so," Valerie answered. "That thing was more like a monster or something. Right?"

Joe nodded. He wanted very badly to get the hell away from there but didn't want to sound too scared. Besides...whatever that thing had been, it was gone. It had apparently needed to return to the water. Maybe it was like a fish, in that it needed to be underwater to breathe.

"Maybe we should get back home," Valerie said, echoing Joe's thought. "I need to try to hide these wet clothes."

"Same here," Joe said, wondering how he was going to get this past his parents.

"And that thing," Valerie said. "We can't tell anyone, can we? We'd get in trouble."

"Yeah," Joe agreed. "It would be like turning ourselves in to our folks."

This knowledge sat between them, heavy and as tangible as the fireflies that continued to dance around them, unaware of the horrors that had occurred under their specks of orange light.

"Come on," Valerie said, standing up and offering her hand again.

Joe took it and felt her still trembling. He used what courage he had left (most having been drained by the thing that had come out of the water for them) and interlocked his fingers through hers again. She gave his hand a squeeze and started walking. There was speed in their step as they left the field and the old speedboats behind.

"You okay?" Joe asked as they stepped back onto Kerr Lane.

"Yeah. Just...shaken up. I don't see myself sleeping tonight. Or tomorrow."

"Same here," he said, trying not to sound as terrified as he really was.

When they neared Valerie's cabin, she stopped and faced him. The night seemed to grow still around them, even the owls and loons falling quiet for a moment.

"Thanks," she said. "If you hadn't pushed me down, that thing...,"

"It's okay," he said as she trailed off.

They stood facing one another in silence, looking at each other with a pointed aloofness that only teenagers that have not yet had their hearts broken are capable of. Joe wanted to kiss her and he was pretty sure that she would let him if he tried. But the gravity of the situation was off. They were both still filled with a terror that had not yet worn off. Joe fought the intense urge to take that one step forward and put his mouth on hers and, instead, gave her hand a playful squeeze.

"You got a phone?" he asked.

"Yeah. Dad finally let me have one for my last birthday."

"Will you text me tomorrow? Just to let me know you're okay?"

"Yeah, of course."

They pulled out their phones and exchanged numbers. As he entered her number, Joe realized that it was the first time a girl had ever given him her number.

"How about we meet tomorrow at the shed?" he suggested when their numbers had been exchanged.

"I have no idea what Dad has planned tomorrow," she said. "So I don't know what time."

"Just show up," Joe said. "I'll be there. I'll wait. Or text me."

"I think I'd rather show up," she said. "The mystery of it all is really cool."

"Yeah, I think so, too."

She smiled at him and Joe released her hand, not sure how much longer he could resist himself. He was surprised when she leaned forward and kissed him on the cheek.

"Thanks for meeting me tonight," she said. "And, you know, saving my life."

He could only smile in response. "Good night," he said.

She headed towards her cabin and Joe watched her go.

When he headed back to his own cabin, the loons, crickets, owls and other night creatures seemed more pronounced. The forest seemed alive. And although most of the sounds were pleasant, Joe couldn't help but hear that slithering noise in his head, the sound of some unnamable creature from the dark waters of the lake that had sprung up on the shore to devour him.

FOURTEEN

Ted Wylerman parked his service truck in the driveway of one of the more luxurious homes that sat on Clarkton Lake and instantly felt depressed. The cabin was owned by the Carter family, one of the wealthiest in the area. They rented their home out from time to time when they spent months overseas in Paris or London or wherever the hell they vacationed when they got tired of the beautiful lake view offered from their enormous back deck.

The weekly rent for the cabin was more than Ted's monthly mortgage payment. He knew this because he had inquired about it as a goof last summer. Looking at the house, Ted simply didn't understand how someone could put so much money into a home: the pretentious trees by the front stoop that looked like something out of *Alice in Wonderland,* the big marble *C* over the front door, and the elaborate stone walkways that led to a porch that was twice the size of Ted's bedroom.

He knew no one was home. The Carters had headed out two days ago, lining up wealthy renters that were scheduled to come in tomorrow. He knew all of this because Mr. Carter had told him so three days ago when he had visited Ted's office and asked to have his floating dock fixed.

Ted cast a glance beyond the immaculately cared-for lawn and to the elegant pier that stretched twenty-five feet into the water. The dock sat at the end of it, looking bare without the Carter's speedboat and pontoon boat anchored to either side. Ted took the sidewalk that wound around to the back of the house. There were three sidewalks, all leading around the property and connecting in the back at the huge grilling porch. With each step, Ted wondered how much spent money he was passing…from the landscaping to the stone walkways.

Working on properties like this always depressed him. He knew the Carters fairly well and knew that Mr. Carter was some sort of hotshot professor that wrote books and was hired to give lectures.

Mrs. Carter was some sort of online savant and had a very successful graphic design company that she ran out of her very large house.

Good for them, Ted often thought. But of course, he didn't mean it. Despite the hard feelings, Ted was the sort of man that had no problem owning up to his own shortcomings. Rather than attend college, he had partied in nearby towns, smoked too much pot, and got fired from too many part-time jobs. The way he saw it, he was lucky to be the assistant manager at Dock Doctors, one of only two dock-repair companies in the large lakeside community that thrived in Clarkton.

It was, for the most part, easy work. Based on what Mr. Carter had told him about the dock, this would be a repair that Mr. Carter could have probably done himself. But why do it yourself when you could afford someone else to do it? It was a luxury that Ted knew he'd never have, but he supposed he understood it.

He crossed the back yard and came to the small pier. Like the house, it had been designed to look like something from a much more pristine location. The posts nearly looking Roman and the wood along the pier and the dock had been recently sanded and stained. Beyond that, it looked like a miniature model of the long fishing piers at the beach. Benches sat to both sides in two different locations, along with cute wooden tables affixed to the pier.

Ted reached the end of the pier and came to the dock. Mr. Carter had said that it was lopsided, the right end dipping into the water at an angle that had nearly caused him to lose his balance and fall into the water on a few occasions. As he stood fully on it, Ted saw that he hadn't been exaggerating. The angle was harsh and any movement on the dock seemed to send the right side of the dock dipping into the water.

Ted's first thought was that one of the float barrels underneath was in need of repair. This would be an expensive fix, which was great for business, but it would also be a pain in the ass. Most fixes were relatively simple and could be fixed with a special kind of Styrofoam. These jobs were often way overcharged, but the customer was always happy with the quick repair time.

Based on the angle of the dock's dip, Ted was pretty sure this wasn't going to be the case. He was going to have to get in the water to check it out, something he had been hoping to avoid when coming out to the Carter residence.

Just to make sure, he lay down on the right edge of the dock, carefully hugging the side so he didn't fall in from the tilt. His two hundred pounds caused the dock to dip down even more on the right side, making it a bit awkward to stick his hand in the water and try to feel along the base of the barrels submerged in the water. He had to extend his arm all the way, his shoulder stretching over the side of the dock, to securely rest his hand on the curved surface of the flotation barrel.

He ran his hand along the side, not feeling any obvious dents or holes. He knew this meant nothing, as even the smallest of dings could slowly let in enough water to cause the sort of unbalanced position the dock was currently in.

Ted inched his way along the side of the ramp, running his hand along the barrel underwater, feeling for any sort of fault in it. As he neared the center of it, he thought he felt a sizable dent but could not find any puncture with his fingers. He felt around a bit longer, making a note of the location.

He moved on, heading to the far end of the dock, still crawling along on his stomach with his right arm submerged in the water.

When he felt something wrap around his arm, it happened so fast that he wasn't aware of what had happened until he felt himself being pulled forward.

He cried out as he fell from the dock and into the water. The scream was promptly cut off by a mouthful of lake water. He slapped out his free hand, trying to grab onto the dock, but he was being pulled under too fast. All his fingers managed to touch was the slimy underside of one of the barrels.

He tried pulling his arm free of whatever had it, but it was useless. He could feel whatever it was coiling around his upper arm, climbing up it and tightening its grip at the same time. He slapped at the thing, trying to find purchase. And through it all, he did his best to make sense of what was happening while not choking on the lake water that was going down his throat.

Could it be a snake? A huge *snake?*

It was a possibility, but he was pretty sure a snake would have tried biting him rather than wrapping up his arm and pulling him under.

He was able to grab on to part of the thing's body as it continued to pull him down and away from the dock, but the body was slippery and he couldn't dig his nails in.

Then, just as he realized that he was running out of breath, Ted's feet touched the bottom of the lake. It felt spongy through his shoes and it was difficult to gain much traction. Still, the moment he felt this, he dug his toes in as best as he could and pushed himself forward against the force of the thing that was pulling at him.

He glided forward and upwards easily enough and the sudden surge in his momentum apparently caught his attacker off guard because its grip loosened for just a moment. Sensing this, Ted pulled his arm away and instantly started swimming for the surface. He was sure that at any moment, the thing would wrap around him again. He *did* feel it reaching out for him, something soft yet insistent slapping at his back.

Ted swam faster, his lungs burning and his guts on fire with fear. When he broke the surface, he found himself only two feet away from the Carter's lopsided dock. He took two huge swimming lunges for it, sucking in air in a huge gulp. When his hand landed on the wood, he jerked himself up at once.

He was halfway out of the water when he felt a vice-like grip on his waist. It jerked him down, but he kept his grip on the dock, pulling up and screaming in pain.

The thing was squeezing him tight, continuing to tighten and pull against him like the Indian Burns he had been given as a kid in grade school. He felt something dig into his back, tearing through his shirt and slicing into his flesh. He screamed, still trying to pull himself away.

But then he felt the thing slap at the side of his face. It reached around, caressing his head for just a moment before latching on with the same force it was applying to his waist and back.

Before the thing clamped down on his head, he saw a dirty white color that was broken by what looked like brown-tinged suction cups. He had just enough time to think of octopi and squids before the white became black, covering his eyes and squeezing.

Ted tried to scream but the tentacle was already over his mouth. It squeezed at his head while he continued trying to pull himself up onto the dock. It was squeezing harder now, hard enough to where Ted was certain that a few of his ribs had broken. But that pain was nothing compared to the pressure he felt in his head as he felt himself giving up, the muscles in his arms no longer able to pull at the dock for safety.

When the thing squeezed harder at his head, his jaw shattered and several teeth splintered and cracked. Again, he tried to scream, but there was nothing. He couldn't breathe, couldn't move...

He let go of the dock, unable to fight anymore.

Before he went completely under, the pressure against his head became too much.

There was a crunch and a wet popping sound that left the side of the Carter's dock covered in blood and chunks of grey matter.

These remnants, left to dry and rot in the summer sun, were the only traces of Ted Wylerman anyone would ever find.

FIFTEEN

Joe was sitting on the couch with his earbuds stuck in his ears, listening to the bruising electric sounds of a band called Death Blow. He was staring at the ceiling and thinking about Valerie. He kept seeing her smile—those sparkling white teeth and those thin lips—and wondered what her lips tasted like.

He was in the middle of such speculations when Mac plopped down beside him. She was grinning with the same sly undertones that Joe was accustomed to seeing on their father's face whenever he had a secret that he couldn't wait to tell. Mac tapped insistently at Joe's leg, trying to get his attention. He managed to ignore her for about thirty seconds before it was clear that she had no intention of stopping.

"What?" Joe said, annoyed, pausing the music.

"I know what you did," she said, the smile still pasted to her face.

"What are you talking about?" he asked, ready to tune her out and ignore her again. Even now, his mind was already drifting back to Valerie, whom he was meeting in less than two hours.

"The other night," Mac said. "I didn't see you go out, but when you came back in, you woke me up. I know you snuck out."

Joe pulled his earbuds from his ears and scowled at her. Sure, he was mad at her but he was also upset with himself. He thought he'd been quite stealthy, but apparently not.

"And?" he said.

"And I want to know where you went."

"None of your business," Joe said angrily.

"I want to know. And I want you to show me where you went. If you don't, I'll tell Mom and Dad."

"Why are you telling me now?" Joe asked, wondering what sort of evil schemes an eight year old might be capable of.

"Because I'm getting bored," she said. "The lake is fun and all, but it's getting boring. I really wish Dad would rent us a boat for a few days."

"He will," Joe said, hoping to seize this opportunity to swerve the conversation. "Just give him time. He's really busy. You think you could get up in skis or do you just want to tube?"

Mac shrugged and quickly returned to her point. *She's good,* Joe thought. *She's going to be a handful when she gets older.*

"I'll tell them," she said. "Unless you show me."

For a terrifying instant, Joe thought of the thing that had come out of the water and nearly devoured him. He could easily still see its leathery hide and its impossible black mouth. He thought of Mac standing before it as the thing brought its weight down on her. She was a pest and could be a little bitch at times, but he loved her more than anything on the planet. Thinking of Mac in the same vicinity as that monster made his heart sag. It also made him brazenly protective in a way that he was unfamiliar with.

"I'm not going to show you," he said.

"Then I'll tell."

He believed her right away. She was not really old enough to know how or when to bluff. As much as he hated to do it, he knew of a way to get out of this without causing too much trouble and inconvenience. He had to act fast, though; past experience told him that Mac wouldn't wait long before running to their folks with the news.

"I snuck out to just hang with a friend," he finally admitted.

"You don't have friends here," she pointed out.

"Well, I made one. We hung out. We caught fireflies."

Mac's face lit up at this. "That's awesome. I want to go!"

"I don't think we're going to be doing that anymore," Joe said. And then, before he knew he was going to say it, he added: "It was sort of scary."

"Is this friend a *girl?*" Mac asked slyly.

"It's none of your business."

"It's not Mom or Dad's business, either," Mac said. "But I bet they'd love to know."

There's no way out of this, Joe thought. He was furious with her but in a small way he actually respected her for being able to blackmail him so efficiently. And besides…he did sort of relate to her claim of being bored with the lake. After eleven days, she was already starting to get bored. It was slowly starting to lose its charms with him, too. But now that Valerie was part of the picture, it had gotten much more interesting.

"Yes. She's a girl," he finally answered.

"I want to meet her."

"You won't shut up unless I agree, will you?"

"That's right," she said, the sly smile coming back to her face.

"Fine," Joe said. "I'm meeting her in two hours. If Mom and Dad will let you, you can come with me. Tell them you want to ride your bike with me or something."

The delight on her face almost made Joe not care that she was infringing on his time with Valerie. She was too damned cute for her own good sometimes.

"Thanks, Joe," she said, leaping on him and hugging him.

"Don't thank me," he said. "This is blackmail. I'm only letting you come because I don't have a choice. I don't *want* you to come."

"Oh," she said, as if she had temporarily forgotten the whole point of coming to him. She then furrowed her brow and did her best to put on an angry appearance.

"Two hours," Joe said. "You better not make me late."

She nodded and leaped off the couch, skipping towards their room. Joe watched her go, smiling. She was really smart for an eight year old and even though he acted like she irritated him most of the time, he knew that she was pretty cool as far as little sisters went.

He plugged his earbuds back into his head and zoned out with thoughts of Valerie again, a rather stark contrast to his music of choice. Thinking of Valerie made him feel weird in a way he had heard about and had even experienced with another couple of girls in school, but never to this degree. He thought of what her hand had felt like in his and how oddly romantic the aftermath of seeing the monster had been. They'd shared panic and fear and that had linked them in a way he wasn't quite able to understand.

He wondered what it would be like to see her this time, two days after their encounter with the thing. He wondered if things would be different and, if so, if there would be a stronger connection or some sort of fissure between them. Mac would be along this time and there was no telling how *that* would change things.

He tried to bring his mind back to the feel of her hand and the way they had looked at one another as they had parted ways. All of it was electric, like a surge to his head and heart.

But it was also all ultimately tainted by the sight of the creature rising up from the lake, nearly paralyzing him with fear. And it was that image that stayed with him until he got up from the couch to meet Valerie an hour and a half later.

***

Mac was waiting on the porch steps when Joe walked outside. She looked up to him with a knowing smile and Joe could only roll his eyes. They wasted no time and started off together, Joe on his bike and Mac on her little pink bike that would have to be replaced next year. As it was, Mac's knees nearly hit the handlebars every time the pedals came up, the chain housing creaking like an old floor board. Joe looked down longingly at the rusted bolts where the training wheels had once been and frowned.

She's growing up too fast, he thought. *This must be what parents feel like to watch their kids getting older.*

Watching her on the bike made Joe understand that he himself was on his way out of childhood. It was more than just recalling how quickly *his* eight-year-old moments had passed him by; it was seeing how quickly his little sister was growing up. She had gone from training wheels to solo riding far too quickly and was now about to grow out of her first bike. She'd gone from hesitantly jumping into the deep end of the pool back home to waiting impatiently for her turn on the diving board. How in the hell had that happened so fast?

She was humming one of the songs from *Frozen* as she rode alongside him. He wanted to be angry with her but couldn't bring himself to do it. They had a secret between them now and it made him feel closer to her, maybe even more protective. His dad had told him not too long ago that he'd end up caring a great deal for

Mac as they got older and he wondered if this was the beginning of that.

Mac had held her end of their little act up well. When Joe had asked his mom if he could go out on his bike, she had agreed but only if he would take Mac as well. He'd acted as disappointed as he could manage and he was pretty sure she'd bought it. His parents usually had pretty good bullshit detectors but they seemed to be off this summer. Joe supposed it was the fact that they were dealing with whatever issues were between them—issues that Joe had started to sense less and less over the last few days.

Maybe the little vacation to this middle of nowhere lake was repairing whatever was wrong between them. If they had mended fences and worked things out, they'd done it all in private because Joe had been none the wiser. He hoped they were okay now or at least on the way there.

When he and Mac pedaled their bikes by the driveway to Valerie's cabin, he looked to the yard. She was nowhere to be seen and her dad's truck was parked where it usually was. He hoped she was already at the little shack waiting for him. With that thought in his head, he quickened his pace. His bike picked up a slight wobble and the humid air whooshed by his head.

"Hey!" Mac shouted. "Not so fast! I can't keep up!"

Joe thought about how he had crashed on this very road not too long ago and certainly didn't want the same thing to happen to Mac. That's just what he needed—Mac to go home with a busted nose or some missing teeth while he was supposed to be watching after her.

He slowed down and then brought the bike to a halt at the footpath that led to the shack. He looked behind him and saw Mac trying her best to catch up. She was slightly hunched up over the handlebars, pedaling as fast as she could. Her tongue was sticking out between her lips as she put extra effort into the last few pumps of her legs. Joe couldn't help but smile. If she pedaled any harder, the bike would fall apart.

Then, further off behind her, he saw Valerie step out onto the road from her driveway. She turned in their direction, hesitated for a moment, and then started forward. Joe felt his heart start doing cartwheels and he felt an impossibly wide smile spread across his face.

Mac pulled up alongside him, panting for breath and red in the face. She looked up to him, confused. "Why did we stop?" she asked.

"This is it," Joe said, his eyes still locked on Valerie. She had now broken into a jog to reach them and as far as Joe was concerned, she was running entirely too slow.

"This?" Mac said, looking into the woods. "This little path?"

"Yeah," Joe said, barely aware that Mac was even talking to him.

Mac turned around then, hearing Valerie's approaching footsteps. Mac gave her a curious glance and then looked up to Joe. "Is that your *friend?*" she asked.

"Yes," Joe said. He wondered if this was going to result in hours upon hours of being teased by Mac. He wouldn't put it past her. It would be a shame, though; he was really starting to like the little brat.

"Hey there," Valerie said as she came up alongside them.

"Hey," Joe said, finding it hard to not look at her. Her hair was in a ponytail today, revealing the entire shape of her face. He found himself focusing on odd parts: the curve of her jaw, the soft flesh between her neck and shoulders, and the perfect shape of her ears.

You're losing it, he thought to himself.

He managed to look away and then back down to Mac. "Valerie, this is my little sister, Mackenzie."

"Well hey there," Valerie said. "You were riding that bike pretty hard, huh?"

"Yeah," Mac said proudly. "It's hard, too. I'm getting too big for it."

"I saw that," Valerie said, giving Joe a quick smile.

"Sorry for bringing her," Joe said. "I didn't have much of a choice. She heard me come back in the other night and threatened to tell our folks if I didn't let her come along."

Valerie looked down to Mac and put her arm around her. "I would have done the same thing," she said.

Mac giggled and then looked to Joe. "Yeah," she said. "I like her. She should be your girlfriend."

"Jeez, Mac!" Joe was petrified but the smile on Valerie's face made it okay.

"I *should* be," Valerie joked. "But I don't know. Your brother's a little clumsy. I'm not sure if he's my type."

Joe's eyes grew wide as they teamed up on him. But when Valerie turned her back to him to look Mac in the eyes, her right hand found his and gave his fingers a squeeze. He squeezed back, understanding that this was all in good fun. She was trying to make Mac feel at ease and maybe even ensuring that Mac now became a part of their secret meetings. If she could do that, Joe felt certain that Mac would never go tattling to their folks about his secret.

"Should we show her the shack?" Valerie asked.

"Sure," Joe said, trying to find the same playful enthusiasm Valerie was putting on. It felt fake on him, though. He figured he'd let Valerie run with it. Meanwhile, he'd stand by pouting because his little sister was soaking up all of Valerie's attention.

The three of them walked down the footpath and came to the shack. Mac took a moment to look at then grinned. Sure, the place had a creepy vibe to it but it also had an irresistible *you-probably-shouldn't-go-in-there* vibe.

"Cool," she said.

"It is sort of cool, huh?" Joe said.

Mac walked a few steps ahead, inching closer to it. "What's in there?"

"Just old dried up fish guts and fishing stuff," Valerie said. "I think it used to be an old fishing cabin. People would catch fish and gut them and clean them in there. There's a pitchfork in there, too. I think that must have been used for frog gigging."

"What's frog gigging?" Mac asked. Joe was listening attentively, as he had never heard of such a thing, either.

"It's gross," Valerie said. "People would go through the woods and along the banks of the lake looking for frogs. They'd gig them with a pitchfork and then take the legs home and eat them."

"That's disgusting," Mac said.

"It really is," Valerie said. "My dad said he did it a few times as a kid but he never liked the taste of frog legs. He always just liked killing frogs with a pitchfork."

"Sounds like your dad has some issues," Joe joked.

"Oh, let's not open *that* box right now."

Mac stepped closer to the shack, peering in through the partially opened door. She then turned back to Joe and asked, "Can I go in?"

"If you want," he said. "Just watch your step."

"I will," Mac said, already sliding in through the doorway.

Joe and Valerie stood in front of the old building as Mac carefully stepped inside. When she was fully inside and out of sight, Joe felt a flutter of worry.

"She's cute," Valerie said.

"Yeah, I guess she *can* be," Joe said.

"Does she follow you around everywhere?"

"Not really. Every now and then she'll get in these moods where she wants to do whatever I'm doing...but not so much anymore."

"And she knows you snuck out, huh?"

"Yeah. And that sucks, because I was sure I had been really quiet."

Valerie started walking towards the far edge of the cabin, towards the back where a clear view of the lake could be seen through the scraggly trees. Joe walked along beside her and with arms that felt like wobbling jelly, he reached out and took her hand. Their fingers interlocked as they headed down closer to the water.

"I had a nightmare about that thing last night," Valerie said. "It ate you and then came after me. I fell down and just before it fell on top of me, I woke up."

"That's terrible," Joe said.

"We really saw that thing, didn't we?" she asked.

"Yeah."

"Still no idea what it was?"

Joe had spent the last two days thinking about it but could come up with nothing. He'd even done a little internet research and never found any satisfactory answers. The best he could come up with was that the thing had been some enormous mutated eel but he knew that wasn't right.

"No idea."

"I almost told my dad," Valerie said. "I know it would have basically been telling him that I had snuck out to meet you, but...I don't know. It seems like the police or someone should know that something like that is out in the lake."

Joe only nodded. She had a good point but he couldn't imagine going to his parents with news like this. First, as Valerie said, he'd basically be turning himself in. Secondly, he wasn't sure if his parents would believe him.

"I know one thing," Valerie said.

"What's that?"

"I won't be getting back in the water for a while."

"Same here," Joe said.

"Something else happened in the nightmare," Valerie said, turning to look directly at him. "Only, this thing happened before the bad stuff...before it actually became a nightmare."

"What was it?"

She gripped his hand a little tighter and took a step towards him. Their eyes were locked and there was no more than a foot of space between them.

"We were standing in the field of fireflies," she said. "I caught one and when I did, you came up to see it. When I opened my hand, it flew away and when I looked up to see it...you kissed me."

"Yeah?" Joe said.

"Yeah. It was nice."

His stomach felt like something had exploded in it and his heart was a thrumming coil of electric wire in his chest. All the same, his body did what it wanted to do. He leaned in, seeing that she was doing the same. Just as she closed her eyes, their lips no more than two inches apart, Joe thought: *this is it, this is it, oh God, don't blow this...*

"Hey, Joe!"

He jumped at the sound of his name. His body felt as if it was burning. He was embarrassed but more than that, he was disappointed. He turned to see Mac standing at the edge of the shack, looking at them.

"What?" he asked with venom in his voice.

"There's an old snake skin in here!"

"Great! Pick it up and wear it as a scarf for all I care!"

Still holding his hand, Valerie sighed. "It's okay," she said. "She didn't know. She didn't mean to."

"Yeah, I know, but..."

"Don't be such a turd!" Mac screamed.

"Mac...I'm warning you..."

"Alright," Valerie said, turning her attention to Mac. "Show me this snake skin." With that, she tugged at Joe, leading him back towards the shack.

"Don't give in to her," Joe said. It was meant as a joke but the words came out with an edge. All he could think about was kissing her. He didn't care if Mac had found a live snake and was skipping rope with it...

Valerie smiled at him and tugged him along. In a whispered voice he would hear in his head for the rest of the afternoon, she said: "We'll get another chance. I promise." And as Joe's mind reeled with that information, he felt himself being led back towards the shack on legs that felt like rubber.

SIXTEEN

The little bass boat was at least twenty-five years old and looked even older. The engine had been replaced twice and there was a patch in the right side. It was a Weld-Craft model and was only one step up from the aluminum deals that every sucker on the lake had stored in their garage. Through its many years spent on Clarkton Lake, it had taken Wayne Crosby and Al Crabtree on nearly two hundred fishing trips.

Neither of the men was sure who the boat belonged to. It had been swapped back and forth between countless games of poker and lost sports bets. It typically stayed anchored at the small dock behind Al's house but had also spent a few drunken weekends anchored to a rock on the bank behind Wayne's house.

One week, after snooping around in George Galworth's back yard under the cover of night, Wayne and Al loaded the boat up with their fishing supplies: two rods, a small Styrofoam container of night crawlers, an old battered tackle box, a cooler loaded down with a case of beer, and Wayne's little handgun—something Wayne never went fishing without ever since a copperhead snake had struck at him on a bank over twenty years ago. It was a puny little Ruger .22 that fit neatly in the bottom corner of the tackle box.

It was two in the afternoon when they headed out from Al's dock. They had a particular destination in mind, a small cove-like dent in the lake that meandered into a stream underneath a heavy canopy of trees. It sat over two miles away from Al's dock, giving the two old men ample time to start drinking and whining about the current state of Clarkton's summer tourists.

It didn't take long for their conversation to turn to what had been their topic of choice over the last two weeks. They were still hung up on those speeding government trucks. And while a great deal of time had been spent discussing them and the odd track they had seen in the sand when they had snuck into George's back yard, they had exhausted just about every theory. They had both come to the lackluster conclusion that it had something to do with either an environmental thing that they would never care about, or some sort of crime—a murder perhaps. But if neither of them had picked up anything from the grapevine down at The Wharf about such a thing, murder or any other sort of foul play could likely be ruled out.

"You have any idea what George Galworth did for a living?" Wayne asked as they started to close in on their fishing spot.

"Not really," Al answered. "Something with the government, I think. Or maybe military. He was rarely out here, you know. From what I understand, his house on the lake was like a second home for him. I think he spent most of his time out near Alexandria or somewhere else up north."

"So then it might not be all that strange that government vans were sitting in front of his house," Wayne said.

"Or," Al said thoughtfully, "that could make the whole thing worse."

Wayne shrugged and opened up his second can of beer of the afternoon. "This is going to turn out to be one of those things no one is ever going to find out about. Sort of like those military helicopters that kept flying over the lake three summers ago."

"Those were marijuana helicopters," Al said.

"The hell they were," Wayne said. "And besides, I don't think military choppers fly around looking for pot."

"What else would they have been?"

"I don't know. Hence no one ever finding out."

"I always forget that you were one of those conspiracy guys," Al said.

"Just because I think the government lies about everything doesn't make me a conspiracy nut. You want a conspiracy nut, go talk to that loon on the other side of the lake—the ham radio enthusiast with Alex Jones bumper stickers all over his truck."

They both had a laugh at this as Al guided the little boat towards the edge of the lake. Ahead, the lake spread out ahead of them, the far banks barely visible. Some of Clarkton could be seen over that mile and a half or so of water and then there was the open lake to all sides. But instead of heading to the wide open lake out there, Wayne and Al were headed into a slight bend ahead, a curve you couldn't see until you were right on top of it. They'd fished here several times before and knew that it was a hotbed for catfish.

Al pulled the little boat into the cove and then carefully swung it around. The back of the boat was facing a marsh-like coupling of muddy lake water and stubborn trees that had not yet figured out that they were not resting on solid ground. The trees had a lazy sort of slant to them, leaning away from the lake and back towards the surrounding forests.

Both men cast their lines out back towards the lake, one on either side of the boat. The *plop* of their weights striking the water was almost perfectly in sync. That was another of those sounds that exemplified summer for Wayne. Along with a can of beer being popped open and the clanging of a good game of horseshoes, the sound of a perfectly cast line plopping into the water was what summer was all about. Sure, as a younger man he supposed women were in there somewhere, too. But the divorce (and maybe even the marriage five years prior to the divorce) had made Wayne care nothing about women. He'd still sneak a peek at a pretty tourist here and there but even that satisfaction was a fleeting one that ended up making him angry.

"So this is retirement, huh?" Wayne asked. "I kind of like it. What's today? Tuesday?"

"Tuesday indeed," Al said.

"Feels like a Saturday. You ever get tired of this?"

"Of what?" Al asked.

"Of every day feeling like a Saturday."

Al let out a dry laugh and shrugged. "I've only been retired for a year and a half," he said. "I'm not exactly a seasoned veteran at it."

"Man, what were you doing with all of that spare time before I retired?"

"Spending time with my wife," Al said.

"You poor man."

"Watch it."

Wayne held up his hands in mock surrender. He then took a hearty gulp from his beer and started reeling his line in.

"All jokes aside," Al said. "What do you plan to do now? I can't imagine you not working."

"Hell if I know," Wayne responded. His line was reeled in and he held the rod thoughtfully for a moment. "I've been retired for five months now and I honestly have no idea."

"No hobbies to keep you entertained?"

"None."

"Any good books you want to read?"

"I hate reading."

"Well then," Al said. "I guess it's just horseshoes for the foreseeable future."

"And there's nothing at all wrong with that," Wayne said with a smile.

But there *was* something wrong with that, although he'd never tell Al he felt that way. It pained him to know that his life was so empty that he had no ideas on how to fill the rest of it. Without work, what the hell was he supposed to do? He wondered if the guys down at the hardware store would be able to use an old fart for part-time help. It was a sad thought but for now, that's all he had.

Wayne brought his rod over his shoulder, ready to cast the line back out. He clicked the release and flicked his wrist forward for the cast. As he did, the boat seemed to shudder beneath his feet. It was so strong that he lost his footing, along with his grip on the fishing rod. It went sailing from his hands and landed in the water about ten feet in front of the boat.

"What was *that?*" he asked.

Al was holding on to the side of the boat, gripping his pole tightly. He was snickering a bit at the sight of Wayne's pole in the water but it was clear that it was also concerned about whatever had happened to the boat.

"Catfish?" Al said, only half joking. They'd seen some monsters pulled out of this lake and the idea wasn't *too* farfetched.

Wayne felt something wet and cold at his feet. He looked down and saw that the bump along the bottom of the boat had knocked his beer over. It had splashed on his toes and was soaking into his cheap flip flops.

Before either of them had the opportunity to speculate further, the bump came again. It was harder this time, actually rocking the boat.

"That's not a catfish," Al said with concern in his voice.

"No, I don't think so," Wayne said. "So then what the hell *is*—?"

His words dropped flat as something jumped up out of the water. It surfaced on Al's side of the boat and slapped hard against the side. Wayne barely saw it—just long enough to see a weird serpentine shape and something grey and glistening. The aluminum body of the boat made a hollow drum-like sound as the thing struck it.

Al jumped back, his rod clattering to the floor of the boat. He wheeled around to look at what had leaped out of the water, but it wasn't there.

"What was it?" Al asked.

"I don't know," Wayne said. "I barely saw it. It looked like…I don't know…like a big-ass snake or something."

"No way that's a snake," Al said. He was backing away from the edge of the boat but also trying to cautiously peer out into the water.

Whatever had hit the boat, it had alarmed Wayne enough to throw open his tackle box. He removed the first drawer completely and pushed aside a bunch of stringy plastic lures to get to his Ruger. For so long, it had gone unnoticed and had been little more than extra weight in the bottom of the tackle box. Having to retrieve it made him feel entirely too uneasy.

As his hand fell on it, he heard the noise of something breaking the surface of the water again. This time, the boat was partially turned in the water roughly forty-five degrees or so as the thing struck the side while it breached.

Wayne drew the gun up and the moment he had it out of the tackle box, Al was screaming.

Wayne saw what was happening, but his body locked in place for a solid two seconds as he tried to make sense of it.

Something had come out of the water—the same something he had caught a glimpse of no more than ten seconds ago—and struck the boat again. This time, though, it had come partially into the boat. Only, it didn't seem the creature was interested in the boat at all.

Instead, it was wrapped around Al's chest.

And while the thing *did* resemble a snake, Wayne started to think it looked more like an eel or a leech instead...only an enormous version of either one and, somehow, abstract in the way it was built.

By the time Wayne was able to move, the unnamable thing was pulling Al off of the boat. Al's feet actually left the floor and were in the air for a moment as the thing pulled him back. He screamed again but it was cut off when he was pulled into the water with the eel-like thing. There was a violent splash as the thing fought against Al's attempts at escape, followed by a loud knock at the side of the boat.

Wayne stumbled forward on shaking legs, the Ruger held out in front of him. Having seen the thing that currently had his friend hauled underwater, the little Ruger felt suddenly stupid and useless. It was loaded with three bullets but he thought he might as well be firing a child's cap gun.

Still, he had to try something. He went to the front of the boat and got there just in time to see Al's arm come shooting out of the water. It slapped blindly at the side of the boat. His fingers fumbled along the slick aluminum and Wayne reached out to take his friend's hand. He was able to make the connection, grabbing his hand and seizing it tightly. He pulled backwards and was relieved to see Al's head pop up above the surface.

But the thing was not giving up so easily. Another part of it came out of the water and wrapped around Al's shoulders. It then seemed to slither around behind the back of his head and came to the front. It wrapped around Al's jaw, covering everything from his nose down. Al stared at him with wide eyes that looked both terrified and utterly confused. He was trying to climb up onto the boat but was immobilized in the water as the thing continued to hold him by his shoulders and the lower part of his face.

The moment the monstrosity was latched on, Wayne felt a surge of strength from it. He nearly lost his grip on Al and knew that he wouldn't be able to hold on much longer. Knowing that it was risky, Wayne leaned forward and extended the Ruger out towards the water. He held it directly along the surface of the creature where it held Al around the shoulder. Wayne saw it tighten up at the feel of something on its skin. As it tightened, it drew Al down again and his head started to go underwater.

Grimacing, Wayne angled the Ruger as far away from Al's shoulder as he could and pulled the trigger. The Ruger made a clapping noise and, despite its small size, kicked in Wayne's hand with surprising authority. The flesh of the thing was peeled away in ribbons. Blood and white gore went flying, some spattering alongside the boat.

The thing instantly released Al but another part of it (*or*, Wayne thought, *maybe it's all the same piece and its long enough to seem like it has multiple appendages*) came up on Al's right side, searching for something else to grab onto.

Wayne saw it clearly for the first time. The skin of the thing wasn't too dissimilar from the color of a catfish but it looked more like some large tentacle from a sea monster, acting of its own accord. There were puckers along its underside, white grey and glistening.

Wayne wasted no time. He aimed as best as he could, the barrel no more than six inches away from the thing, and fired again. He hit it a little off of center, but the result was good enough for him. The slithering thing sank quickly into the water, disappearing just as quickly as it had appeared.

Wayne dropped the gun and used both hands to reach into the water for Al. He grabbed both of Al's wrists and pulled as hard as he could. He drew Al up out of the water and then fell down, nearly falling ass-first out the other side of the boat. Al was hanging halfway in the boat and scrambling in the rest of the way. He was taking in deep hitching breaths as he climbed in. Once his entire body was inside, he simply lay along the floor for a moment, shuddering and coughing.

"You okay?" Wayne asked, getting to his feet and locating the Ruger.

"No...don't know," Al said, clearly still frazzled. "Wayne, what the *hell* was that?"

"I don't know," Wayne said. "I've never seen anything like it."

"Get...get us out of here. Now."

"Absolutely."

He wasted no time, heading to the back of the boat and giving the pull-crank engine the little bit of strength he had. It took four tries, his muscles jittery from what he had just witnessed, but the little engine finally came to life. As he got behind the wheel, he also did his best to look Al over for any serious injuries. Other than having gone about ten shades paler than his usual lake-tanned self, he seemed to be okay.

"I've got my cell phone," Wayne said. "Do I need to call an ambulance?"

"No. Just get me home."

It looked like Al might start crying at any moment and that broke Wayne's heart. He looked away and out to the water as he rocketed the boat ahead as fast as it would go. On a few occasions, he looked back over his shoulder, sure that he'd see an impossible shape chasing after them.

With the small steering wheel in one hand and the Ruger in the other, Wayne sped back towards Al's house. He tried to come to a conclusion as to what the creature had been but came up empty. It was either some impossibly big leech or eel...or something completely unheard of.

Either way, there seemed to be a monster of sorts residing in Clarkton Lake.

And suddenly, the black government vans started to make a little bit of sense.

SEVENTEEN

Joe had it bad. He hated to admit it, but he had it *really* bad.

He had it so bad that as he strolled down Kerr Lane with the weight of the night pressing down on him, he didn't pay attention to his surroundings as he had done on his first trek out at night. Instead, he was looking at his cell phone. The white light bounced up into his face and anyone that might have passed him (which was no one, as it was 11:30 at night) might have thought he looked like a phantom.

He was looking at the screen and reading the text message he had received half an hour ago. It had come from Valerie and read: Can you meet me at the shack?

Mac had been asleep when his phone had buzzed by his bedside. He had almost been asleep himself; the only thing that had kept him awake was thinking of Valerie. So when he received the text, he'd wasted no time. He was dressed and had his shoes on within two minutes. He'd then sat on the bed and listened to some music. He thought about texting Ricky Marshall to let him know that he could go see Devilsgut as much as he wanted. Meanwhile, he, Joe, would be meeting up with a beautiful girl in the middle of a humid summer night.

Joe had made his exit the same way he had before. He didn't much care if he woke Mac this time. She was in on the secret now and he doubted she'd do anything to mess it up. It made her feel special, almost like a big kid. She hadn't come out and said this, but Joe could tell.

He came to the spot where the little footpath started, shining his phone towards it to make sure he was in the right spot. He recalled what Valerie had done the last time he'd come out here to meet her, creeping up on him from behind and scaring the hell out of him. He didn't think she'd do it again, but he wasn't sure. He looked around cautiously and then headed down the path.

He'd been too excited about seeing Valerie to allow thoughts of the monster to slow him down. But now, as the trees started to crowd in around him, Joe began to feel fear for the first time since slipping out of the bedroom window. He hurried down the path until the dark shadowed shape of the cabin came into view. He headed directly for it, suddenly certain that the thing from the water was waiting for him in the leaves or maybe even over his head, waiting in the branches to leap down on him with its dark mouth and slimy underside.

"Hey there," came a voice.

It was soft and sweet and instantly recognizable, but Joe jumped anyway. He stopped walking and looked ahead. He could just barely see Valerie's shape against the side of the cabin. She was walking towards him and as she drew closer, he started to see her a bit from the scant moonlight that fell through the branches.

"Hey," Joe said.

"Sorry to text you so late," she said. "But I wanted to see you and...well, that's about it."

"That's fine," he said.

She took his right hand in her left one and they simply stood there, looking out to the dark lake. Joe's heart was thundering in his chest and every inch of his skin seemed to be on fire.

"So," Valerie said, "Dad and I went into town today. He ran into one of his friends and they started talking. I overheard them talk about some guy that does dock repairs that was killed three days ago. He was fixing a dock when it happened. Dad's friend said that he'd heard it was like some vicious attack—like an alligator or something."

"I didn't think alligators lived around here," Joe said.

"They don't."

"Oh," Joe said and understood what she was insinuating. "You think it was the thing we saw?"

She shrugged and stepped closer to him. He was new to all of this but his body seemed to respond to her in a way that it had been designed to do. With his right hand taken, his left arm found her waist.

"Do you think we should tell someone?" he asked.

"I don't know," she said. "We'd get in trouble and…really, would anyone believe us?"

Joe didn't think so. And honestly, in that moment, the monster was once again the last thing on his mind. Valerie was so close to him that he could smell her shampoo. "Probably not," he said.

"It's sort of scary, isn't it?"

"Yeah," Joe said…but it wasn't the monster from the lake that he was scared of. It was something else—some push he felt within his heart that seemed to drag the rest of his body with it. "Are you okay?" he asked.

"Yeah. I'm just not—"

And then he was kissing her. He had no idea that he was going to do it until he started moving slowly forward. He knew that it was clumsy at first, especially because he was interrupting her. She had not been expecting it and he honestly had no idea what he was doing. But after a few seconds, they caught up to one another and she was leaning into him. There was too much for his mind to take in: the feel and taste of her lips, the feel of her hand coming up and resting along his side, the soft little sigh she made, and the spark of unexpected electricity that shot through his body in a chaotic ricochet of energy.

Not wanting to overdo it, Joe pulled away. He immediately wanted to do it again but figured he should get her reaction first.

"Okay," she said. "Maybe I'm not *as* scared now."

He looked into her eyes and thought he saw the same sort of feeling that was coursing through him. She took his other hand now and pulled him closer. "Can we do that again?" she asked.

He didn't bother answering with words. They were kissing again and the forest seemed to dissolve around him. This time, she took the lead. They got into sync quickly and when he found her tongue darting in to touch his, the spike of energy that was still riding the waves inside of him seemed to burst into a heat that his body could not contain.

In the back of his head, he knew that there was good reason to be alarmed about the death of the man that had been killed while fixing a dock. If it really *had* been the monster that had come lurching after them through the field of fireflies, who knew how many others it might kill? Who knew *what* something like that was capable of?

Still, thoughts of the monster or whatever it had been faded quickly as their second kiss grew longer, especially when Valerie's hand went to the back of his neck and lightly caressed him there. It was clear that she'd kissed someone before and, perhaps, for extended periods of time. But that wasn't something that Joe wanted to think about; it was nearly as bad letting thoughts of the monster from the lake invade his head.

Joe kissed her under the fragmented moonlight and, for the moment, not at all afraid of the darkened lake that sat just to his right or the deadly secret it might be hiding.

EIGHTEEN

Less than two miles away from where Joe Evans was experiencing his first real kiss, a more experienced couple was also enjoying the summer night. It was the sort of summer night that so many country and southern rock musicians had written songs about. The moon was nearly full, the heat of the day was still sagging on the lake, and the cooler was filled with beer. It sat in the back of Jeremy's truck, the ice sloshing around in a half melted state as he pulled it out to the edge of the opened tailgate.

Kelly watched him open the lid up and fish two beers out of the cooler. He popped the top on one of them and handed it to her. She took it and sipped, her eyes never leaving Jeremy. The rest of that summer night equation came in the thrum that spun through her heart (and, if she was honest with herself, that place located just a bit south of her center) when she was with Jeremy. While they'd been dating for a little over a year and a half and had been sleeping together for a little over a year, that little thrum of electricity was new. She supposed it could be love, finally sprouting up in her heart for him. The truth of the matter was she had no idea *what* it was and she wasn't about to ruin their summer worrying with it.

They sat on his tailgate and looked out to the lake, sitting in the spot she knew full well they would be sitting on when the Fourth of July rolled around. This was their own little private spot, the place where they had watched the fireworks last year and then created their own in the back of this very truck, sandwiched between two blankets.

How they had managed to keep this place a secret was beyond her. It seemed perfect and really wasn't all that well hidden. It sat off of Poor Boy Road, down a gravel road that she'd been told was reserved for state trucks. Why state trucks needed to get down here for was beyond her, though. The road dead-ended a quarter of a mile from where they sat and the only attraction the entire road held was a pair of old concrete blocks and discarded wooden docks that were going to rot. There were areas like this all around the west side of Clarkton Lake; they were nothing more than little holes in the middle of all the vacation homes that had been set aside for projects the state or private owners had started but abandoned.

Kelly supposed the creep-factor of this particular location kept others away from it. That was fine with her. While she did her best to present herself as a sophisticated eighteen year old that would be getting out of Virginia and going to college in Boston in two short months, she was glad to have Jeremy to herself. Lately, he'd been making her feel like a little school girl with a crazy crush.

Being that she was leaving for college in two months meant that these intense new feelings for him were coming at the worst possible time. And that was one of the primary reasons she hadn't told him how she was feeling. She wasn't going to screw up her last two months with him.

"You okay?" he asked.

His voice caught her off guard. She'd been lost in her thoughts, looking out to the lake she had grown up around. Her entire childhood was built around that lake; the thought of heading off to college and leaving it behind was brutal all of a sudden.

"I'm good," she said. "Just zoned out."

"Thinking about college again, weren't you?"

"Maybe."

"You can talk to me about it, you know."

"I know."

This was something of a new development in and of itself. They had never bothered trying to make their relationship out to be some grand romantic thing. They had started dating because they had been madly attracted to one another and how they had put off sex for the first few months of their relationship was beyond her. But once they had crossed that line, it had become the center of their relationship. Everything had been about sex to both of them. While their friends had partied and went out to the movies, they had locked themselves in their bedrooms. Or, if both of their parents had been at home and no bedroom was available, they'd taken up their time along the winding dirt roads around Clarkton Lake. That was how they had come across this particular spot, in fact.

Because of their intense focus on sex, Jeremy's recent interest in getting to know her was out of nowhere. Maybe it was because she would be gone soon. They made no promises to one another and it was basically an understood reality that once she went to college, their relationship would be over. Maybe he wanted to get to *really* know her in the time they had left.

Or maybe he was feeling what she felt, too. Was it love, perhaps, starting to blossom between both of them? She wasn't sure she wanted to know. She figured they needed to talk about it eventually. But not tonight. It felt too perfect—the temperature, the cold beer, the tranquil lake beckoning from less than twenty feet away.

Given that, she thought she knew how to distract both of them from the looming subject of her leaving.

She scooted down from the tailgate and gave him a long lingering kiss on the lips. She then took another sip of her beer and set it down. "I think I feel like a swim," she said.

"Want to go back and get our bathing suits?" Jeremy asked.

She shook her head and smiled, playfully biting her lip. She slowly took off her shirt and tossed it at him. She then removed her jeans as well, sliding out of them and then throwing those as well.

With just her bra and panties on, she turned away from him. She reached back and undid her bra. It dropped to the ground and she looked over her shoulder at him, grinning devilishly.

"You coming?" she asked.

Jeremy answered by removing his shirt and quickly hopping down from the tailgate with a speed that nearly cartoonish. When she saw him unbuttoning his pants while slowly walking towards her, she started to giggle. She raced to the water, bending over slightly and nearly tripping as she slid out of her panties.

Naked, Kelly ran down the bank and into the water. She let out a gale of laughter as she made it out to her waist and then leaped in. When she came back up, she turned and saw Jeremy, now just as naked as she was, leaping into the water.

They met in the water, submerged to their shoulders, with their feet grazing along the muddy bottom. She laced her hands around his back and he placed one hand on her hips, pulling him tight to her and lifting her slightly. She kissed him then, surprised that in their time together, they had never done this before. Sure, the water was unsanitary but every now and then you had to ignore those things and just have fun.

The idea that they only had two months left together made it easier to take the risk. She did her best not to think about it as she kissed him in the water, their naked bodies pressed firmly against one another. But it remained there like a ghost in her head. She was going to Boston and he was staying here. It had been his choice to not go to college and while she hadn't understood why, she had not pressed it. They had not been serious…just someone to hang out with, drink with, and sleep with while high school came to an end.

But now there were these new feelings and that was complicating things. But what those feelings *weren't* complicating was the sex. Even now, as they kissed and grinded against one another, she thought she might explode from the anticipation of having him start. The water and the muddy lake floor was creating a challenge for him and she smiled against the kiss. He smiled, too and before long, they were laughing.

But then he gave her a curious look, as if she had said something that had offended him.

"What?" she said, wondering if he had also started to think that doing this in the lake might be gross.

Jeremy answered in a horrendous scream.

He pulled away from her quickly, swatting at the water as if it were attacking him. As he beat at the water, he fell under for a moment, his eyes wide. He then popped back up almost right away, still screaming and now choking on water.

Kelly was splashed in the face and right away, she knew that something was wrong with the water. The musky and earthy smell she had come to know the lake by was different. There was something bitter to it now, something almost familiar that made her start to panic.

"Jeremy?" she asked.

"Out! Get out! Something just bit m—"

He screamed again and this time she watched as he was jerked underwater. He did not fall this time, slipping in the muck along the bottom. He was *pulled*. As he went down, he was jerked backwards, towards deeper water. Kelly screamed for him as she watched him get pulled under, the night making the water seem more sinister than ever. She saw one of his arms come flailing out of the water, slapping blindly at it. She reached out and took it, pulling him forward.

His head came up, his mouth opened in a scream of pure horror and pain. She had never seen such a look on his face and it broke her heart. She continued to pull at him and just as she thought she had a good grip on him, pulling him forward with ease, she saw something rise up out of the water.

It looked like a stump, but it moved like a snake. She saw it for only a moment as its body broke the surface of the water in twin humps. She saw the flesh of it in the weak moonlight and could make no immediate sense of it. She thought of an octopus and as the thought crossed her mind, she desperately wanted to get out of the water.

With fear sparking inside of her heart, Kelly watched as the thing went back underwater with a splash. Again, her face was splashed with water. This time, some of it went into her mouth. The taste of it clued her into what had been different about the water when she had been splashed the first time.

There was blood in it.

She tasted it, strong and coppery in her mouth, as Jeremy was again pulled back out. She continued to pull on his arm but her feet were slipping along the muddy floor. Her head went under once and when she was fully submerged, she lost her grip on Jeremy.

She swam up to the surface and started screaming for him immediately. He was five feet away from her, his arms paddling madly at the water. She tried reaching out for him again as she headed for the shore, but could not reach. He was yanked under again and the look of terror on his face as he went under made her feel helpless.

"Jeremy!"

His head bobbed to the surface right away. It was covered in blood and his eyes were wide with shock and horror. He opened his mouth as if to reply, but not a single word made it out. Instead, that stump-like thing came out of the water behind him and wrapped itself around his head. She could see nothing more than Jeremy's hair as it tugged him under the water.

This time, even Jeremy's extended arm was submerged. Jeremy was gone and something in the darker corner of Kelly's heart told her that he was not going to come back up.

Kelly turned and finished splashing her way back to the shore, screaming and crying. She felt a wave of panic coming on that she was certain would cripple her. So she simply repeated his name to keep it at bay, saying it like a mantra of sorts: "Jeremy...Jeremy..."

She finally reached the muddy shore and ran for Jeremy's truck. She was barely even aware that she was naked, not bothering to stop for her clothes. She was only worried about the cellphone sitting on Jeremy's dashboard. If she could get to it fast enough, maybe she'd be able to save him.

She made it to the door and opened it. She got one foot into the truck and then felt a million hornets stinging her back.

She cried out and nearly fell backwards. She grabbed on to the door, trying to keep herself up and get away from whatever was at her back. She saw the faintest reflection of what was happening in the driver's side window, which was partially rolled down to let in the summer breeze while they drove.

The thing from the water was on her back. It clung to her with what looked like small black holes all along its underside. The very sight of this made her mind quake, issuing up the dredges of insanity. She shrieked and then felt the thing tug at her. It was violent, and she had a fleeting image of a bug being sucked up by a vacuum cleaner. That's how much pressure this thing was applying to her.

She was unable to hold on. She fell out of the truck and hit the ground. She instantly felt the thing wrap around her entire body. After that, she was pulled back towards the water. She felt her bare backside scraping against the ground as she fought for breath. The thing was crushing her and she could not seem to draw in a breath. She smelled the thing around her—fishy and also like the smell of copper. She found it harder to breathe and the world slipped away from her. She slapped at the ground but could find nothing to stop herself from being dragged away. Her fingernail tore as she clawed for purchase in the dirt and grass.

The thing grew tighter around her body and breathing became impossible. By the time she heard the water splashing around her, she also heard something splinter and crack. An explosive pain in her left side told her that this was her ribs being shattered and splintering in several pieces.

She didn't even feel it when the thing pulled her fully into the water. By then, she tasted blood in her throat and she was desperate for air.

The pressure eventually let up and she was released. It was then that she realized that she was in the lake, underwater. She tried swimming away but the pain was too much. She made two half-hearted strokes towards what she thought was the surface and then her body gave up. Something inside of her trembled and popped.

The water grew darker and darker and there was nothing else.

In her final conscious moment, Kelly felt something brush against her back. She secretly hoped that it was Jeremy, reaching out for her...a simple and foolish dying wish. It was a wish that came true, though. Jeremy's hand did indeed slide across her back as she died. That hand, however, was attached to a mangled wrist and nothing more.

NINETEEN

It was just after nine thirty in the morning when Scott Miles parked his rental car behind the painfully generic county police car. There were three police cruisers parked in the small field, but the cops themselves were all standing on the other side of the gravel road, looking out to the lake. There were seven in all, five by the edge of the lake and two standing by a truck that was parked alongside of the road. They looked to be examining something on the driver's side door.

As Scott parked, all seven of them turned their heads in his direction. One of the policemen started immediately towards him, waving him away. Scott opened his door and reached for his ID before the man—the local sheriff, he assumed—could get good and pissed off.

Scott flashed his ID just as the cop reached the car. "Sorry to get you moving," Scott said. "My name is Scott Miles. I'm with the FBI."

The sheriff paused for a moment, clearly baffled. "Why in the hell are you out here?" he asked.

"Two teens are missing, correct? Likely dead?"

"Yeah," the sheriff said, looking back out to the lake. "We *know* one of them is dead because we found his arm and right foot. But we're guessing that this is just an animal attack. Everything we can see points to it. No need for the FBI to get involved, with all due respect."

"Normally, I'd agree," Scott said, now also training his eyes out to the lake. "But there are some other things to be considered."

"Like what?"

Scott eyed the sheriff, trying to size him up. He looked to be about fifty and showed all the signs of being a stereotypical southern hard ass. Scott had no doubt that if he didn't get to the point soon, this man would lose his cool and start raising hell. That in and of itself would not bother Scott at all. But it *would* make this process much harder. So Scott levelled with the man as best he could.

"I've been here at Clarkton Lake for a little less than a week. I've been listening to the chatter on my police band radio. I know about the abandoned fishing boat floating thirty yards off of the shore in a little cove two miles away from this very spot. The boat belonged to a man named Brett Yates, did it not?"

"It did," the sheriff said. He was impressed and a little off his game now, and he did nothing to hide it.

"Mr. Yates has been missing for a few days, right?" Scott asked.

"Eight days. Yeah."

Scott left it at that although he knew more. He knew that Yates had been reported missing by his family five days ago and, from what Scott could decipher from conversations on the police scanner, the discovery of the boat was causing the PD to assume the worst.

"And what about the dock repairman that died at the Carter residence three days ago? Another animal attack?"

"That's the theory," the sheriff said. "We've called the game warden and she's out looking for any leads right now."

"What sort of leads?" Scott asked.

The sheriff looked to the ground, as if embarrassed. "Alligators. Maybe a bear or wolves."

"You don't sound too confident," Scott said.

"Mister, I'm not. I don't know what in the hell is going on. But I know we need to find out soon or word of this is going to get out and we're going to have a very scary summer."

"Could you please get me in touch with this game warden?"

"Absolutely," the sheriff said, pulling his cellphone out and immediately scrolling through the numbers. "If you can help us get this under wraps before more people die, I'll do anything you ask."

Scott saved the game warden's number into his phone and then looked to the pickup truck the two officers were still studying.

"You mind if I look around a bit?" Scott asked.

"Help yourself."

Scott did just that. He walked to the truck, standing behind the officers as to not get in their way. There were a few small splatters of blood along the edge of the opened door but nothing else of note. He then turned around and looked at the area behind him. Ankle-length grass covered an area of about five feet before it dipped down slightly towards an area where the grass tapered off and gave way to a small slip of sand that served as the bank.

The trundled path that had been pressed into the grass was easy to spot. Scott walked to it and hunkered down for a better look. There were a few more splatters of blood along the path, but it was not the blood that bothered him…not specifically. What made his stomach feel as if it were going to bottom out was the fact that he'd seen a path identical to this on the day he had first arrived at George Galworth's house.

Only now it was much bigger. The width of the thing had easily tripled in size.

Scott stood back up and saw that the sheriff was standing to his left, slightly behind him. He was also looking to the path that had been etched in the grass and the look on his face was a perfect accompaniment to the fear that was beginning to spread through Scott.

"Did the game warden see this?" Scott asked, nodding to the path in the grass.

"Yeah. And when she saw it, she looked just like you do right now."

"Did she say anything about it?"

"No," the sheriff said with a nervous chuckle. "As a matter of fact, she stayed quiet. She just said she'd get back to me."

That was all Scott needed to hear. "Thanks for your time, Sheriff," Scott said, walking quickly back to his car.

"How about you?" the sheriff asked.

"What do you mean?" Scott asked, already opening his door.

"Do *you* have any ideas?"

"No," Scott said. "No, I don't."

Yet as he got into his car, he was thinking about the deeper parts of the ocean, where a darkness so black exists that men couldn't begin to imagine it. He then thought of the pictures he had seen of the interior of the sub that George Galworth had been stationed on and tried to imagine something that could have caused such a scene living in this quaint little lake.

When he exited the field and pulled back out onto Kerr Lane, Scott realized that this might be out of his control. He might be too late to stop this and that was *not* the sort of news he wanted to deliver to Roger Lowry.

With a hand that wanted to tremble, Scott pulled out his cellphone and dialed up the game warden.

TWENTY

The game warden was a stout woman named Susan Lessing. When she met Scott at a local diner called The Anchor, she smelled of cigarettes and looked like she was both mad and tired. Given recent events in her area, Scott couldn't blame her.

She met him in the back booth, as he had requested. When she sat down, he saw relief pass over her face, like someone that was finally able to sit down after running a marathon. Scott assumed that Susan hadn't been able to get much rest over the last few days.

"Agent Miles, right?" she asked.

"Yes," he said, extending his arm over the table. "Pleased to meet you."

"Are you?" she asked. "You were very vague on the phone and I'm not quite sure why you needed to speak with me. The local sheriff is a nitwit, but he should have been able to get you all the information on the murders that you need."

"The murders are just that," Scott said. "*Murders.* They can't be prevented. I'm more interested in stopping the thing that is doing the killing."

"I'm working on trying to figure out what that is right now, Agent Miles."

"That's why I contacted you rather than working with the sheriff. I already know what's doing the killing. I want to share the information with you, but it's highly classified and I have to ask that once I tell you everything I know, you can't tell anyone. Not your husband, not your pastor, not your best friends. *No one.* I'd have to have you sign a document to verify your agreement to this."

Susan Lessing eyed him suspiciously and he could feel the scrutiny in her gaze. She was trying to figure out if he was lying to her or not.

"Okay, I'll bite," she said. "What is it?"

"A group of marine biologists and a small think-tank within the bureau are almost positive that it's an unknown creature that lived somewhere within the Aleutian Trench. It got here after hitching a ride in the body of a marine biologist that was part of an expedition that was attacked by a much larger version of the creature currently residing in your lake."

"What do you mean *in* the body?" Susan asked. There was fascination on her face that, quite frankly, scared Scott a bit.

"No one is sure, but we think it works like this: somehow, the eggs of the creature get into a host—a human body. The eggs are quite small and black, not much larger than a flake of pepper. Once inside the body, one of the eggs sort of latches on and starts to grow rapidly. After that, the embryo develops. The period of gestation is somewhere between five and seven days. Based on what we've seen, the creature hatches inside of the human body and then comes out through the mouth."

"That's disgusting," she said. "And you're certain of this?"

"I'm certain of nothing," Scott said. "But I've seen the photographs from the scenes of the deaths as well as footage of a ruined vessel that barely made it out of the sea in one piece. One of the men on that expedition had a summer home out here. His name was—"

"George Galworth," Susan interrupted.

"Yes. How did you know?"

"It's a small town, even when the vacationers are running the place. I meet most of the folks that come in through here during the summers. George is easy to remember because of his profession. He's the only marine biologist I ever met." She paused here for a moment and then frowned. "He's dead?"

"Yes."

"And you think this thing is responsible for the other deaths over the last few days?" she asked.

"I'm almost certain of it. I came from the most recent scene less than an hour ago. I saw a trail in the grass that resembles the same one I found behind George Galworth's house several days ago."

"The one that looked like a big snake?"

"Yes," he said. "But the one I saw this morning is much bigger than the one I saw at George's place. This leads me to believe that the thing is still growing just as fast as it did while gestating in a body."

"So how do we catch it?" Susan asked.

"I'm trying to get creative. As you might imagine, a case like this has a tight lid at the FBI. It's especially hush-hush because the doctors that cleared the survivors of the expedition to the Aleutian Trench *knew* that there was something in them. They let them go because they thought it would be a great research opportunity."

"That's messed up."

"It is. But this isn't the time to question the morals of the people I work for. I need to stop this thing and I have very few resources. If you could help me, I think we might be able to find it and kill it."

"What can I do for you, then?"

"I need to rely on your knowledge of the area. Based on what we know about the creature, it's assumed that it likes confined areas that are extremely dark and quiet. I need to know where there might be an abundance of nooks and crannies. Also, the thing that makes this creature so dangerous is that it appears to prefer areas near the shore. My guess is that this is strictly for easy access to food."

Susan was quiet for a moment and Scott could all but hear the gears in her head going to work. After ten seconds or so, she said, "I know of at least eight places that fit all of those descriptions. Nooks and crannies close to the shore."

"What sort of access do you have to trail cams or security cameras?" Scott asked.

"Not much in the way of security cameras, but I can get you just about as many trail cameras as you'd need."

"That's a great start," Scott said. "Do you have a few hours to help me set cameras up in the locations you have in mind?"

She laughed nervously, nodding her head. "If you're telling me the truth, consider me at your disposal until we kill this thing."

Scott reached beneath the menu had brought out a sheet of paper that he had been hiding the entire time. "Before we start, I need you to sign this confidentiality agreement. I'm sure you understand why something like this is considered sensitive to the government."

Susan took the paper, read it, and then took a pen out of the breast pocket of her shirt. "Not just the government," she said. "But this whole town. News like this would dry up the tourist boom pretty damned quick. You don't have to worry about me running my mouth, Agent Miles…even though I could easily say that this can be pinned on the selfishness and irresponsibility of the men you work for."

She paused here, as if hoping this would bait Scott into an argument. When he remained quiet, she went on.

"I think word might already be spreading," she continued. "Half the town knows about Ted Wylerman already—the poor man that died while trying to fix some rich asshole's dock. Then yesterday I got a call from a local old-timer that swears that his best friend was pulled out of a boat by something that looked like an enormous leech."

"Did the friend die?"

"No," Susan said. "The other man—Wayne Crosby—says he shot the thing two times and they were able to get away."

"But apparently, if the deaths of the teens from last night are any indication, the shots didn't kill it."

"I'd assume not," Susan said, scanning the document she had been given.

She scrawled her signature on the appointed line and then slid the paper back over to Scott. He took it, folded it up and then placed it into his pocket.

"Can you start right now?"

"In a minute," she said. "I need coffee first. This has been one long day and it's not even ten o' clock yet."

Scott nodded and thought: *It's only going to get longer.*

TWENTY-ONE

Joe's first nightmare involving the monster from the lake was a doozy. Even as it unfolded, his sleeping mind was somehow aware that it was a nightmare but he did not wake up. That's probably because it did not start out like a nightmare at all. In fact, it started out like one of those dreams that often had Joe waking up in a flush, hurriedly checking the sheets,

In the nightmare, he and Valerie were lying in a huge field, kissing in the grass. The night was pitch black around them. Fireflies flickered here and there, casting a golden light down into them. He was kissing her along the curve of her neck like he had seen guys do in some of those cheesy romantic movies his mom watched sometimes. Her hands were at his back, going up his shirt. The feel of her hands on his skin was mesmerizing and the fireflies seemed to glow in tandem with the electricity that seemed to flow between them.

"Joe?" Valerie had said in a breathy whisper than had ticked the side of his face.

"Yes?"

"It's here."

"What's here?"

"That thing...it's here. And it's hungry."

Joe pulled away from her. Or, rather, he *tried* pulling away. Her hands clenched together at his lower back and he could only pull himself up a small amount. When he did, he found himself looking down into the face of a waterlogged corpse. Valerie's face was pale and eaten away along her cheeks, which were bloated and purple. There was mud and muck in her hair from the bottom of the lake. One of her eyes was missing and when she smiled lovingly at him, lake water and mud trickled out of her mouth.

"It's here," she said again. "And it's hungry. It won't hurt...you'll drown before it eats you. And drowning isn't so bad."

She pulled him down to her and he tried to fight away. But then she was kissing him and as much as he wanted to pull away, he couldn't stop. Her tongue was cold and rancid. When it left his mouth, it left something behind. Something that squirmed, wriggled, and tasted like fish.

Revolted, he was finally able to pull away. When he turned to run, the leech monster was there. It was standing on its tail and hulking over him. It was at least nine feet tall and its shadow was darker than the night. Its mouth was even darker than that, opening into a squeal of hunger.

Joe turned to run but when he did, Valerie reached out and grabbed his ankle. Her hand was cold and rotten but she displayed impossible strength as she jerked him to the ground. She then crawled on top of him and trailed kisses around the side of his face. More lake water came out of her, trickling down his cheeks and along his lips.

He opened his mouth to scream but the thing was falling on them. It wasn't cold, as he thought it would be, but warm and inviting. The suckers along the bottom of its body latched on to him and the stinging sensation was only brief. Valerie had been right; it wasn't so bad.

He felt himself being pulled across the field and towards the lake in its warm embrace. And all the while, Valerie was kissing him, whispering into his ear: *"It's hungry and it won't stop until we're dead..."*

That's when Joe jerked awake in his bed.

He came awake so fast that he nearly fell into the floor. He was covered in sweat and his heart was hammering in his chest. He looked across the room and saw Mac sleeping peacefully with Mr. Scraps tucked under one arm.

As he glanced around the room, trying to force his panicked mind and heart to realize that they were safe in the cabin and not out in the water, the nightmare replayed in his head. He felt like had *had* to remember it and relive it because maybe then he could also convince himself that the monster wasn't real. He and Valerie hadn't *really* seen that impossible creature come lurching out of the lake, had they? No...because things like that just didn't exist.

But still, the logical part of his mind still cowered behind the part that had been spooked by the nightmare. *Well, whether it exists or not, you saw it,* his brain told him. *And so did Valerie. So yeah, I'd say it was pretty damned real.*

When he was sure that he was calm and collected, Joe reached out to the bedside table and grabbed his iPhone. It was 2:06 and he saw no missed texts from Valerie. He didn't know if she slept with the sounds on her phone off, and he really wasn't all that worried about it in that moment. He texted her, trying not to think of her as the dead and rotting thing that he'd seen in his nightmare.

Pretty bad nightmare about that thing from the lake, he typed in. Hope you're doing okay. Thinking about you a lot.

He waited a few moments to see if she'd text him back but his phone remained silent. He guessed that meant she was sleeping. That was good—maybe it meant she wasn't having any more nightmares.

He lay back down but realized that his mouth was dry. Although it had been nothing more than a dream, he could swear that he tasted lake water and a faint trace of fish in his mouth. He got out of bed, figuring a glass of water might make it go away. He quietly left the room, taking a final peek back at Mac to make sure she hadn't stirred awake.

He tiptoed through the hall and to the kitchen. He grabbed a glass from the cupboard and filled it with water from the sink. He drank it slowly, still not liking the idea of having *anything* in his mouth after the nightmare. But the cool water seemed to make those imagined tastes leave his mouth and he finished the glass quickly. He set the glass down in the sink and started back to his room.

That's when he heard the voices. He stopped and stood motionless for a moment. Because of the frazzled state of his nerves due to the dream, he automatically assumed that the voices indicated something bad. But as he cocked his head to the side and listened to them, he realized that he the voices were both familiar.

His parents were whispering from somewhere very nearby. This made no sense, as their bedroom was nearly on the opposite side of the cabin. He turned to see if they were maybe lurking behind him with the intent of playing a joke on him or something, but the kitchen and hallway were empty.

He looked to the picture window behind the dining table and saw the briefest flicker of light. He stepped towards it and when he saw the shapes of his parents, he stopped.

He was embarrassed at first but then realized that they weren't doing anything that would scar him for life. If he had to guess, they had recently finished doing such a thing, though. They were laying together on one of the big lounge chairs on the back deck with a blanket over them. Maybe they *were* still doing…well…doing *that*. Joe didn't think so, though, because they were actually talking.

He stepped away from the window and pressed himself against the wall. It was hard to hear everything they said through the glass, but he was able to catch the tones and inflections of their voices. And the important thing is that they sounded happy. They were laughing. In fact, at one point his mother started giggling in a way that reminded him of how Mac sounded whenever she started laughing and couldn't stop.

Realizing how creepy it was that he was essentially spying on his parents after they'd probably just had sex, Joe stepped away from the window and headed back to his room. He felt a momentary pang of joy at the sight of his parents so happy together. It was a joy that increased as he got into bed and noticed the flashing light on his phone. He picked it up and saw that he had a message from Valerie.

That sux. Sorry about the nightmares. Thinking about you too. Cabin tomorrow at 4?

Smiling, Joe typed in: See ya there.

When he pressed Send, he was again struck by just how badly he was falling for this girl. It made him feel weak…but in a good way.

He put the phone down and lay down in bed. When he closed his eyes, the nightmare wasn't very far from his mind. But thoughts of seeing Valerie tomorrow began to dwarf it as he managed to find sleep once again.

TWENTY-TWO

Wayne knew something was wrong with Al. It had been three days since his friend had been pulled into the lake by a creature that he still couldn't put a name to. Al had been a little distant and very quiet. He'd spent most of the day after the incident in bed. When Wayne had called to check on him, Kathy had answered the phone and requested in a not-so-polite way that Wayne give him a few days to recover.

Now, though, two days after being pulled into the water, Al looked like he was on the mend. They were in Al's back yard, taking up their usual positions around the horseshoe pit. The only noticeable difference was that Al was not drinking from a can of Coors as he usually did. Instead, he had a bottle of vitamin water sitting in his lounge chair as he went about the business of taking Wayne to task at a game of horseshoes.

"What did the doc say?" Wayne asked. While he would never admit it to anyone, he was extremely grateful to have his friend safe and sound. He'd spent that first night after the attack trying to imagine the sort of person he'd become if he didn't have Al to spend time with.

"He said I'm fine," Al said. "My blood pressure was up a bit, but that was to be expected from the scare I had. There's a mark of some sort on the back of my neck from where the thing latched on, but the doctor cleaned it up and said there are no signs of infection."

"Good," Wayne said.

"What's good is that you had that nubby little pistol with you," Al said. His voice was grave, taking on a serious tone that freaked Wayne out a little bit. "If you hadn't shot that thing, I'd probably be at the bottom of the lake right now."

"You don't know that," Wayne said.

"Yes, I do. I felt that thing…it was strong as hell and it was not about to give up. If you hadn't shot it, I'd be dead right now. I know it. Kathy knows it. And we're both extremely grateful."

"Thanks," Wayne said quietly, not sure how to take the gratitude. He couldn't remember the last time someone had sincerely thanked him. For that matter, he couldn't remember the last time he had done something worthy of such thanks.

Wayne took his turn, tossing a horseshoe slightly left of the peg. It landed with a thud in the sand.

"I'll be honest with you," Al said. "Kathy didn't want you over here. She thinks I should be in bed, recovering."

"Is that what the doctor said?"

"The doctor said to take it easy for a few days. He's worried about the stress levels and all of that." He gave a roll of the eyes as he took his place to take his turn. He tossed his horseshoe and it landed directly in front of the peg. So far, there had been no musical *clinks* of the shoes hitting the pegs. That alone was enough to indicate that both men were distracted and off their game.

"You heard anything from the game warden yet?" Al asked.

"Not a thing. She assured me that she'd look into it and I think she meant it. There's been some other things, you know. Word around town is that some dock repair guy died a few days ago. He was a bloody mess when they found him out at the Carter house. All anyone knows is that *something* attacked him. There was a teenage couple, too…both dead. They still haven't found all of the boy."

"Damn," Al said. "Kathy was telling me that weird guy Brett Yates is missing. Someone found a little rowboat that he owns just floating around by itself nearly two weeks ago."

"You think whatever it was that we saw is doing all of it?"

A look came over Al's face when he nodded and Wayne suddenly thought that maybe Al *should* be resting inside. The man looked like a ghoul, his eyes glazed over and his mouth drawn tight.

"Yeah," Al answered, and it was clear that he was remembering what it felt like to be in that thing's grip—to have it clinging to him, covering part of his face as it tried to pull him beneath the water.

"You okay, Al?" Wayne asked.

Al nodded, his gaze no longer glassy. He bent down slowly to pick up a horseshoe and looked at it longingly. "I don't know," he said. "Look...I'm going to be honest with you, so you better not use this as joke ammo later on, got it?"

"Sure."

"That thing scared the hell of out me. It was so bad that my bladder let go when it had me in the water. The last two nights, I've woke up from nightmares. Last night, I cried like a baby. Kathy is scared for me and the only reason she didn't put up an argument about you coming over today is because she thought it might do me some good. But...something's wrong with me. I think it's a mental thing, really. Physically, I feel fine. A little tired, maybe."

"I'm sorry, man," Wayne said. "I had no idea..."

"I know. I didn't *want* you to know. But just thinking about the lake makes me terrified, like a kid scared of the boogie man. I really appreciate you being so concerned and all but I need to take a break. Let's try this some other time, okay?"

"Sure. No problem, man. I...well, I was scared to death, too. I thought you were dead the moment that thing came up out the water and got you."

"I did, too."

"Why don't you call me when you're ready to hang out?" Wayne said. He did his best to sound serious, something he knew he was terrible at doing. "And if you need to just talk through it, give me a call."

"I will. Thanks for understanding."

Wayne nodded and watched Al grab up his vitamin water and head for the front porch. Wayne tossed the horseshoe he had been holding in his hand. It barely landed within the box. He looked up to the porch and watched Al go through the screen door and into his house.

Wayne picked up the little red cooler he always brought to Al's (the same cooler that had been on the boat when the thing had attacked Al) and started walking towards Kerr Lane. He only made it a few steps before he heard the screen door opening. He turned, wondering if Al had already changed his mind.

Instead, he saw Kathy coming down the steps. She crossed the yard and met him in the driveway. She looked just as tired as Al had looked but there was also a smile on her face.

Without saying anything, she approached him and gave him a hug. Wayne was pretty sure it was the first time she had ever willingly touched him. Awkwardly, he returned it as best he could. He caught sight of the veggie garden beyond the back corner of the house and wondered how much time she'd spend out there in the coming days while Al was on the mend.

"Thank you for saving him," she said.

He waited until she broke the hug before responding. "It wasn't a problem."

Kathy looked to him like he was a stranger that she was trying to learn to trust. She had been very pretty when Al had first met her and a lot of that younger woman still existed behind the growing wrinkles and grey hair. Her age showed mostly around her eyes, where the crow's feet were deep and pronounced.

"Do you know what that thing was?" she asked.

"I have no idea," he said. "I know it wasn't a snake or an alligator. It looked like a leech or…I don't know…just like some random sea monster, you know?"

"Do you think Susan Lessing and the police are taking this seriously?"

Given what had nearly happened to her husband, Wayne didn't see the point in going down the checklist of deaths and disappearances that he and Al had just reviewed to prove his point. "Yes," he said. "When I spoke to her on the phone, it seemed like she is taking it very seriously."

"Good," she said. "Now, Wayne, can you do me a favor?"

"What's that?"

"I hope you know I mean nothing by this, but I think you should stay away for a while. This shook Al up more than I think he'd let you know. Let him deal with it for a while. I thought you coming over today would help him but the look I just saw on his face when he came inside was…well, it was haunting."

"That's fair," Wayne said. "I told him to call me when he's feeling better. I think I'll stick to that."

"Thank you."

"Sure."

"Could you do me another favor?"

"Maybe," he said.

"Stay off the lake until this thing gets figured out. I hate to be the protective hen, but that's what I'm going to be. Al thinks a lot of you and if he lost you…"

"I know."

She smiled and looked him in the eyes directly. "Stay off the lake, Wayne."

"I will."

Kathy gave him a kind nod of approval before turning around and heading back for the house. She hurried up the stairs and back into the house without looking back at him.

Wayne looked sadly at the horseshoe pits and the strewn shoes. Then, hefting the minor weight of his cooler, he started back towards his house. Within seconds, he knew he had lied to Kathy.

He was already making plans to break the second promise he'd made.

TWENTY-THREE

As Scott had expected, it had been a massive pain in the ass to get the trail cameras set up in the way he needed. Susan had made the issue a top priority with the local PD and even then, he didn't get the set-up he wanted until nearly twelve hours after having lunch with her. Back in DC, this job could have been done in less than an hour...maybe two, given the travel time between the sites where the cameras were being set up.

Still, in the end, it was a nice set-up and as effective as he could have hoped for. Susan had even brought a laptop from her office to give him an extra screen. After making some calls to the DC office to get remote help with the technical set-up (an area he was not at all adept in), he ended up having eight trail cameras to view on three different screens—his own laptop, Susan's laptop, and the television that was mounted on the cabin's living room wall. The tech guys had walked him through the set-up over the phone and had even handled some via screen-sharing from DC. They set it all up so that he could easily switch any trail camera footage of interest directly to the television's screen.

That had been two days ago and so far, he'd seen nothing of interest. He'd watched a ton of fishermen come and go, unaware of what lurked in the waters around them. He hadn't even had so much as a single scare—not even some large fish breaking the water or a floating branch or log that could be misconstrued to be some sort of lake monster. In the two days that had passed, Scott had started to feel like one of those idiots that were constantly examining footage on the internet, sure that they had spotted the Lochness Monster.

He wished there was a better way to go about doing this. Essentially, he was waiting for one of two things: for the creature to surface for a moment so he could rush to the location and hope it had not moved too much, or to see the creature attack and probably kill someone, hoping he could make it to the location on time before the monster got its fill and went elsewhere.

There was also the fact that he had no way of knowing if the damned thing was going to pop up at any of the locales where the cameras had been placed. Susan had gone an extra step and conferred with a local fishing expert, asking for locations that matched the specifics Scott had given her in the diner—in the darker nooks and crannies but close to banks or, at the very least, shallow water.

Three of the locations they had selected were thin coves that meandered off of the lake and created muddy little creeks. One of these was the exact spot where two elderly men had encountered the thing three days ago—one day before the cameras had been set up. Another of the cameras had been set several feet up a tree and provided an expansive view of a small pool of water that fed into the larger regions of the lake. This view also took in the sight of the opposing bank about seventy-five yards away, lined with trees that showed the occasional speck of Kerr Lane through their branches. Scott figured he was looking at a portion of Kerr Lane that sat no more than a mile away from his own cabin. The other four cameras were set up at seemingly random locations. One was setting along the bank of an old set of piers where Susan said older men would meet for beers between fishing, back when the open container laws had been a little more relaxed out on the lake. Another had been set up at the Carter residence, on the very same dock Ted Wylerman had died on while trying to repair it. The theory here was that the thing would come back to the scene of a previous meal, hoping for more.

The other two had been set up at the end of old piers that Susan's fishing expert claimed were good catfish holes. They were taking a gamble, assuming the thing might feed on some of the larger fish in the lake if it got impatient looking for humans.

This was how Scott had lived for the last two days. He'd glared at the screens, no better than some common agent running surveillance. If he took a break to use the bathroom or just to rest his eyes, he had to rewind the footage on all of the recordings just to make sure he hadn't missed anything. Susan had come by a few times to help him out but she seemed mostly bored and unimpressed with the plan. Honestly, Scott was starting to feel the same way.

As that second day wound to a close, he was borderline ecstatic when Susan knocked on the door. The woman talked a lot and she had a deep southern accent that crawled up his spine like barbed wire when she said certain words. But he needed some sort of company other than the occasional rant-filled phone call from Roger Lowry.

He answered the door and saw that she had brought him fast food. He took it gratefully and started eating right away at the small coffee table in front of the couch that he had come to know all too well.

"Still nothing, huh?" she asked.

"Nothing," he confirmed.

"You want to think about swapping the cameras to some other places? I can think of a few more, but these were the most promising ones."

"We might want to," he said. "Can you have someone do that tomorrow?"

"Sure thing. I do think we should keep an eye on the cove the old men were attacked on, the Carter pier, and the one up the tree, though. You get more coverage on those and two of them are sites we know the thing has come to before."

"That's fine," Scott said, wolfing down the burger he'd found in the fast food bag.

"Your guys in DC getting antsy?"

"Yeah. And I am, too. Two full days with staring at screens with nothing to show for it. I take it there have been no calls from the police about another attack?"

"Not a single one. I even called twice today just to check."

They were quiet for a moment as Susan looked to the screens. "You know, I could probably talk the local PD into sending another set of eyes out here to help you."

"Thanks, but the fewer people that know about this, the better. If you could just dupe them into believing there's *something* killing people, that would be enough. Just enough to have them sort of patrolling the major roads that go by the lake to keep an eye out."

"They're already doing that," she said. "Some think it's a gator that somehow found its way up from a swamp in Louisiana or something. That's stupid, of course. A few others think it might just be a forest animal lurking near the shore. Maybe a bear or a rabid bobcat or something."

"Are there bears out this way?" he asked.

"Very few. But yes, they do make it out here. Strays that have wandered too far away from the mountains."

"Huh," Scott said. He found it interesting just because it was something to think about other than the screens in front of him.

"How long do you think your supervisors will let you keep doing this?"

Scott shrugged, cramming the last of the burger into his mouth. "I have no idea. Probably as long as it takes. This is...well, this thing is bad."

"I know. I saw the pictures," she reminded him. "Anyway...you need a nap or something?"

"No thanks. I'm going the opposite route and keeping the coffee going. You're welcome to stay and have a cup."

"I think I will," she said. "No offense, but you look a little stir crazy. You look like you could use the company."

"Yeah, I guess I could," Scott said.

He sipped from the soda that had come with his meal and sat back on the couch. He looked to the eight different squares on the screens in front of him, hoping for some sort of change in the scenery.

There continued to be nothing, just minor events. A bird swooped down by the camera installed in the tree, pecked at something, then flew off. A small fish leaped from the water and splashed back down. A small boat could be seen in the distance of one camera, pulling a late-afternoon skier behind it.

Scott sighed, the screens taunting him. With all of the questions about what this thing was, where it might be, and when it would attack next, there *was* one thing Scott knew for sure: he was good and tired of this damned lake.

TWENTY-FOUR

Three days passed.

They passed in the way summer days on the lake tend to: in a humid haze of buzzing insects, the nagging itch of sunburn, and sunsets that seem to strangle the night for as long as possible. A handful of vacationers left the lake while new ones came in, hauling campers and recreational vehicles like jet skis and ugly golf carts. It happened quietly and without much fanfare, as it did every summer around Clarkton Lake.

Wayne Crosby watched it all from his front porch. He spent a lot of time there, perched in an old folding chair that was starting to rot away along the bottom. He spent a great deal of those three days drunk and grumpy. He had not yet heard from Susan Lessing about the creature that had nearly killed his best friend. Even when he called her office and left messages, there was nothing.

From his porch, Wayne listened to some of his favorite music while drinking more beer than he had since his thirties, back when he'd finally had to admit that he had created a nice and complicated drinking problem for himself. It had been the first real hit to a marriage that would fail nineteen years later. But he didn't bother thinking of that failed marriage or even about how easy it had been to fall back into that black hole of drinking in order to solve his problems as he sat on his porch.

Instead, he thought about some unnamable monster rising up out of the lake and trying to kill his friend. He thought about an overweight and incompetent woman game warden trying to hunt such a thing down and it only made him drink more. He was not a sexist man, but he knew Susan in an off-hand sort of way. She was known around the community for half-assing things and delegating the nastier and more complicated parts of her job to those beneath her. Wayne didn't see how someone of her skillset and drive was going to find and kill the monster he and Al had seen out on the lake.

146

With such thoughts heavy on his mind, Wayne sat in his deteriorating chair, smelling the cooking meat from grills everywhere around Kerr Lane and thought about how one might track down such a creature.

He had an idea that, when he was extremely drunk, seemed like a good idea. But during those little slivers of sobriety in the morning, it seemed stupid and dangerous. He pondered this idea like some great philosopher while he watched vacationers and locals alike come and go. He would, on occasion, look to the west, towards Al's house. He wondered how his friend was doing and if there was anything other than staying away that he, Wayne, could do to help.

But he decided to keep his word and stay away until he was called upon. He stayed away and continued to refine the simple plan he kept revisiting in his head. It was a plan that, by the end of that third day, started to seem so simple that he could no longer find a reason *not* to go through with it.

And really, that was the scariest thing of all.

***

While Wayne Crosby got a pretty good grasp on the goings-on around Clarkton Lake by simply sitting on his porch, there was one thing that he did not see during those three days. What he did not see was the quickly growing relationship between a vacationing fourteen year old from New York City and a fifteen-year-old semi-local girl.

It happened night after night, and sometimes during the afternoon when the boy's sister tagged along. If you asked either of them, they would likely tell you (rather naively) that they were falling in love. And maybe they were. Rural summers by the lake have a sort of magic to them, the sort of thing kids imagine exist in faraway lands where maidens are rescued from towers and brave knights can win wars all by themselves. The mosquitoes and stifling heat mute that magic from time to time, but it's not nearly enough to stop young love.

And because Wayne did not see these two falling in love no more than a mile and a half away from his porch, he also had no way of knowing the fear they shared. It was a fear that was very similar to his own—a fear that was born of something deep in the water, without name or shape.

These teenagers felt the fear, too; like Wayne, they had seen it.

It was nearly strong enough to get in the way of their raging hormones, their thunderous hearts and the stubborn chemistry of first loves.

And that, they would both realize later, was probably why things went as badly as they did.

PART THREE

SUMMER'S
END

TWENTY-FIVE

Even with Mac tagging along by his side, Joe was still as happy as he could ever remember. They were walking down Kerr Lane, towards the shed that he had come to know and love so well over the last two weeks. The last two times he had come here during the day, Mac had insisted on coming with him. He would refuse but she would threaten blackmail like usual. So there was nothing he could do to keep her away.

Joe had wondered if it would be so bad for his folks to know that he had met a girl. His dad might even be happy and, although Joe would never admit it to anyone, he had been seeking something for him and his father to bond over for quite some time. Still…confessing to a summertime romance with one of the semi-locals would only make this vacation more awkward and Joe didn't think he could handle that.

His mother was under the impression that he and Mac were simply getting along better than usual. She had even gone so far as to credit it to the vacation and how it was bringing them all closer together. The hell of it was that Joe actually *didn't* mind Mac glued to his side as he made these walks down Kerr Lane towards the shed. She never really got in the way and there was something about the way she looked at him that he liked. He supposed it was respect or appreciation for being able to spend time with her big brother. It made Joe feel more grown up in a way he didn't fully understand.

So yes, maybe the vacation was bringing the Evans family closer together. His parents certainly seemed to be repairing whatever damage they'd been dealing with. Joe still thought about accidentally seeing them on the back porch several nights ago, wondering just how late he had been from seeing something that could have easily traumatized him for life.

There had been a few good times on the lake with all of them, back when Joe had still been getting in the water. They'd also had some borderline cheesy moments on the back porch with dad's guitar and grilled burgers and hotdogs. All in all, it had not been the misery he had assumed it would be.

Of course, Valerie had a lot to do with that. He knew that they only had another four or five weeks or so of their…whatever they were calling it. He tried not to dwell on that or if Valerie was now his "girlfriend" or not. Mac had already taken to calling Valerie his girlfriend when they were alone and he was okay with that.

Actually, he rather liked it.

The footpath came into view and Joe felt that tug at his heart—a warm sort of surge in his chest that instantly got him excited. He saw that Mac was glad to be there, too. She went off ahead of him, sprinting. This would be only the third time the two girls had hung out, but Valerie made a point to be nice to her. It irritated Joe a bit because Mac was stealing some of his time with Valerie, but he also thought it was cool. It showed the sort of person Valerie really was.

Today, when they reached the shack, Joe saw that Valerie was sitting in the back of the old aluminum boat out near the edge of the lake. The idea of her being so close to the water scared him, but he didn't want to let it show. The canoe sat beside it, anchored by time alone, and seemed foreboding, almost like a coffin beside her.

"Hey, Valerie!" Mac said, skipping far ahead of Joe. Joe sped up, not wanting to seem too anxious but also unable to resist closing the distance to her as quickly as possible.

Valerie turned around and waved at them. She slid out of the boat and took a few steps towards them.

"You going for a boat tide?" Mac asked her.

"Not in one of these old things," Valerie said. "Too dangerous."

"Yeah, they look old," Mac agreed. She ran her hand curiously along the wooden surface of the canoe. It made Joe more than a little uneasy.

Valerie's eyes found Joe's over Mac's head. Just looking at her in such a way made Joe want to start kissing her. Between now and when the moving truck arrived five weeks from now to pack all of their stuff up, Joe wanted to kiss her every second of every day. He knew his buddies back home would ask if anything else had happened between them. They would be referring to sex—a word that Joe and his friends all tried to avoid actually *saying* at all costs, preferring terms like *doing it* or *banging* instead. To call it *sex* inferred that they might actually know what they were talking about.

Sex had never crossed Joe's mind; he knew he was a little young to actually hope for it and, honestly, was perfectly happy with nothing more than kissing, holding hands, and enjoying the way his hand felt on her hip when they were standing close together.

"Hey, Mac," Joe said. "Go poke around the shed for a while."

"No way. I'm not going to leave you just so you guys can make out."

"Actually," Valerie said, "I'd like to talk to your brother. Nothing you'd be interested in. Can you let me talk to him for about five or ten minutes, just the two of us?"

Mac let out a little sigh, accompanied by a pouting sort of frown. It was a combo that worked wonders on their dad. But neither Joe nor Valerie were moved by it.

"Fine," Mac said. She didn't sound too disappointed. "I'm going to go down and check out the boats...maybe splash around in the water."

"No!" It was out of Joe's mouth before he could stop it. He could feel the fear rising up in him and wondered if Mac had heard it in his voice.

Mac looked startled to have heard such concern in his voice. She took a step back, giving him a curious look. "It's okay," she said. "I won't go in past my knees."

"If anything happens to you, Mom will kill me," Joe argued.

"I'll be safe. Yikes, don't throw a fit about it."

"Mac..."

He would have argued further, but then Valerie's hand was in his. She held it loosely, sort of caressing his fingers. Far back in his mind, he saw a vision of the monster rising up out of the lake and slapping its odd-shaped body on the shore, devouring Mac. But it seemed unlikely, maybe because it was daylight now or maybe just because nothing felt as if it could go wrong with Valerie's hand in his.

"Just be careful," he said. "And don't go out past your knees."

"Duh!"

Joe rolled his eyes as Mac turned her back to them, making her way down to the boats where the water met the shore in a smooth brown dip. He watched her for a moment and when he turned back to Valerie, she was already leaning in to kiss him. He met her slowly and they shared a long kiss. It was the sort of kiss that still felt new in a sense because they were still beginning to learn things about one another. She pulled him close to her and when he put a bit more intensity into it, she let out a breathy little sigh.

When she pulled away ten seconds later, Joe felt dizzy. He steadied himself by taking both of her hands and making sure to stand still.

"So, I have some not so great news," she said.

The dizziness faded and everything came snapping back into place. "That doesn't sound good."

"It's not terrible," she said. "It's just not good."

"Well, what is it?" Joe asked. He wondered, not for the first time, if there was something in the female DNA that didn't allow them to get straight to the point. It was not a cruel observation, but one that he had legitimately wondered about in secret as he had tried to learn more about the opposite sex.

"Dad's having some inventory issues at work," she said. "We're leaving in two days to go back home. If it's *really* bad, we're going to stay."

"Well, that sucks," Joe said plainly. His heart felt as if it were cringing.

"But even if it *is* bad, we'll still come back up on the weekends."

"Still…"

"Hey, it's nothing to worry about right now. Don't let it get you down."

"I'll try not to," he said with a smile.

"There's something else I've been thinking about," she said.

"What's that?"

"Well, in three weeks, you'll be back in New York and I'll be back home. It's a little town called Bower, a little over an hour away from here. I Googled it last night. That's almost eleven hours. And I know there's Facebook , Skype, FaceTime and e-mail and all that, but…this won't work, will it?"

It was something Joe had also thought about and, surprisingly, had come to terms with. This thing between him and Valerie was a *for now* thing. It would end in five weeks, when he would be headed back to New York, crammed into the family car with his mom, dad, and Mac. It felt like a very grown-up thing to think about. Maybe that was why he was taking it so well.

"No, I don't think it will," he admitted.

She frowned, but there was something playful about it that drove Joe crazy. She looked down to the ground and said: "So what do we do, then?"

He knew it was a playful sort of bait, and he gladly took it. He took her gently by her hips and pulled her to him. They kissed again and this time there was an energy and heat to it that he hadn't felt before. It took him by surprise and almost scared him a bit, but the feel of her against him and the taste of her mouth was enough to kill off any fear.

That changed, though, when he heard Mach screaming for help.

It was just a scream at first, but then she included his name.

"Joe! Help!"

Joe broke the kiss instantly and had a fleeting second where he became perfectly aware of what his sister meant to him. He would gladly have pushed Valerie to the ground if she tried to hold him away from helping his sister to continue kissing him. Thoughts of the monster from the lake popped up into his head and a scream rose up in his throat.

But when he turned to see what had happened, he settled down a bit. In fact, he started to feel the barbs of anger. Irritated laughter bubbled out of his throat as he looked towards the two old boats.

"Mac…"

She had gotten into the old rickety canoe and was now floating away from the shore. Somehow, she had managed to move the boat from the bank without making much noise. She was now floating in the water, and had made it about ten feet away from the shore before bothering to call out to them.

"Joe, please help!" She was near tears, her eyes wide and filled with fear.

"It's okay," Joe said, aggravated. "Is there an oar in there?"

She looked around the bottom of the boat as it continued to drift further away. "No!"

"Damn it," Joe said.

"Oh my God, I'm sorry," Valerie said. "There was one in there earlier this summer but I swiped it for Dad. An antique sort of thing…"

"It's okay," he said. "How would you know my idiot sister would do something like this?"

He looked around for some solution, not liking the thought of simply wading out into the water. She was far enough away where the water was likely over his head by now, meaning he'd have to swim out to her.

Valerie took his hand and led him down to where the aluminum boat sat along the bank. "There's on old wooden oar right here in this one," she said, stepping into the old fishing boat. It was so decrepit that it groaned under her meager weight.

Every ounce of his heart begged him to not get into the boat. He knew the monster was in this lake somewhere. And yes, it was a large lake but after having seen that thing, it was easy to imagine that it could be lurking anywhere, just out of sight and ready to come after absolutely anyone. Yet, his heart also demanded that he get his ass out into the water and save his sister.

"You stay here," Joe said.

"No. You might need help."

Joe looked out to Mac, now crying and looking to the sides of the boat. Joe could tell that she was starting to form her own plan—a plan, he thought, that might include jumping out and swimming for the shore.

"No, Mac," he shouted. "Stay there. We're coming to get you."

He had no idea what to do but didn't want to seem clueless in front of Valerie. With her sitting inside and picking up the plastic oar, Joe grabbed the boat along the front end and started to push it into the water. The boat slid easily across the sand, the front end of it plopping down into the water. With another shove, it moved easier still and Joe was able to march it all the way down into the water.

Valerie held out her free hand and helped him climb into the boat. It rocked far too much for his liking as he got inside but he was able to sit down without falling on his backside. Again, it groaned under their weight and Joe wondered when someone had last taken this old heap of junk out on the water.

Right away, Valerie started rowing. They moved in little jerks of motion, heading forward and quickly closing the distance between the two boats. The boat would drift to the left after every stroke but Valerie compensated very well, keeping them on a mostly straight track towards Mac.

"Done this before?" Joe asked, impressed with the nearly mechanical way she managed to push the boat along without much force.

"A few times," she said with a smile.

Joe looked ahead and saw that Mac was no more than fifteen feet away. She saw them coming and her crying subsided a bit. "I'm sorry, Joe," she said in a little whimpering voice.

"It's okay," he said, carefully standing up so she could clearly see him. "Just hold tight. I don't know how you managed to get out there without realizing what had happened, but—"

He was interrupted by a cracking noise that was followed by a peculiar metallic creaking and crushing sound. It was almost like a soda can being crushed. By the time he even thought to look down, he felt water cascading over his feet.

"What the hell?"

When he had stood up, his weight had caused a small portion of the old rotten floor of the boat to buckle and crack. The crack was a foot long and about half a foot across. Water was coming in at a steady rate, funneling to the front of the boat and starting to cover the floor.

"That's bad," Valerie said, her voice shaky with worry.

"What can we do?" Joe asked. He was no longer too concerned with looking clueless in front of her now. All he knew was that his feet were already covered in water and Valerie's once-powerful strokes in the water with the oar didn't seem to be moving them along very far.

"Nothing," she said. "We're going to have to jump out."

Joe looked back to the bank. It was less than twenty feet away but that was far too much water between them and solid ground as far as he was concerned. *Not that it would matter much,* he thought. *That thing will come* out *of the water for you if it needs to.*

"Let me see this," Joe said, taking the oar from Valerie. She gave it over willingly and slid aside to let him row.

As he put the oar into the water, he could actually hear the water gurgling in through the hole in the bottom of the boat. The water was nearly to his ankles now and when he stroked the oar through the water, he could feel the added weight of the water. He glanced ahead and saw that while they continued to close in on Mac, she was still several feet away. He figured if he could just get them close enough to where he could reach out and grab the canoe, they could climb into it and join her.

With his third stroke of the oar, that seemed less likely. But he wasn't going to give up...not with Mac out there alone in the canoe and with Valerie watching him. He put all of his strength into his next stroke and it felt as if the boat barely moved.

Meanwhile, the water in the boat went over his ankles.

"Joe, we're sinking, "Valerie said. "We're sinking *quick.* "

"I know," he snapped, trying not to sound too mean. "If I could just get a little closer..."

He tried another stroke but he couldn't even manage to give the oar the full breadth of the stroke. With a curse, he pulled the oar back in and looked to Mac. She was maybe three arm lengths away. He could *maybe* jump to her boat, but it would be close. And even if he landed in the water, the canoe would be easy to reach.

The idea of jumping into the water terrified him, but he had to do it. There was no other way. For a moment, he thought about just letting her float to the bank on the opposite side, but it was at least thirty feet away and he'd have to ride his bike all the way over there, looking for some access point to get to her.

There were no other solutions. He had to jump.

"I'm going to jump," he told Valerie. "Can you do this with me?"

"Yeah," she said, although she looked just as scared as he did.

He took her hand and then looked out to Mac. He could now *feel* their boat sinking, going down fast with the added weight of more and more water.

"Mac, you stay right there and don't move," Joe said loudly. "Our boat is sinking, so we're going to come into yours, okay?"

Mac only nodded and went as still as a statue as she waited. Her little canoe now seemed to be drifting away impossibly fast, headed in the direction of the opposite bank.

Joe looked back to Valerie. "You ready?" he asked.

"No. But let's do it anyway."

He gave her a nervous grin, gripping the oar in his left hand and using his right hand to hold Valerie's left one. There was no counting to three or steely gazes of encouragement; they just acted. Joe heard Valerie make a small fearful sound as they jumped out of the boat and into the lake together, hand in hand.

They splashed down into the water at the same time. Panic spiraled through him as his head went under.

This was made worse when, less than a second later, he felt Valerie's hand get pulled away from his grip.

TWENTY-SIX

Joe came up to the surface, his heart pounding as terror slammed at its walls. He still held the oar in his left hand but his right was empty. He looked around in horror, gripped with a fear unlike any he had ever felt. That monster could be anywhere in this lake. It could be directly below him, waiting in the muck and murk at the bottom. It could be coming for his legs with that black mouth and—

Through the fear, Joe realized that he was directly beside Mac's boat. She was looking down into the water with something like amusement.

"You okay?" Mac asked.

"Yeah, but I don't see Valerie..."

But then he did. She came up from the water by the edge of their still-sinking boat. Her eyes sprang open and she gasped for breath.

"What is it?" Joe asked. "Are you okay?"

"Yeah. My stupid foot hit the side of the boat and I fell in."

She swam towards him, looking embarrassed but still visibly scared, too. Joe waited for her and helped her along the edge of the canoe.

"How do we do this without tipping the boat over?" Joe asked.

"Very carefully," she answered. "I'll pull myself up and the boat is going to rock. But when I get most of my back up on the air, I'll try to throw a leg up over the side. If you can give me a boost after that, I think we'll be okay. Mac and I can pull you in once I'm inside."

"Sounds good," Joe said, tossing the oar into Mac's boat. "Let's hurry."

Valerie gripped the side of the boat and everything unfolded just as she had explained. When she pulled herself up, the boat rocked considerably. Mac let out a little yelp of surprise and slid to the opposite side of the boat. This actually helped a bit, as the weight of the boat shifted. When Valerie raised her leg up, Joe used one hand to take her hip and the other to leverage against her backside. He hoisted her up, pushing himself underwater in the process.

When he felt Valerie's weight leave his hands, he swam up instantly. He was waiting for that monster to attack at any moment, maybe pulling his limbs off like it had allegedly done to that poor dock repairman.

The moment he grabbed the side of the boat, he felt Valerie take his hand. Noticing the plan in action, Mac also came over to help. The two girls worked together, getting him halfway out of the water. The canoe tilted a bit but not dangerously so. With a careful pull upwards that caused both girls to lose their footing, Joe fell into the boat.

He lay there for a moment, letting the rocking of the boat settle. He sat up slowly and when he did, Mac hugged him in a way she had not dared in several years. It was the hug of a toddler that idolized her big brother. Completely out of the blue, Joe found himself getting misty eyed. He pushed the emotion away as quickly as he could, mortified at the thought of crying in front of Valerie.

"Mac, what were you thinking?" he asked.

"I wasn't...I mean, I didn't mean to. I just stepped in and it started floating. I thought it was cool and fun at first but then I was too far away from shore and I...I—"

She started crying then, burying her face in Joe's shoulder. He noticed the way Valerie was looking at him and knew that there was no need for him to be embarrassed about Mac's reaction. Valerie was looking at him with the same sort of approval his parents gave him whenever he decided to help Mac with something like tying her shoes or putting a puzzle together.

"I'm sorry, Joe," Mac said. "I really am. Don't be mad!"

"Ah God, Mac. It's okay. Don't worry about it."

She pulled back to look at him and the sight of the tears in her eyes made him feel wretched. Had she been *that* worried he'd be mad?

"What about your clothes?" Mac asked. "They're wet. Mom and Dad might get mad."

"We'll tell them we found a pier somewhere and I fell off," he said. "It's okay."

"You sure?" she said, still not sure whether to trust him or not.

"Yes, Mac. I'm su—"

Something broke the surface of the water about three feet away from the boat. Joe's words died in his throat as he and Valerie looked in that direction. All they saw was the splash of water and the briefest glimpse of something going back under. The splash had been a decent one, much larger than the little ripples he had seen on the few occasions where he had seen a small fish leap out of the water.

Just a big fish, Joe thought. *That's all. Just a fish. Maybe a bass or a catfish.*

"That was a pretty big splash," Valerie noted.

"Yeah," he said, still looking at the space in the water.

"It's just a fish," Mac said, still wiping her tears away. "Why do you guys look so scared?"

"I'm not," Joe said, pretty sure that he *did* look terrified.

"Want me to row us out of here?" Valerie asked.

"No," Joe said. "I've got it."

He picked up the oar he had thrown into the boat moments ago and hesitated. If whatever had made the splash was something other than a fish—if it was indeed that nightmarish thing he and Valerie had been chased by—then an oar in the water might attract it. The alternative, though, was to remain floating out here in this boat until they reached the opposite bank.

"Joe?" Valerie asked.

"I know, I know," he said. *Just a fish,* he thought. *Just a big fish.*

He put the oar in the water and managed to clumsily turn it around. Valerie looked a little amused but said nothing about his struggle. When he finally had the canoe turned around and headed back for their bank, he stroked forward. He looked ahead and their bank looked like some shimmering island. That's how badly he wanted to be back on the ground. Even the sight of that old shack was like seeing a glimpse of Paradise.

The simple act of re-directing the canoe had calmed Joe's nerves. He had saved his sister from floating further out into the lake and hopefully his ability to pick up the mechanics of rowing so quickly was impressing Valerie. Aside from having to lie to his folks about why his clothes were wet, this potentially disastrous event had turned out okay.

Feeling the weight and fear slide right off of him, Joe put the oar into the water and stroked ahead, sending the boat gliding closer towards the bank.

He looked back to Valerie and saw that she still looked a little spooked. If he didn't have the oar in his hands, it would have been a great time to hold her hand and tell her that he would protect her. He could tell her that he'd never let anything happen to her, even when he was back in New York. He'd tell her that he was pretty sure he was falling in love with her and that meant he would—

"What's that?"

Mac's voice broke his daydream as he brought the oar up for another stroke.

"What's *what?* " Joe asked.

Mac pointed into the water slightly behind them and to the left.

By the time Joe saw it, it was too late.

He saw the slithering shape angling quickly towards them. Part of its mottled back had breached the surface, creating a sort of M shape above the water. That shape was only there for a moment because as it drew within five feet of the canoe, it brought its head out of the water.

"Joe…" Mac said.

He heard absolute fear in her voice, the cold sort of fear that exists only in children that are still convinced the Boogeyman is real, that he does live in their closets, and he has a taste for the flesh of frightened boys and girls.

Then he heard Valerie behind him, her voice mingled with Mac's. "Oh God," she said with a sharp intake of breath.

When the head of the thing was out of the water, it brought more with it and it propelled itself at the boat. Joe had just enough time for one single thought before it struck the boat.

No, that's not right, he thought. *The thing we saw was smaller than this. This thing is almost double the size of what Valerie and I saw.*

His attempt at reason died as the monster slammed into the back of the canoe. The collision made a hollow sort of sound and jolted the boat forward. Mac nearly fell into the water, but Valerie, now screaming in terror, managed to catch her.

Part of the thing—the head or at the very least its top portion, Joe assumed—was now in the canoe, coming into the back. Its head was pointed, but not in an angle. It was dulled and had a curve to it. It lifted the upper most part of its body up and slapped around the boat. When it rose up, Joe saw the slit where that dark mouth was. Seeing it again nearly made him freeze in terror but the screams of the two girls standing between him and the monster kept him from losing it.

Knowing of nothing better to do, Joe acted heroically before he realized he was doing it. He stepped in front of Mac and Valerie and brought the oar back like a baseball bat. His arms felt like steel rods as he swung the oar around as hard as he could. It connected with the thing's head, making a wet smacking noise. When Joe drew it back, a mucus-like substance connected to the oar and the thing's body. The blow seemed to stun the monster, so Joe drew back again. This time, the thing dodged him and when Joe's swing continued its arc and hit the side of the canoe, the monster struck out, rocketing forward.

It knocked Joe off of his feet and when he landed on his back, he struck his head hard on the side of the canoe. He saw black tendrils in his vision, but he blinked them away as best he could. He got to his knees and saw that the head of the thing had kept shooting forward. It had wrapped around Valerie's leg and she was now crying *and* screaming. People in horror movies didn't scream like this; there was something painful and shrill about it, the type of sound that you expected to hear in an asylum.

Mac was cowering against the other side of the boat, doing all she could to get as far away from it as possible without jumping into the water. Her eyes were wide and unblinking and she wasn't moving much.

At the front of the boat, the thing continued to pile in. It slithered into the boat quickly and as it filled the length of it, Joe estimated that creature had to be at least seven feet long—and that's just from what had come out of the water.

Acting as quickly as his overworked mind would allow, Joe managed to get to his feet, drawing up the oar again. The thing's grip on Valerie was stronger now, having now wrapped itself around her leg up to the knee. She was slapping at it and trying to grab it, but her hands kept sliding off in the slick substance along its skin. She was shrieking and looking at Joe, her eyes pleading for help.

Joe screamed then, and started to wail on the thing. He now lifted the oar like an axe, bringing it down on the thing as if it were a log that needed to be split into firewood. He screamed in fear and fury, raising the oar and bringing it down in blow after blow. He lost all thought and meaning behind the strikes, simply attacking on some primal instinct to save Valerie.

The thing responded by flailing wildly. Part of its rear tried knocking him down again. Joe sidestepped, almost falling out of the canoe, and instantly redirecting his attack.

He started stomping on it, hoping to inflict as much pain as he could. But it was like stepping on a wet floor, the traction on his shoes slipping. He did see that the thing had lost some of its grip on Valerie now, maybe because of the beating he was giving it. Spurred on by this, Joe reared back and delivered the hardest blast with the oar yet. He slammed the oar down in what he thought was its center.

The oar's paddle splintered into several pieces, leaving Joe with a makeshift spear in his hand. He stumbled as close as he could get to Valerie, now holding the shattered oar like a dagger. The monster squirmed, it head coiling around in search of him as it was preoccupied with Valerie.

"Joe," Mac said, her voice in a high-pitched whisper from the far end of the canoe. "I want to go home. Let's go home now, Joe…"

Still, she was unblinking. It killed Joe to see her like that. He felt the fury and desperation mingling into a ball of raw emotion in his guts. That energy radiated through him, soaking into his muscles.

He gripped the broken oar and dropped to his knees again. Beside him, Valerie continued to struggle. She tried to form words but each one died in a scream of panic, each one punctuated with the certainty that she was about to die. The thing was all the way up her leg now, starting to wrap around her waist.

From his knees, Joe brought the jagged end of the oar down onto the body of the thing. He had to give an extra thrust once he made contact, but he managed to bury the splintered wood into the thing's greenish-grey hide. When the wood was in, Joe jerked it left and right. A black substance came out of its body, spilling out in a thick pool under its body and along Joe's knees. This spurred Joe on and rather than bringing the oar up for another blow, he held it down, pressing it hard into the bottom of the boat, ensuring that he had the monster pinned down.

The reaction was slow, but the thing finally responded as most creatures with the will to survive usually do. It released its grip on Valerie and instantly started to retreat. Only, when it tried to slip out of the boat, it was trapped by the oar. For a single moment, Joe thought he had bested the damned thing. He had pierced it and now it was trapped on the boat. Joe could do as much damage as he wanted to now.

He had just enough time to think this was really the case when the rear of the thing came sailing through the air. Joe saw it a little too late but in just enough time to prevent the thing from covering his entire head. Instead of wrapping its tentacle-like body around his face, it simply slapped him along the forehead. The weight of the thing was massive and Joe went to the floor of the boat again, his head aching tremendously.

He rolled over right away, realizing that he had lost the oar when he'd been blindsided. He saw Valerie sprawled out along the bottom of the canoe, shuddering and weeping. Meanwhile, the monster was slipping out of the boat, sliding out along the side.

And on its way out, its thick body had trapped Mac along the backside of the canoe. It slithered along her body as it escapes and, in doing so, instinctively started to coil around her.

"No," Joe croaked.

He got to his feet, seeking out the shattered oar. He found it behind him, took its now slimy handle in his hands, and took a step forward. When he did, he slid in the vicious fluid of what served as the monster's blood. He nearly fell again, dropping the oar into the water as he managed to keep his balance. He reached out to Mac and pulled her to him just as the monster had started to tighten around her. Joe felt the strength of it in the last moment, trying to claim her legs. They both fell, tripping over Valerie and falling in a heap.

The monster slipped completely out of the back of the canoe.

Or so it seemed.

It didn't take Joe long to understand that the thing was still inside the canoe. It was so long that the back of its body was still in the front of the boat even through its front half had exited out of the back and was now underwater. At the front of the boat, the backside of the thing was making quick slithering motions. It was wrapping itself around the canoe in the same way it had wrapped itself around Valerie's legs. Joe could hear the canoe creaking, the boat being squeezed beneath the thing's weight and strength.

The canoe was tugged hard to the right as the creature moved deftly underwater. Joe recalled how quickly the thing had moved when it had come after him and Valerie that night in the field of fireflies. That, plus its strength, made Joe pretty sure that it would have no problem at all with either crushing the canoe completely or pulling them underwater.

"It's going to crush the boat," Joe said.

"Or try to pull us under," Valerie said, echoing Joe's other thought.

"We have to jump out," Joe said.

"No," Mac wailed. "No."

"If we don't it'll kill us," Joe said.

"But it can get us in the water, too."

"Probably," Joe said. "But at least we have a chance that way. Right?"

"Yeah," Valerie said.

As they spoke, the head of the monster reappeared. It started slapping at the rear of the canoe, nestling itself around it in the same way the front was currently being claimed. Joe could feel the weight of the thing on the boat. The bottom buckled and cracked as the monster continued to squeeze.

"I can't get in the water," Mac said. "It'll get us."

The boat creaked again. Up front, the side cracked down the middle. Water started to trickle in. Two seconds later, that trickle was a steady stream.

"We don't have a choice," Joe told Mac. "Just hold my hand and we'll be okay. We'll swim back to the shack. And it's right there...maybe fifteen feet away. We can do that. The thing is distracted with the boat."

"But I can't."

"We'll have a head start," Valerie said, trying to help Joe convince her. "By the time it's done with the boat, we'll almost be there. Okay?"

Mac nodded, but let out a deep gasping pout. Joe hugged her to him as the boat made another cracking noise. Joe was pretty sure the entire body of the thing was wrapped around the boat. He counted three coils of it at the front of the canoe and one thicker one at the back. Meanwhile, they stood near the center as the boat was being crushed all around them.

Joe brought Mac to him and kissed her on the forehead. "I'll get you over there," he said, nodding to the pointing station. "But we have to go *now*. You ready?"

Yes," she said, still crying.

"You?" Joe asked Valerie. She gave a nod in response.

"Now," he whispered.

And once again, Joe found himself jumping into the lake. Only now, he knew without a doubt that the monster was there. It was there and it was bigger than he had known it before. It was bigger, it was stronger and it was hungrier.

They hit the water and even before he came up with his sister's hand in his own, he was swimming as hard as he could. He didn't dare look back. But even still, he could hear the canoe. It was cracking, creaking, splintering.

Beside him, swimming as well as she could (which wasn't very good at all), Mac continued to cry. Valerie came up beside them and they worked together to keep Mac afloat.

The shore was now about twelve feet ahead of them. Then ten...then eight. Joe kept his eyes focused on the old shack and hoped it would serve as some sort of safety.

Behind them, there was a chilling crashing noise. Joe couldn't help it—he looked over his shoulder and saw the boat being snapped in half. It broke into three pieces, one of which flew a few feet into the air. Splinters and dust formed a small cloud that settled over the water. Then the monster was slithering over the remains of the boat and quickly darting under water.

Joe let out a moan. The shore was now six feet away. He took another stroke forward and felt instant relief when his feet touched the bottom. He pushed himself forward, hauling the two girls with him as he splashed out of the water and towards the shack.

He looked back again and saw nothing—only the lake and shattered remains of the canoe. But somewhere between their bodies and those flecks of wood, he knew their deaths were speeding towards them somewhere in that murky lake water.

TWENTY-SEVEN

The cabin was starting to reek. There was a thick mingling of Chinese food leftovers, garbage that needed to be taken out, and the overall smell a place tends to take on when the inhabitant is being unproductive. Only, Scott didn't *feel* like he was being unproductive. Starting at these damned screens for the better part of a week was causing some of the worst headaches he'd ever had. He was tired, he was listless, and he was frustrated.

And truth be known, he wasn't quite sure when he had last taken a shower.

Still, there were a few positives to the situation. For instance, there had been no reports of violent deaths around the lake. The only death in the last four days had come from a drunk driving incident on the outskirts of Clarkton. No deaths meant no extra guilt from not having found the creature. Of course, it also meant that the next attack could be right around the corner.

He was starting to wonder if the old man on the fishing boat had mortally wounded the thing. Susan had told him that the man— Wayne Crosby, if he remembered correctly—claimed to have shot the creature with a Ruger .22. Being that the creature seemed to have not been active in the last few days, it was worth considering.

The other positive was that Roger Lowry seemed to have accepted that his "clean-up man" was holed up in a cabin in the remote lakeside community of Clarkton, Virginia. Roger understood the waiting game and knew that this slow surveillance process was essentially the only way to find the creature. The only alternative was to send a specialist of some sort that had a background in marine biology, or maybe even a whole FBI team with a diving background. But that meant spending more bureau dollars on a case that, when all was said and done, would be buried under so much paperwork that no one in their right mind would ever dig deep enough to find out what had happened. It was also a case that less than a dozen people were aware of, so there was also the level of secrecy to be considered.

As long as Scott sent in his reports twice a day (at lunch and just before he went to sleep), Roger seemed happy. Scott assumed that after another week or two, there would be talk of relieving him with another agent, but if that week ended up being as long as this one, Roger wasn't even going to waste his time with such hopes.

He was looking around the cabin, wondering if he should maybe take an hour to clean the place up, when he saw a small wooden boat go wafting out into the water on one of the screens set up in the living room. At first glance, he thought nothing of it and turned his attention to the overflowing garbage can in the kitchen. But just as he turned his head, he saw that there was only a single passenger in the boat and it looked to be a little girl. Closer inspection revealed that the boat was a small canoe.

He went to the laptop the screen was being displayed on and maximized it, temporarily blocking out the other feeds on the screen. He then switched it to the television screen, giving him a forty inch view of the scene.

The camera he was viewing was the one that had been set up several feet within a tree along one of the banks not too far away from his cabin. The little girl was a good distance away from the bank, having crept onto the screen from the left. Scott could see the tree line on the opposite side of the water, assuming the girl had come from the bank on the opposite side of the cove. There seemed to be no activity along the tree line, making the sight of this young girl all alone in a boat a little alarming. She looked to be no older than ten, but it was hard to be certain given the angle of the camera and the distance between the girl and where the camera was perched. She was a good seventy feet away and was little more than a detailed speck on the screen.

The scene was more alarming still when the girl got to her feet and starting to yell. There was no sound, as the cameras had no audio capabilities, so her little screams were totally silent as he watched. She was looking slightly to her left, peering somewhere off the screen. And as she continued to shout, her little canoe continued to drift slowly closer towards the trail cam.

The more responsible part of him thought about calling the local PD to go out and check on things. But he also knew that this could be some sort of elaborate play between the girl and one of her friends. If this was the case, the only thing worth looking into were the irresponsible parents.

He held off for a while, although he found that he was already holding his cellphone in his hand. Scott was not one that typically relied on gut instincts but he felt something instinctual slipping in behind the control as he watched the girl and her little wooden canoe drift closer to the camera. As she got closer, Scott saw that she seemed to be settling down into the canoe again but was still looking to someone or something off camera. He could also see her more clearly now and he was certain that this little girl was no more than ten years of age—probably younger than that.

After another minute or so, Scott saw another boat come into view, coming from the same direction as the little girl. Again, the distance made it hard to tell, but he thought this boat was a basic aluminum fishing boat. It was old but it came across the water quickly. There were two people in it and when Scott squinted at the screen, he felt pretty confident that they were kids, too. These looked a little older. There was one boy and one girl; the girl was rowing and making pretty good speed. Scott wondered if this was a bullying situation or some sort of rescue attempt. He looked back to the little girl and saw that she looked a little more relaxed. He began to get irritated with the screen, wishing he were there in person to watch it play out. It was so hard to judge correctly when his subjects were no larger than three inches on the television screen.

As he continued to watch, something went wrong. The two kids in the aluminum boat had stopped rowing. The boy was standing up and looking out towards the younger girl. The older girl in the canoe was trying to row but didn't seem to be going anywhere.

Scott started to almost absently pull his contacts up on his cellphone as the boy took the oar from the girl and tried rowing closer to the canoe. By the time the two older kids in the canoe had decided to leap out of their boat, Scott had figured that it was sinking. He watched the older kids amble into the canoe with the younger girl and his gut reaction was stronger than ever. Sure, the older kids had come to the little girl's rescue; that much was clear now. But seeing the older two jump into the water...well, something didn't seem right about it. They were moving with a sort of urgency that spoke of fear and survival. Maybe he was jumping to conclusions as he watched the tiny people play out their scene on the TV in front of him, but he was pretty sure the older two were scared of something.

Figuring it was better to be safe than sorry, Scott pulled up Susan Lessing's phone number and tapped it. As it rang in his ear, he watched the older two kids get situated in the boat with the younger one. The boy started working to turn the canoe around in the direction the canoe had drifted from. A few feet away, the aluminum boat continued to sink, now almost entirely submerged.

"Yeah?" Susan said in his ear.

"Susan, I've got a potentially dangerous situation out on Kerr Lane...on the opposite side of the lake from where the trail cam in the tree is situated. There are three kids—a younger girl and what looks to be two teens. I'm not sure yet but...well, maybe head over this way."

"Sure. I'm in the car now. I'm maybe five minutes away from your cabin, actually."

"Great. It might be nothing, but these kids, they..."

"They what?"

Scott saw two humps break in the water. It looked exactly like a snake rippling through the water, only the size was off. This would have been a *big* snake.

"Shit. Susan, I think we've got a sighting. I'm watching it right now."

"The monster?"

"I think so. It—"

And then he saw it rise up out of the water and attack the canoe. Even in a tiny form on the laptop screen, it was terrifying.

"Kerr Lane," Scott barked. "Now!"

"Oh God," Susan said. "Okay. Give me about five minutes."

With his cellphone still by his ear, he grabbed up his gun from the coffee table. Just feeling the Sig Sauer in his hands made him feel like he was finally doing something productive.

Scott was already figuring the time it would take him to get there. He figured he was a little less than a mile away from the place where the kids had gotten into the water. Hauling ass in the car down Kerr Lane, he could probably get there in a minute and a half.

Seems quick, he thought. *But I'm pretty sure those kids will be dead by then...*

With that thought haunting, Scott ran to his car.

In the seconds between opening and closing his door, he heard screams coming from somewhere off the lake.

TWENTY-EIGHT

Wayne opened his bedroom closet and shoved the few clothes he had on hangers to the side, revealing the dusty back corner. The Remington had been propped up in that corner for more than two years now. The last time had used it had been for some lazy turkey hunting two falls ago. Since then, he'd thought about selling it and had even tried to pawn it off on Al a few times.

But it had remained here, in his closet. It was the second gun he'd ever purchased, long before his little snake-scare had convinced him to buy the Ruger a few years back. He looked at the Remington for a few moments. It was a very common twelve-gauge model but Wayne felt as if he was looking at a weapon of great power—even more so when he reached in and took it out.

He figured a few blasts from this would do a hell of a lot more damage than the Ruger.

The plan he had concocted was a flimsy one. He knew this, but it was all he had. It was the only thing he could come up with that would make him feel like he was doing something productive in order to find and stop whatever had come up out of the lake and nearly killed Al. Sure, they had called the game warden but he knew that meant nothing. Even if it went as far as the police, the local PD would do nothing more than set a few cruisers on the roads with instruction to keep their eyes peeled.

Anyway…what else was he going to do? Sit around his house, get drunk out of his mind, and stay awake as long as possible to stave off the nightmares he'd been having of the monster from the lake?

Hell no. He'd rather be out there on the lake looking for it.

The trusty Weld-Craft boat that he and Al had shared back and forth over the years was tied up behind his house, anchored to a stump on the bank. He'd taken it on the day he'd raced Al home, terrified with every inch of water it carried him across. Even on that first evening when Kathy had assured him that she didn't need any help in taking Al to the doctor, Wayne had sat on the uneven stump he'd anchored the boat to, watching it float a few feet out from shore. He'd stared out beyond the boat, wondering about what the hell he and Al had just seen.

That had also been the moment when he had started to wonder how one might kill such a thing.

Wayne walked across his back yard, noting that he really should cut it, as it was just about up to his knees in some places. He carried only the Remington, not even bothering to pretend that he intended to do any fishing. No, he was going to head right back out to the little cover where had and Al had encountered the thing. It was a big lake and he figured the best place to start looking for a strange creature was in an area it had been seen at least once. He'd also heard the story about the dock repairman, so Wayne figured if the cover offered nothing, he'd scoot on down to the Carter residence and float along the bank.

When he cranked the Weld-Craft's engine, he felt odd not having Al with him. He also felt strange not having a cooler of beer with him. As badly as he wanted one, he knew that he'd need all of his concentration and patience if he had any hope of finding the thing that he had already started thinking of as a monster. He wanted a beer so badly that he nearly cut the boat off and headed back to his house to pack his cooler.

Before the urge grew too strong, he untied the boat from the dock post and started out onto the lake. The Remington lay flat in the floor, sitting in an area where the monster had slithered across seven days ago. He looked to the shotgun from time to time as he covered the two miles between his house and the cove that he and Al had been frequenting since their thirties. As he hit open water for a while, he realized how pathetically alone he felt in the midst of all of this water without Al in the boat with him. He passed by a boat packed out with what looked like a family of four with the older child being pulled behind the boat on a wave-riding tube. The kid was hollering for his dad to go faster and Wayne could hear the engine buzz a bit more as his father obliged.

He thought about his ex-wife and the family they had often discussed having. Then there had been the fertility issues, then his drinking, then her affair, then *his* affair, and that had been that.

Somehow, thirty years of marriage had passed by unhappily and a divorce had been waiting at the end of that long and knotted rope. He often tried to tell himself that this post-divorce life—especially now that he had retired—was a new and exciting chapter of his life. And while that was true, that chapter was still included in the same shitty book he'd been reading his whole life.

My mind wonders like a stray dog when I get by myself, he thought. *That can't be good...especially not for an old borderline-alcoholic fart that is discovering just how alone he is while he's driving a boat with a shotgun as a passenger...*

Luckily, the cove came into view on his right. When he spied it, he instantly became afraid and slowed the boat considerably. The engine puttered him along and it took everything within him not to grab the Remington right away. He coasted into the cove and then angled the boat to the place where he and Al had been sitting when they'd been attacked.

He killed the engine and simply floated there. He sat still, his hands itching for a beer more than ever now. The sense of loneliness only increased as he sat in the cove, the trees from the bank towering over him like they might snatch him up at any moment. The world was silent other than its natural noises: birds singing somewhere nearby, the buzzing of distant boats and the cheerful noise of a child shouting elsewhere on the lake—perhaps the same kid he had passed several minutes ago, still enjoying the tube ride behind his family's boat.

Wayne sat and he waited. His mind kept going back to his ex-wife and it made him angry. Her name was Theresa, but he had stopped referring to her as such years ago, calling her only *my ex-wife* in all conversation and even in his internal thoughts. He wondered where she was now. What was she doing and where was she living? He had her number. He could find out. He could—

He heard the kid yelling again and this time it sounded even further off. But no...this was a different voice. And while he wasn't certain, he didn't think the voice sounded all that happy.

Cocking his head in that direction, Wayne listened closer, waiting to hear the kid again. He knew that sound often travelled across the water in a weird way, so there was no way to tell *exactly* what he was hearing or to accurately pinpoint where it was coming from.

The shout came again. This time, he heard two voices and he now knew without a doubt that one of them was afraid. Not only that, but whatever the scared one was saying sounded a hell of a lot like *"Help!"*

He felt certain it was coming from his right, a good distance away. He nearly did nothing, content to sit there and do his lazy monster hunting. But who was to say anyone else would respond to the call for help he'd just heard? Wayne knew that he was far from a Good Samaritan, but he also wasn't a hapless asshole that would let a kid scream for help without at least swinging by to see what was wrong.

Another scream came darting across the lake and this time there was no word to it; it was just a scream.

Hearing it, he thought his first estimate had been off. The scream wasn't too far away at all. It was coming from the direction of Kerr Lane, directly to his right and less than a mile away.

Wayne cranked the engine to life again. When the boat got moving, there was nothing slow or hesitant about his driving this time. He blasted the boat across the lake, staying fairly close to the bank, and wished Al was there to tell him to slow this deathtrap down. He couldn't remember the last time he'd opened the boat up like this. It felt good in an odd way, even with the uneven tremble of the engine vibrating through the back of the boat.

He leaned into the wind as it ruffled the little bit of hair that was still on his head. As the boat skipped along the water, a look of steeled determination came across his face. It was drawn so tight that within several seconds, it could have easily been mistaken as a smile.

TWENTY-NINE

When Joe was completely out of the water and rushing up the bank, he nearly lost his footing and fell flat on his face. The only thing that kept him up was the pull of Mac's light yet insistent weight, pulling him ahead. Their hands were still linked and she was a few feet ahead of him, displaying speed that Joe had never seen out of her. To his right, Valerie was also running up the bank, reaching out for his other hand. He took it and they ran towards the cabin in a staggered chain.

They had made it no more than five feet up the bank before he heard the light but noticeable splash in the water behind them. Joe turned and saw the exact same thing he had seen on the old boat ramp a week or so ago, the night Valerie had asked him to come out and catch fireflies with her.

The monster was coming out of the lake and now that the water wasn't completely hiding its shape, Joe saw that it was easily twice the size it had been the first time he had seen it. Even on the land, it seemed to be moving along as if it were swimming, raising up the front portion of its body along with a portion in the center and pulling itself along. But as its entire body came out of the water—what, Joe thought, was easily ten feet long now—it went flat to the ground and started to slither like a big snake.

And when it did this, it moved *fast*. There was no way they could outrun it. They probably wouldn't even make it back up onto Kerr Lane before the ugly thing caught up to them and fell on top of them—just like he'd seen in his nightmares.

So the old fishing shack was their only hope. And that, he knew, was a flimsy hope at best.

"Go!" he screamed. "Get in the shed!"

But Mac was way ahead of him. In fact, she was so far ahead of him that he had to completely outstretch his arm just to keep from losing his grip on her. The shack loomed less than ten feet ahead now and looking at it, he wondered how much shelter it would provide. The boards were old and weak, the ceiling was lopsided, and he knew the door likely wouldn't close securely.

Still, it was better than nothing and was probably their best shot at staying alive as long as possible.

Beside him, Valerie screamed. He looked over to her and saw that she was okay for the time being. She had looked back to the monster for the first time since coming out of the lake and was reacting at what she saw. It was still slithering towards them, sending leaves, twigs and other fallen debris flying. It left a clearly strewn path behind it, highlighted by a clear substance that looked very much like mucus.

As he looked back towards it, he felt his right arm take a sudden jerk to the left. He looked ahead and saw that Mac had reached the shack. She was running to the left, where the doorway stood. Reaching it, Mac let go of his hand once she was in the presumed safety of the little building.

He followed along, pulling Valerie with him. He peered back over his shoulder and saw that the thing was catching up at an alarming rate. If the shack hadn't been an option, he was pretty sure it would be on Valerie's heels before they got halfway up to the road.

He knew that their only hope was to cower in the shack, hoping its weak structure would hold up against the thing long enough for it to retreat back to the water like it did the first time it had nearly killed him. He couldn't remember how long that had been. Thirty seconds? Maybe forty?

He came to the edge of the shack and took a hard turn to the left, just as Mac had done. With Valerie's hand still in his, he skidded to a stop, realizing that he was about to overshoot the doorway. He halted and leaped into the dank interior, realizing for the first time that they would essentially be trapped. At least outside, there was plenty of room to run if the thing made some kind of mistake. But in the shack, their only hope was in the questionable strength of the wooden walls and the door.

Valerie's hand was still in his and he gave it a tug, hoping to help her along. She came in through the door with a scream and the moment she cleared the frame, Joe reached out to shut the door. He pushed it as hard as he could, the hinges shrieking as the warped door and the frame rubbed together.

Just before he gave it a final push that he hoped would at the very least take the door to the edge of the frame, the bottom of the frame was suddenly filled with what he assumed the head of the monster. It came in a fast and fluid motion that once again reminded Joe of a very determined snake. It instantly found Valerie's leg again, as she was the closest to the door, and wrapped around it. Valerie screamed a high-pitched wail and fell to the dirt floor.

Not knowing what else to do, Joe pushed hard on the door. It moved considerably and pinched the first quarter or so of the creature's body between the door and the frame. Realizing that it was caught, it restricted a bit, tightening its body and trying to draw back. Joe let out a scream and shoved hard against the door one more time. It moved only slightly, wedging the thing's body in even more.

This time, it drew back considerably and let go of Valerie's leg. Still, Joe shoved on the door, hoping that maybe the old wood would puncture the thing's skin or, if they were very lucky, tear right through it.

The monster managed to pull away completely, slinking quickly through the door. Joe was pleased to see that the thing was hurt in the process; its flesh peeled back in much the same way human skin might be peeled back in a violent scratch. He saw the white meat beneath and more of its black flowing blood.

Joe let out a string of curses that he had never spoken out loud in front of Mac as he gave the door one final shove. It took some effort, but he managed to get the door to fit almost completely into the frame. He wasn't sure if the door or the frame was causing the problem, as both were considerably warped and out of shape, but he hoped the force it had taken to shut it meant that it would be equally hard to get it open.

With the door closed, he ran to Valerie and saw that her leg was inflamed and red. She was wincing against it, a tear slipping from her eye.

"Are you okay?" he asked.

"I think so," she answered. "It just burns."

Joe then went to his sister and took her in his arms. "You okay, Mac?"

She nodded, but frowned. He could tell that she was on the verge of breaking down into a crying fit. He'd seen it out of her several times before but it was usually because she wasn't getting her way or because she'd been disciplined. He had no idea what this fit might be like and had no interest in letting it happen.

"Look, we'll be okay in here," he told her. "That thing is just like a fish. It needs water to breathe. It will have to go back to the water after a while and—"

The side of the shack shook violently as something slammed into it from outside. This was instantly followed by the sound of the thing slithering around the corners of the place.

Joe looked around for a suitable place to look outside without putting himself in harm's way. He found two slats on the left side of the shack that had about three inches between them but it wasn't quite enough to see anything of substance. As he tried to get a good vantage point, the monster slammed into the side of the building again. This was a harder attack and Joe's heart sank when he heard the sound of splintering wood. The old tool rack along the front of the shack was jarred loose from the wall and came clattering down to the ground.

Joe saw the old pitchfork among the clutter and went to it. Valerie thought it had likely once been used for frog gigging. What they were up against was much worse than even the largest frog he could think of, but he had to go with what he had. He grabbed up the pitchfork and found that it was so old and worn that it felt like nothing more than a heavy toy in his hand.

"Joe..." Mac said.

He went to her and held her close, the pitchfork still in hand. "I know," he said.

Valerie slid over to them, still on her backside and extending her wounded leg out.

"Maybe if we scream loud enough, someone will hear us," she said. "My dad's cabin is *so* close."

This thought seemed to depress her more than relieve her. Joe knew the feeling; to be so close to someone that could help but still be in such danger seemed almost ridiculous.

"We can give it a try," Joe said.

As if sensing what they were about to do, the monster attacked the shed again, this time from a different side. Joe watched the door shudder in its weak frame. The bottom of it popped out a little. From overhead, dust and dirt wafted down from the force of the attack.

"Okay, start screaming," Joe said.

All three of the screamed at the top of their lungs. Their voices were desperate and terrified, coming out of the tiny shack like the wailing of lost ghosts. Whether or not anyone heard, they did not know. They simply continued to scream as they waited for the next attack on the shed.

After thirty seconds of yelling, after which time Joe's throat had started to get sore, a thought occurred to him. He stopped screaming and looked back out of the thin space between the slats he had used earlier. There was no sign of the monster and it had not attacked the building in nearly a minute. Maybe it had gone back to the water.

Or maybe it was slithering quietly around the edges of the cabin, waiting for them to assume that they were safe so it could spring on them when they stepped out.

"Hold on," Joe said, making a *stop* gesture with his hand. "Stop screaming. If we're quiet, we might be able to hear when it heads back to the water. If we can be *sure* it's going back to the water, we can get out of here. If we start running for the road while it's headed for the water, we could probably make it to the closest house."

"You think?" Valerie asked.

"It's worth trying," he said. "If it hits this shack a few more times, it's going to break through the walls."

She nodded. "Sure. Let's try that."

"I don't know, Joe…" Mac said.

"I don't either," he admitted as he took her hands. "But it's the only plan we have right now. Okay?"

"Okay," she said. The look of trust she gave him made Joe feel like a grownup. He felt like the man in charge, the one responsible for getting these two girls out of this stupid old shack alive and in one piece. And although he felt silly holding the pitchfork as their only means of protection, he still held it as if their lives depended on it.

He walked over to the crack in the wall between the two slats and peered out. He couldn't see the area a foot or so in front of him and beyond that, he was offered a very obstructed view of the lake. There were too many trees in his way to make sense of anything. The fact that he couldn't see the monster did little to comfort him. As far as he was concerned, the fact that he couldn't see it simply meant that it could be hiding at the door.

But it needed to get back to the water, right? Based on his first encounter with it, this seemed like a reasonable assumption.

"Do you see it?" Valerie asked.

"No. I can't see *anything*."

He turned around and looked at the door. It had been hard to close it, so he figured it would also be hard to open it. And if it made all of the creaks and squeals it had made upon closing, the monster would surely hear it.

Joe had no idea what to do. He peered back through the slat, back to the lake, praying to hear the sound of something easing back into the water.

Behind him, Mac started to cry. It was a soft sound, as she understood that staying quiet might be their best bet at survival. He turned to look at her and saw that she was covering her mouth with her hands. Her tears ran onto her fingertips and pooled there.

"Mac, it's okay," he said.

"Please," she said between gasps for breath. "Let's go home."

"We will," he said. "We will. I promise."

"Now," she said.

"I'm trying…"

As he said that, he heard the slithering noise again. It was coming from the right side of the cabin, the side that held the door. It was slight but fairly consistent. The thing was on the move, and it was moving at a steady pace. The question, of course, was whether it was circling the cabin or heading back down to the water before the air suffocated it.

Giving up on his useless peeking spot, Joe glided over to the door. There was the smallest fraction of light coming in from the bottom where the door wasn't fitting securely in the frame. Joe looked down to the spot, getting down on his hands and knees to do so. He looked to the little section of light—no larger than the size of a quarter—and felt despair well up within him.

He could see a fraction of the thing as it moved along the base of the shack. It was moving quickly, its body looking like some smooth and glistening oil along the underside of the door. Joe wondered if it was circling the shack, looking for any sign of weakness.

"Joe?"

Valerie's voice called softly from behind him.

"It's still there," he said.

"You're sure?"

"Yes. It's right here along the d—"

Suddenly, it stopped moving as if in response to Joe's voice. Joe stayed where he was, watching that small bit of it through the hole in the bottom of the door. *How long can this damn thing stay out of the water without dying?*

It was a desperate thought, one that seemed to fill his head in a repetitive shout. He assumed this was because he knew that their only chance of escaping was taking advantage of the thing's weakness. But even then, it moved so fast that he didn't know if they'd be able to get away.

"What is it?" Valerie asked.

"What's wrong?" Mac followed up, her tears making her voice sound thick and broken.

"It's not moving. It's—"

A loud banging noise seemed to explode right out of the air directly in front of him. The door shuddered in its frame, popping out slightly. A large crack formed along the bottom, racing up like a backwards lightning bolt.

Joe fell back on his rear end as the girls screamed behind him. He scrambled back, unable to get to his feet. He looked back, making sure Mac and Valerie were okay. Mac was crying at full force now, but it was unlike her usual bouts of crying. There was horror in the sounds that came out of her mouth now. Hearing her like that made him both terrified and pissed off.

In front of him, the thing struck the door again. This time, the entire bottom section of the door popped out, the right corner splintering and almost falling away from the rest of it. The monster darted its head in but the broken bit of door was not enough to allow it a full entrance. It drew back quickly, its slithering noise now louder and without stealth as it backed up to reach charging speed again.

"It's coming again," Joe said, now on his feet and holding the pitchfork almost like a shield. "When it hits the door, run through it. Right away. Okay?"

Valerie nodded but Mac looked to be frozen. She was still weeping but her eyes looked to be unblinking as she stared at the place where the monster had been only seconds ago.

Joe got back to his knees and looked down through the hole that had been partially created along the right side of the door. He could just barely see the thing coiling up around itself and then charging forward. It was close, surely no more than ten feet away, and its speed was uncanny.

"Here it comes," he said.

And then the door to the shack seemed to blow inward. There was a cracking sound that was almost like a comical *pop* as two of the door's three hinges were blown off. Splinters of wood hit Joe in the face as the bottom of the door exploded and the thing came charging in.

Joe rolled to the right and felt the slimy side of the thing against his arm. He finished his roll just in time to see Valerie doing as he had been instructed. She reached towards the door before the entire length of the monster was inside the cabin. She jumped over it and darted into the forest.

After that, Joe lost sight of her. His eyes were on Mac. She was still frozen but now her face had contorted into something that was almost feral. She was literally frozen in panic as the thing went charging after her.

Joe lunged for her, not sure what he was doing. Rather than grabbing her and pulling her away (which he knew he didn't have time for), he shoved her hard against the far wall. The charging monstrosity missed her, lashing through the air where the little girl had been standing less than a second ago.

Mac struck the far wall and started screaming again. Joe knew it was inviting death to think such a thing, but his only hope now was that the thing would turn back for him. Maybe it would leave Mac and come racing back to him. Then Joe could only hope he could manage a few good strikes with the pitchfork.

The thing slowed itself before striking the wall and then Joe was both terrified and relieved when the thing did exactly what he had wished. The upper half of its body turned and seemed to study him with eyes that Joe could not see. The thing's flesh seemed to expand slightly and then contract, as if it were breathing. It drew back a bit, arching to strike and Joe was given another glance of that wretched slash of a mouth that had haunted him since the night he and Valerie had caught fireflies. It opened that mouth twice and Joe was pretty sure it was somehow tasting the air, figuring out where it needed to strike.

And then it was coming at him. Joe looked into that mouth, vaguely aware of the bowl-shaped suckers along its underside.

"Run, Mac," Joe said, unable to take his eyes away from the thing.

Behind him, he could hear Valerie screaming.

He brought the pitchfork up and stabbed out at the monster as it closed the distance between them. The monster moved at the last moment and only one of the prongs at the bottom of the pitchfork pierced it. Most of the thing's weight slammed into Joe and he was knocked to the ground.

As the thing started to fall on him, Joe saw Mac freeze again, a look of shock and surprise on her face behind the thing.

Then there was a sound like an explosion and the monster was on top of him.

After that, darkness.

THIRTY

Scott brought his car to a hard stop, slamming on the brakes. A cloud of dirt and dust billowed up around the sedan as he opened his door. His hand instantly went to his hip where the Sig waited. When he was out of the car, he stood motionless for a moment, listening.

It took no time at all to hear signs of distress. He heard a girl screaming from very close by. It was coming from directly ahead of him, a shrill sound of terror. Scott went racing in that direction, the Sig raised as he went bounding through the forests in the directions of the screaming.

As his eyes fell on the shack a few yards ahead of him and the teenage girl running out of it, he heard an approaching engine roaring down the road. Susan, he assumed.

He started down towards the shack, not bothering to wait for Susan. The girl that had come running out of the shed was still screaming, staring at either the shack or the lake beyond.

Scott worked purely on instinct, running down into the woods and towards the shack. When he passed the girl, he gave her only a passing glance. He hoped Susan would stop and check on her. For now, he was more concerned with what had caused her screams.

As he neared the old shack, a series of screams came rocketing out of it. It sounded like another girl, probably much younger than the one he had already passed. He came to the door in a sprint and drew his gun up. He took a step in and everything in his body—his mind included—froze for a split second to try to make sense of what he was seeing.

His brain first brought to mind the world *slug*. After that, he thought *leech*. But the truth of the matter was that the thing he saw falling on top of a teenage boy was neither of those things. It was eyeless and without appendages. Its underside—which he saw clearly for a moment as it fell on the boy—was filled with suckers that reminded him of tentacles, bringing to mind one of his favorite childhood novels, *Twenty Thousand Leagues Under the Sea.*

It took that connection to reality to unhinge his mind and muscles. As the boy fell to the ground, the leech-like thing on top of him, Scott looked for a shot where the boy would not be at risk. The boy's head was still uncovered, but it was clear that the head was what the monster was going for. It squirmed and crawled, trying to position its own head over the boy's. The boy fought diligently but the weight of the monster was just too much.

Scott steadied his hand and fired three times into the lower part of the thing's body. The thing responded instantly, coming up off of the boy and rearing back like a snake ready to strike. Scott peered into its horrid mouth for just one second before firing two more times, each shot tearing into the meat of the thing's sickly-white underside.

Black fluid poured out of it as it barreled forward. Scott tried to move out of the way but the thing slammed into him. It was soft to the touch but incredibly heavy. Rather than falling onto him as it had done with the boy, it simply knocked him out of the way. Scott went tumbling into the front wall of the shack, his back smacking into the wood and sending the breath out of his lungs.

Amazingly, the monster went slipping out of the doorway. The gunshots had apparently hurt it enough to make it give up on its latest meal. Scott watched the length of it trail out of the shack, still not quite sure what he was seeing.

At his feet, the boy was rolling over and getting to his feet. He looked around as if in a daze. On the far side of the cabin, the little girl he had heard screaming before he entered ran to the boy, crying hysterically. The boy took her carefully into his arms and looked back to Scott.

"You have to stop it," the boy said, looking desperately to Scott. "It's going back to the water. It's just like a fish, I think. It can't stay on land for so long."

"Stay here," Scott said, drawing a painful breath. He turned to head out of the shack when he heard two loud gun blasts that made him jump. He looked out of the doorway, up towards the road. He saw Susan standing in a shooter's stance beside the other girl. She held a shotgun up on her shoulders, looking towards the shack.

"I'm coming out," Scott yelled, not wanting to wander into her line of fire.

He stepped out as Susan came rushing down the hill, the shotgun still held up. "It's making a run for the water," Susan said. "I shot the damn thing…I know one of the shots hit it. But it just kept going."

Scott only nodded, already turning towards the lake. The thing was moving along the ground, making strange U shapes along its belly as it crawled along. He could clearly see the place where Susan had landed one of her shots. A large chunk of meat along its center was bleeding more of the black stuff he had seen spill from its body in the shack.

"Kids, I need you to stay where you are and not move a muscle," Scott said loudly back into the shack. He then looked to Susan and said: "Light it up."

They stood together and fired at the thing. Scott knew that every shot he fired landed true but the thing kept moving. It was now less than five feet from the water and Scott emptied his clip into it, stepping forward and closing the distance with each shot. The thing's body shuddered with each round that pierced it and although its movements slowed, it still continued to move.

"To hell with this," Susan said. She ran forward, pumping a new round into the shotgun.

"Careful," Scott said.

"Got it," she said. She ran in front of the thing and brought the barrel of the shotgun down.

But the monster was too close to an escape to be stopped. Before Susan could take her shot, the thing lashed out hard to the right, knocking her to her feet. Without so much as stopping, the thing wrapped its lower half around her leg and continued on towards the lake.

Its top portion had reached the water as Susan started to wail and scream. She tried to angle the shotgun for a clear shot but was unable to do so. Scott ran down to her and grabbed her hand. He yanked as hard as he could but the monster only tightened its grip. As more of it went into the lake, moving slower than ever now with Susan's added weight, Scott heard the sound of an approaching boat engine. He looked up and saw a boat speeding towards them. A single man was on board and as far as Scott could tell, he showed no signs of slowing down.

"Give me the gun," Scott said, feeling stupid that he had exhausted his rounds so easily and that he'd left his additional clips in the trunk of the sedan. He looked back to the approaching boat and wanted to yell for the moron to turn around or, at the very least, to slow down.

She handed it to him, stock-end first. When he took it, he remembered that he'd already watched Susan load the next shot into it. He aimed carefully three inches away from where Susan's leg was caught, and fired.

Black goo splattered against his leg as a chunk of the thing's left side was disintegrated. The rear portion of its body went limp for a moment, releasing Susan.

But still, it moved on, slinking further into the water. Only, it was moving oddly now. It seemed to be turning itself in the shallow water and—

Scott realized what was happening a moment too late.

The boy had been right; the thing needed water. In the back of his head, Scott could see one of those e-mails written to George Galworth from KC Doughtry.

It needs water.

And then its upper half was rocketing out of the shallow water and coming directly for him. Scott had just enough time to bring the shotgun up but that was not enough. The monster knocked it out of his hands and then it was on him, the soft and fetid flesh of its underside covering his face and suffocating him.

THIRTY-ONE

Wayne's vision was nowhere near perfect, but even he could see enough of the surreal scene along the bank to know that something unnatural and violent was taking place. The sporadic sound of gunshots was a further indication of this. Then, as he neared the bank and saw more of the situation clearly, he knew he was in the right place. He saw Susan Lessing on the ground and a man standing not too far away from her, pointing what looked to be a shotgun towards the ground. Behind them, three kids watched on, a boy a two girls, unmoving.

There was the roar of a shotgun blast as Wayne drew closer. It made him jump a bit, even over the rough purring of the boat's engine. Within another few feet, Wayne saw the shape on the ground between Susan and the man with the shotgun and his guts seemed to boil.

It was that thing…that *monster.*

Wayne slowed even more, the bank now no more than twenty yards away. As he slowed the boat, he kept his eyes on the scene playing out on the shore. He watched as part of the monster came out of the lake like some weird projectile and knocked the man with the shotgun down on the ground. It wasted no time covering the man's head in much the same way it had done to Al.

Susan started to scream, the noise tearing through the noise of his engine as it scaled down. Sensing the urgency in the moment, Wayne acted before his brain could lock down at the absurdity of it all. The three kids looking on in terror, the screaming game warden, and the man currently with his face covered by some ungodly creature…it was insane.

He closed in on the bank—ten yards, eight, five—and picked up his Remington. He had to move and not think. If he thought about it too long, he didn't know if he would be able to act at all.

He drove the boat directly into the bank, pulling up directly beside the area where the creature was still partly submerged, its backside coiling tightly in the water. The underside of the boat groaned, punctuated by gritty scratching sounds. The engine struck the sand beneath the boat and came to a shuddering halt.

But Wayne wasn't paying attention to any of that. He leaped off of the front of the boat, his knees aching from the effort, as they had not moved so quickly in a very long time. Wayne looked down to the creature and watched as it tightened itself against the fallen man. He placed the Remington directly along what he assumed was the thing's back and pulled the trigger. The thing responded by coiling back. It did not release the man, though; it simply dragged him towards the water.

Wayne pulled the trigger again, loaded the next shot, and fired again. The shots rang out like small thunderclaps across the lake. Black blood-like fluid flowed from the thing's flesh and it finally relinquished its grip on the fallen man. When he was freed, the man backed away on his haunches, coughing and retching between strangled screams.

Meanwhile, the creature waved its upper half around like a cobra seeking where it would strike next. Wayne saw that the thing had taken a beating. He saw at least six gunshots in the thing—a few of which looked to have been close-range shots with the shotgun—and a long ragged scratch along its head. It darted forward towards him, but Wayne held his ground.

He leveled the rifle and fired again. His shot tore into the flesh directly beneath what served as the thing's mouth and it shuddered backwards with the impact. Still, the damn thing was on the move, backing into the water.

"No!"

The sudden voice made Wayne jump a bit and didn't realize who had spoken it until he saw the shape of a small person running by him. It was the boy he had seen standing by the shack. He was running forward, running towards the monster as if his life depended on it.

***

Watching the hefty woman and the man shoot at the thing was sort of cool. There was no way Joe was going to deny that. But at the same time, he could tell that the shots weren't doing enough damage. The damned thing was going to escape back into the lake and they'd never get the opportunity to kill it again. Even his fourteen-year-old logic told him that this would be a wasted opportunity—that they should kill the thing before it escaped.

Joe watched in horror as the thing assaulted the man, slamming into his chest and taking him to the ground. Joe assumed this man was a cop or something; it was obvious in the way he had carried his gun when he had come into the shack. But now, cop or not, he was on the ground with the monster covering his head.

Gunshots won't slow it enough, Joe thought. *Enough shots might kill it, but it'll get back to the lake before they get the chance...*if *they get the chance.*

An idea formed in his head as he thought about narrowly escaping death on the little canoe thanks to the shattered oar. He took Mac by the hand and then placed her hand into Valerie's. Both girls looked at him, confused.

"Please, both of you, stay here and don't move."

"Joe, what are you—" Valerie started, but Joe was already on the move.

He dashed back into the shack, barely aware of the slight droning noise of an approaching boat engine. Now that he was in the darkness of the shack, the place where the thing had pinned him to the ground, his idea suddenly seemed very stupid. But at least it was *something.*

He went to the place where he had been knocked to the ground, his nerves electric. He picked up the pitchfork even though it had proven worthless the first time he'd tried to use it. With the rusty old tool in his hands, he started for the door again as another round of gunshots sounded out from the shore.

Joe got back outside with the pitchfork in hand just as an older man pumped a shot directly into the monster's featureless face, just below the mouth. Joe also saw the thing continue to slither back. It was moving slow now, a clear sign that it had been severely wounded, but wounded wasn't good enough in Joe's mind.

"No!"

He let out the scream of desperation as he ran past Mac and Valerie, down towards where the grown-ups were trying to kill the thing. He passed by the old man and then the woman and neither of them tried to stop him.

"Son," the old man said. "What are you—?"

Joe was well aware that the thing was tracking him as it retreated. Already, at least half of it was back in the water. Joe didn't wait for the thing to come at him, even if it *was* wounded. He brought the pitchfork high over his head and slammed it down into what he thought was the thing's center.

When the forks drove through the monster's flesh and into the soft sand beneath, Joe kept pushing down on the handle, trying to get them to go deeper.

"Damn good thinking," the old man said, coming up next to him. He placed his hands on top of the pitchfork handle, gently nudging Joe out of the way. The man then pushed down hard, letting out a grunt, and the handle seemed to drop another six inches or so.

At their feet, the creature writhed. Its head came less than a foot from Joe's face and he stumbled back, nearly falling.

"I've seen it before," Joe said. "It came after me but after I ran away from it, it gave up. It had to go back to the water."

The man that might have been a policeman was slowly getting to his feet, still coughing. "He's right," the man said, stopping to let out a gagging sound. "Keep it out of the water. It'll suffocate."

Joe watched as the thing tried to pull away from the pitchfork, but it was impaled all the way through and the forks were almost entirely buried in the sand. Joe could see them beneath the thing's stomach as it lifted its body slightly in an attempt to get away.

Joe didn't know if keeping the thing's head out of the water would be enough to do the job, but he thought so. Even now, as he watched it struggle, it seemed to grow weaker. Where it was thrashing about before, it now seemed to only lash out in a blind and lazy sort of way.

The man that might have been a cop came over to Joe and patted him on the back. "Quick thinking," he said. "If you hadn't have done that, this thing might have gotten away."

Joe tried to accept the thanks, but it was hard to do. Standing in the presence of this thing made it hard to think of anything other than the nightmares he was sure to have for the foreseeable future.

"What is it?" Joe asked.

"Dying," the maybe-cop said. "And that's all that's important."

"You're from the government, aren't you?" the old man asked, watching the thing as intently as Joe. "I saw black vans a few weeks ago. I know where they went."

"You and I need to talk later," the government man said. But from the way he spoke, Joe didn't think he'd be doing much talking for a while.

The woman took a few steps towards them. Joe saw tears trailing down her eyes. "I'm sorry," she said to the government man. "You had the shotgun and it had you and—I just froze. Oh my God, I'm sorry."

The government man shook the comment away. He was leaning against a tree and breathing heavily.

Joe watched it breathe heavily, now done with any attempts at fighting. It knew it was done and it slumped to the ground in defeat. It gave one last twitch that traveled the entire length of its body and then there was nothing.

Joe felt something graze his hand. He looked to his side and saw Valerie standing there. He took her hand and drew him to her. She hugged his right side and buried her head into his shoulder while his sister hugged the other side.

They stood in awkward sort of hug and when the government man started asking them questions a few minutes later, Joe did his best to answer them. And when government man placed all three of them into his car to escort them home, Joe looked back down towards the shack. He tried his best to think of the kisses he and Valerie had shared there—of what it had been like to fall in love around that old rustic structure, but all of that was gone now. Instead, there was only the very recent memory of thinking that he was going to die in order to save his sister.

He wanted to feel heroic and he supposed it would be justified. But it was hard to feel like a hero when all he wanted to do was crumple up in his mother's lap and cry.

THIRTY-TWO

Even after the government man—who had introduced himself as Agent Scott Miles—dropped them off at the cabin, Mac would not leave Joe's side. Even when their parents tried to scoop her up to comfort her, she refused. She clung to Joe's arm, saying nothing and barely moving unless she absolutely had to. Joe didn't mind. He played with her hair in a way he knew she liked, hoping it would console her.

He and Mac sat on the couch while Scott Miles and the woman that he had pieced together was the local game warden tried explaining to his parents what had happened. Every now and then one of them would ask him a question and Joe would give a brief answer. The longer he sat there, the more he realized just how tired he was. He had read somewhere that a sudden surge of adrenaline could leave the human body feeling exhausted and he was pretty sure that was what he was feeling.

For most of the conversation, his mom was sitting beside him. She would look at him as if she were studying a painting, looking for some hidden meaning. Joe assumed she was looking for injuries. When she cupped his face in her hands and kissed him on the cheek, he uttered a light, "I'm fine, Mom."

She started weeping at this, something Joe didn't understand. Whether it was his eight-year-old sister, a fifteen-year-old girl that he had fallen in love with, or his mother, he just didn't think he'd *ever* understand women. As his mother made a fuss over both of them, Joe still managed to hear a bit of the conversation taking place between Scott Miles, the game warden (her name was Susan, he had figured out) and his father. He heard Agent Miles saying that the creature that had attacked them was of unknown origin and was possibly a mutation of some kind.

Joe had no idea how he knew it, but he thought Agent Miles was lying. Joe had seen that thing up close on two occasions. Sure, maybe it *was* a mutation. But Agent Miles knew more than he was letting on. Joe watched his dad and wasn't sure he was buying it, either. Maybe he was just too distracted by the fact that his children had narrowly escaped death to really care, though.

As if reading his mind, Agent Miles looked over to him slyly, just out of the corner of his eye. It was the brief sort of glance that Joe had seen grownups give one another far too often. He'd seen it shared between his parents when they talked about Santa Clause in front of Mac. He'd also seen it when they thought they were being clever and sneaky when talking about sex when young ears were around. It was a glance that spoke without words, saying: *We have a secret and it wouldn't do anyone any good to find out about it.*

Joe knew that he could object; he could let them know that whatever had attacked them was a monster of some kind, not just an abnormality or mutation. It was…well, it was something else.

But Joe let it go. The thing was dead. He had watched it die and that was enough for him. As far as he was concerned, its death meant that it never had to be mentioned again.

So he stayed quiet, although he kept feeling that pitchfork in his hands and how easily it had torn through the flesh of the thing. Now that it was all over, it made him feel slightly ill. He pushed it away, thinking instead of Valerie. He wondered what she was going through right now. Susan—the game warden—had dropped her off at her father's cabin moments before delivering them home. She had not been in the house long, so Joe assumed she had given a very boiled down version of the same story she and Agent Miles were giving his folks right now. Joe was dying to know how her father had reacted and if Valerie was in any trouble, but he hadn't dared ask.

Thinking of Valerie and what might become of them within a few days, Joe sat there without saying anything else. He continued playing with Mac's hair and let his mother embrace him softly, like he might break at the slightest touch.

***

It took less than two days for Joe's parents to decide that staying around the lake after everything that had happened would probably do their children no good. It was for that reason Joe found himself walking down Kerr Lane late at night, using the light of his phone to illuminate the road, as it was a cloudy night and the moon was nowhere to be seen.

He'd packed his suitcases with his mother's help. She was still trailing him like a shadow but she was getting better on a daily basis. She seemed to bounce back and forth between her kids, hovering over Joe one moment and Mac the next. Joe was sure that Agent Miles hadn't even told her the entire story—about what that thing had really been. If she'd known *everything*, there was no telling how she would act. He tried to imagine what she'd do if she woke up right now, at 12:25, to see that her oldest son's bed was empty. She'd lose it. She'd freak out and call the police and then ground him for life. His dad would go along with it because when Amy Evans went berserk, Drew Evans did the smart thing and went along with just about anything she said or suggested.

But he had to see Valerie this one last time. Harsh words and punishment from his parents would be worth it. At such a young age, he didn't *really* understand regret yet but he thought that not seeing Valerie again before he left Clarkton Lake would be something he would regret later on in life.

They'd communicated through text messages, deciding to keep it simple and meet on the edge of the road somewhere between their parents' cabins. The conversation had been short and sweet, with Joe simply stating I need to see you. Need to talk.

She had responded with OK. How about on the road between our houses in 15 mins? There had been no subtext and no cutesy emoticons. Things were different now—a fact that was proven in their location of choice.

The mere idea of returning to the shack was horrifying to Joe and *almost* kept him from heading out to meet with her at all. If there was any doubt that his fond memories of that place were now ruined and replaced by feelings of pure terror, that realization had killed it.

Peering through the dark, he saw her approaching. She was also using her phone as a means of light. They closed the distance and when they met, they said nothing. They instantly kissed, their arms going around one another and sharing the sort of kiss that most teens don't experience until under the dimmed lights of a prom or parked on a back road, exploring the backseat of a car.

When they pulled away, Valerie tore the band-aid off. With a simple question, she made Joe's job much easier.

"It's bad news, isn't it?"

"Yeah," Joe said. "We're leaving tomorrow. Dad thinks it's the best thing for me and Mac."

"He's right," Valerie said, taking his hand and pulling him close.

Joe took in her scent, smelling a faint whiff of strawberry in her shampoo and the sweet tinge of summer sweat.

"This was awesome," Joe said, wishing he could think of something better to say.

"It was," she agreed. "It was amazing."

"You know...that word people say when they care a lot about someone..."

"Yeah, I know," she said, kissing him softly on the jaw.

He shuddered and was embarrassed to find that he was starting to cry. But holding her in his arms, he felt a shudder pass through her and realized that she was crying, too. His heart seemed to sag and an intense sorrow weighed heavily on him. He was terribly confused because he was sure he was too young to feel such a thing. Wasn't he?

"Well," Valerie said, pulling back to look him in the eyes. Their noses were nearly touching and even in the darkness, Joe could feel her eyes taking him in. "One thing's for sure...I sure as hell won't forget you. With everything that happened, I don't think it would be possible."

It sounded like such an adult thing to Joe's ears and he understood in that moment that he had grown up considerably in the last few weeks. It wasn't isolated to having met this beautiful girl and tasting love for the first time, nor was it all focused on experiencing true fear and overcoming it in a very adult way. It was all of that put together; it was in how he'd fought to save Valerie and his sister and how he was accepting this pain and sorrow as if it was a normal, expected part of life. It was in knowing that this was not meant to last and that, quite frankly, they *would* forget each other over time. He knew that just as sure as he knew he wanted to kiss her again in that moonless night.

And he did it. He drew her to him and kissed her. He supposed he *did* love her, and that was okay. But he knew how teenagers were. He knew that his parents were right about how he would grow up and mature. He'd meet someone else and fall in love with them and by the time he was married, all childhood things would be forgotten.

But he recalled the fear in his sister's eyes and how that pitchfork had felt in his hands as he had run down to the bank where some unimaginable horror had tried to escape back into the water.

And with that bit of bravery in mind, he continued to kiss Valerie. Somewhere nearby, a dog barked and a loon cried out across the lake. Joe heard it all, as if it were a door being gently pushed shut to keep all the bad things out...and all the promising things inside.

THIRTY-THREE

It took Wayne a six pack and a shot of whiskey to summon up the courage, but he finally decided that he was going to walk down to Al's house to see how he was doing. It had been two days since the gruesome events on the bank in front of the old fishing cabin and Wayne figured his friend might want to know that the thing that had attacked him out on the lake was dead and gone now—and that he, Wayne, had played a part in its death.

That's how Wayne found himself walking up Kerr Lane on a Saturday afternoon, slightly drunk and hopeful for his friend's recovery from whatever was ailing him. He'd kept tabs on the comings and goings around the lake since the events at the shed. That had been five days ago, although every morning since, he could have sworn it had only been the day before.

He knew that the Evans family had left town, headed back to New York. He also knew that Agent Scott Miles had holed up in his little cabin to get some rest and break down his equipment. The last Wayne had heard, Agent Miles was having problems breathing (which made perfect sense to Wayne, as one of the clearest things about that evening by the shack was seeing that monster wrap itself around the poor agent's head). Wayne knew these things because Susan Lessing had told him. She had called him yesterday with no real purpose. She had gingerly approached the topic of the thing they had encountered on the lake but had not dwelled on it. Wayne was pretty sure she had simply called someone else that had been there just to make sure it had really happened and she wasn't going crazy.

But Susan Lessing was the furthest thing from his mind as he walked up Al's driveway. He gave the horseshoe pit a longful glance, hearing those musical *clink*s in his head. He marched up the porch steps and was glad that he was a little drunk; that would make it much easier to deal with Kathy if she was still insisting that he couldn't see Al.

Might have been a good idea to call first, he thought before he knocked. *Oh well...she would have just put me off anyway. Harder for her to do that with me standing right here in front of her.*

He knocked on the door and waited, hoping that Al would answer but pretty damn sure that it would be Kathy.

Twenty seconds passed and no one answered. He knocked again, louder this time. As he waited for an answer, he turned to look at the top of the gravel driveway. Both cars were here, Al's truck parked directly beside Kathy's little Subaru. They were both home but apparently not answering the door.

Maybe Kathy had seen him coming up the drive and was choosing not to answer the door for him. That meant that she had convinced Al to stay quiet, too. That, or it meant that he had gotten worse since the last time they'd spoken.

A bit concerned now, and not really caring about Kathy's concerns at all, Wayne tried the door. He found it unlocked, which was not surprising because no one hardly ever locked their doors around Clarkton Lake. He pushed it open and stood there between the opened screen door and the partially opened front door. He poked his head inside and listened for any sounds but there was nothing.

"Hello," he said. "Kathy? Al? What's going on? You there?"

He waited a handful of seconds but got no response. He stepped into the house and once he was fully inside, he could feel the stillness of the place. Almost instantly, the slight drunkenness seemed to wash away from him, much like it had done when he'd seen the events playing out on the shore that afternoon as he'd sped his boat closer to the horror.

"Al?" he said again, although by then, he was sure he wasn't going to get an answer.

Get out, he thought to himself in a meek voice. *Better yet, get on the phone and call the cops. Something isn't right. You know it. You can feel it.*

That was beyond true, but he somehow found his legs moving forward. He moved through Al's living room. A magazine was opened on the coffee table. A can of Dr. Pepper sat beside it. The entire scene looked like something in a wax museum.

Wayne left the living room, heading left for the hallway where the bedroom was located. He made only a single step before he saw the body on the floor. His right foot paused in mid-step as he stared at it.

"Oh my God," he breathed.

It was Kathy's body, her face turned slightly to the right away from him. After that, nothing else about her made much sense because of all of the blood. It was caked along her chest and splattered against the walls.

A low moan escaped Wayne's mouth and he felt himself falling softly against the wall. He stepped closer, the blood getting richer and more real with every foot forward. There was so much of it, so much blood that the area between Kathy's neck and knees was nothing more than a red mess.

He was so close now that he thought he could smell the blood, rich and coppery almost like a handful of pennies. He took a final trembling step and came to the midway point of the hall. To his left, the bathroom door stood open. He glanced inside and instantly fell back against the wall. A scream tried to crawl out of his throat but his body was too shocked to produce the sound. All that came out was a low whining moan as he clapped his hands to his mouth.

Al was sprawled awkwardly on the floor, his body partially supported due to the fact that his left arm had fallen on the toilet seat and his head had struck the bathtub. His blood-coated face was aimed directly at Wayne, his eyes wide and his mouth—oh God, his mouth...

His mouth looked to have been ripped open, almost like someone had grabbed his chin and pulled own until the jaw snapped and the skin stretched and split. There were fragments of teeth speckled in the maroon blood that was sprayed all over his shirt. There was more blood on the walls and a literal pool of it in Al's lap and on the floor. The white toilet was also stained with it; the tank looked like a morbid Jackson Pollock painting.

But Wayne's eyes went back to that gaping hole where his friend's mouth had once been. Now there was a black cavern of blood and unspeakable suffering.

Wayne felt the scream building in his chest as tears came cascading down his cheeks. But before he could let it out, he heard something. It was the first sound he had heard since stepping into the house other than his little muffled cries.

Something splashed in the toilet.

With a creeping dread spreading through his guts, Wayne leaned forward slightly and looked into the bowl. Something was coiled up inside, something alive and flipping what appeared to be its tail in an agitated manner. When Wayne's eyes fell on it, it froze up and coiled up tighter on itself. It was a much smaller version of the beast he had helped to kill down by the shack four days ago but it still managed to fill almost the entire bowl.

Looking at it, there was a humbling moment where Wayne was sure his bladder was going to let go. He managed to keep control of himself, though. He slowly backed away on trembling legs.

He made it out of the doorway and back into the hall before the thing struck. It came sailing out of the toilet with speed that matched that of the larger creature Wayne was familiar with. Wayne's scream finally came bolting out of his mouth as he took off in a run to his left, back towards the living room.

The thing struck the hallway wall, making a wet *splat* sound. Wayne looked back for only a moment, watching as it rebounded from the wall and hit the floor, already recovering and slithering quickly towards him.

It was fast as hell, already on Wayne's heels. Thinking purely on instinct and not considering the consequences, Wayne reached he still-open front door and collided with the screen door beyond it, thankful that it had not completely closed when he came in. Still, his impact shattered the glass and the edge of the frame caught him in the forehead. He stumbled across the porch, hearing the sound of the snake-like thing also banging it open behind him.

Wayne turned, still running to the porch stairs, just in time to see it leaping from the porch and directly for him. Watching it propel itself without legs was almost like some kind of dark magic. It was going to get him; it was going to wrap around his head just like the larger one had done to Agent Miles and—

Suddenly, the porch was not under his feet. He realized moments after gravity took him that he was falling down the porch stairs. He went flailing down the stairs head first and could actually feel the slimy surface of the thing barely touch the side of his face as it overshot its falling prey.

Wayne struck his shoulder on the porch railing and then hit the last few on his side. He felt a rib crack right around the same moment his left foot bent awkwardly on the ground. He cried out in pain as he hit the ground, instantly scrambling to his knees to find out where the monster was.

He caught sight of it just short of the edge of the driveway. It was still now, stretched out to its full length of about three feet or so. Wayne stayed on his knees, a sharp pain in his side and his left foot screaming in pain. He slowly got to his feet, hobbling on his right foot as it took on almost all of his weight. He was afraid to test his left foot just yet and he knew that if it came down to being chased again, he wouldn't stand a chance.

But to his surprise, the thing started to slink off away from him. It slithered at a steady speed towards the side yard, in the direction of the horseshoe pit. Wayne watched it go, expecting it to turn back towards him with lightning speed at any moment. Instead, it continued on its way, as if it was bored of chasing an old man.

Then he remembered the boy that had come running down towards the water with the pitchfork. The thing had been heading back to the water to breathe…

"Ah hell," Wayne hissed.

Then, in an ultimate ironic twist, he started chasing after the thing. He cried out at the pain in his side and when he finally decided to test the ability of his left foot, he nearly fell on his face. He made it forward in a hobbling sort of run, his eyes still on the creature. By the time Wayne had passed the horseshoe pit, the thing was already halfway through the back yard. Beyond that, there was a thin grove of trees broken by a footpath that led to Al's deck. Past that there was only the open lake.

Wincing, Al trundle forward, doing everything he could to look past the pain. As he finally hit a stride in balancing out the weight on his injured left foot, he saw Kathy's little garden to the right, alongside the back porch. Propped against the side was a rake, a small hoe, and a mid-sized shovel that he supposed any respectable gardener would called a spade.

He grabbed the shovel (or spade, or whatever the hell it was) and continued down towards the trees and the lake beyond. Now that he had found a suitable pace—somewhere between a jog and a sprint—he dared to hope that he'd catch up to the thing. He didn't know if it was because the grass was slowing it down or if it was running out of breath and, therefore, growing weaker, but it seemed much slower now, almost lethargic.

When he reached the bottom of the slight hill in the back yard, his foot was nearly numb, causing him to slow to a hobble. And the pain in his side was so bad that he felt like someone had wrapped barbed wire around his ribs.

The little monstrosity sped up a bit as it got closer to the trees, perhaps sensing the relief of water within the next several yards.

Its renewed speed wasn't enough, though. Wayne closed in on it and raised the spade over his head. It had apparently assumed that the old man it had nearly killed would not be a threat because when it noticed another presence directly behind it, it froze for a moment rather than striking out at once. It had only enough time to coil back into its striking position before the spade came down.

It sliced cleanly through the thing's body. There was very little give to it and it made a sick popping noise as its body was split cleanly in half. Black and clear fluid leaked from its two ends as it writhed in agony. It made Wayne feel sick and the only thing he could do to keep from puking in his dead friend's back yard was to keep stabbing at it.

He cut the two pieces into three and the three into six. He stabbed at the ground several more times, not stopping until the thing that had erupted from Al's mouth and sought refuge in the water of the toilet had been torn into unrecognizable bits of meat.

When he finally stopped and dropped the spade, Wayne was crying. He turned away from the mangled corpse of the thing and started back up the small hill of Al and Kathy's back yard. He planned to go inside and call the police to report the deaths of his best friend and his wife. He had no idea how he'd explain the condition of Al's face and that thought alone set him to weeping uncontrollably.

He made it as far as the horseshoe pit before he had to rest. He fell down on the grass and looked to his left foot. The ankle and upper part of the foot were swelling considerably. His side still stung but even that felt like it was also going numb.

With a trembling hand, he reached out and took one of the horseshoes from its place by the wooden planks that made up the frame. With tears in his eyes, he hefted it towards the opposing side and struck the stake along the front.

Cling.

Wayne let out a moan, picked up another horseshoe and held it close to him. He looked back out towards the lake, glimmering through the trees in Al's back yard.

He remained there, motionless and crying, for the better part of the afternoon.

THIRTY-FOUR

Scott had slept for almost an entire two days straight, recuperating in the little cabin that had eventually become nothing more than a surveillance station. He'd slept soundly through the nights and had stirred awake during the day mainly to eat, use the bathroom, and field phone calls. The calls had come from Susan Lessing and Roger Lowry. Susan was checking in on him and when she spoke, he could hear a sense of distance in her voice. She was in some sort of shock, he supposed.

He was, too. What had happened on the lake had drained him and he figured he would enjoy a stress-induced sleep before the nightmares started to come...which they almost certainly would.

Roger Lowry had calmed considerably after being told that the threat had been neutralized. He'd been grateful in a brazen and abrupt way that only Roger was capable of. He told Scott to get some rest and then report back when he felt up to it. He also suggested that, given the nature of the attack he had endured from the thing, that Scott should maybe see a doctor... preferably one suggested by the bureau when he got back to DC.

Now, after his two days of rest, Scott was doing just that. He had packed up his few things and took them out to the car. He felt refreshed but, at the same time, a little winded. He was finding it a little hard to breathe and felt the beginnings of a migraine stirring in the back of his head. So yes, heading back to DC seemed like a good idea. And after he had settled in, he'd see a doctor if he was still having these breathing issues.

He went through the cabin one final time to make sure he had packed everything and then locked the place up. He went back out to the car and stood by it for a moment, taking his cell phone out. He called Susan Lessing's number, wanting to let her know that he was headed out. The phone rang several times and then went to her voicemail. Scott considered leaving a message but then killed the call.

What was the point in dragging things out? There was only sentiment in such a thing and considering the horror they had witnessed, sentiment seemed useless. The sooner he could disconnect himself from all of this, the better.

As he backed out of the driveway, he broke into a small coughing fit.

He made his way up Kerr Lane, headed for the main stretch of highway that would take him away from this godforsaken lake. When he stopped at the intersection, seeing glorious black pavement ahead, he coughed again. He brought up a considerable amount of phlegm this time. He rolled the window down and spit it out.

He then pulled out onto the pavement, completely unaware of the tiny black flakes that he had spit out into the dirt.

CHECK OUT OTHER GREAT DEEP SEA THRILLERS

MEGA
by Jake Bible

There is something in the deep. Something large. Something hungry. Something prehistoric.
And Team Grendel must find it, fight it, and kill it.
Kinsey Thorne, the first female US Navy SEAL candidate has hit rock bottom. Having washed out of the Navy, she turned to every drink and drug she could get her hands on. Until her father and cousins, all ex-Navy SEALS themselves, offer her a way back into the life: as part of a private, elite combat Team being put together to find and hunt down an impossible monster in the Indian Ocean. Kinsey has a second chance, but can she live through it?

THE BLACK
by Paul E Cooley

Under 30,000 feet of water, the exploration rig Leaguer has discovered an oil field larger than Saudi Arabia, with oil so sweet and pure, nations would go to war for the rights to it. But as the team starts drilling exploration well after exploration well in their race to claim the sweet crude, a deep rumbling beneath the ocean floor shakes them all to their core. Something has been living in the oil and it's about to give birth to the greatest threat humanity has ever seen.

"The Black" is a techno/horror-thriller that puts the horror and action of movies such as Leviathan and The Thing right into readers' hands. Ocean exploration will never be the same."

CHECK OUT OTHER GREAT DEEP SEA THRILLERS

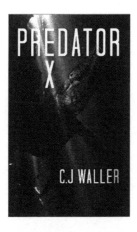

PREDATOR X
by C.J Waller

When deep level oil fracking uncovers a vast subterranean sea, a crack team of cavers and scientists are sent down to investigate. Upon their arrival, they disappear without a trace. A second team, including sedimentologist Dr Megan Stoker, are ordered to seek out Alpha Team and report back their findings. But Alpha team are nowhere to be found – instead, they are faced with something unexpected in the depths. Something ancient. Something huge. Something dangerous. Predator X

DEAD BAIT
by Tim Curran

A husband hell bent on revenge hunts a Wereshark...A Russian mail order bride with a fishy secret...Crabs with a collective consciousness...A vampire who transforms into a Candiru...Zombie piranha...Bait that will have you crawling out of your skin and more. Drawing on horror, humor with a helping of dark fantasy and a touch of deviance, these 19 contemporary stories pay homage to the monsters that lurk in the murky waters of our imaginations. If you thought it was safe to go back in the water...Think Again!

CHECK OUT OTHER GREAT DEEP SEA THRILLERS

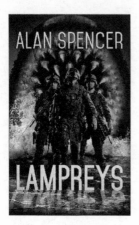

LAMPREYS
by Alan Spencer

A secret government tactical team is sent to perform a clean sweep of a private research installation. Horrible atrocities lurk within the abandoned corridors. Mutated sea creatures with insane killing abilities are waiting to suck the blood and meat from their prey.
Unemployed college professor Conrad Garfield is forced to assist and is soon separated from the team. Alone and afraid, Conrad must use his wits to battle mutated lampreys, infected scientists and go head-to-head with the biggest monstrosity of all.
Can Conrad survive, or will the deadly monsters suck the very life from his body?

DEEP DEVOTION
by M.C. Norris

Rising from the depths, a mind-bending monster unleashes a wave of terror across the American heartland. Kate Browning, a Kansas City EMT confronts her paralyzing fear of water when she traces the source of a deadly parasitic affliction to the Gulf of Mexico. Cooperating with a marine biologist, she travels to Florida in an effort to save the life of one very special patient, but the source of the epidemic happens to be the nest of a terrifying monster, one that last rose from the depths to annihilate the lost continent of Atlantis.

Leviathan, destroyer, devoted lifemate and parent, the abomination is not going to take the extermination of its brood well.

Made in the USA
Lexington, KY
11 November 2016